A PLUME BOOK

THIS IS HOW I'D LOVE YOU

HAZEL WOODS lives in New Mexico with her husband and two children. This is her first novel.

Hazel Woods

This Is How I'd Love You

A NOVEL

A PLUME BOOK

PLUME
Published by the Penguin Group
Penguin Group (USA) LLC
375 Hudson Street
New York, New York 10014

USA | Canada | UK | Ireland | Australia | New Zealand | India | South Africa | China
penguin.com
A Penguin Random House Company

First published by Plume, a member of Penguin Group (USA) LLC, 2014

LIBRARY OF CONGRESS CATALOGING-IN-PUBLICATION DATA
Woods, Hazel.
This is how I'd love you : a novel / Hazel Woods.
pages cm
ISBN 978-0-14-218148-5
1. Loneliness—Fiction. 2. Correspondence—Fiction. 3. Impersonation—Fiction. 4. Chess players—Fiction. I. Title. II. Title: This is how I would love you.
PS3623.O67623T45 2014
813.' 6—dc23
2014014928

Printed in the United States of America
10 9 8 7 6 5 4 3 2 1

Set in Janson
Designed by Eve L. Kirch

For Edward and Margaret

Part One

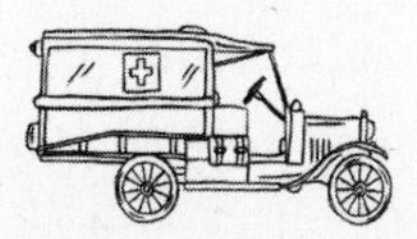

The docks are flooded with deep, black puddles. Men move quickly, their nerves numbed by their hurry. The French steamer awaiting them appears massive and gray and gloomy. Its twin black stacks convey the seriousness of the day. Charles stands shoulder to shoulder with other Field Service volunteers, all of their overcoats darkened by the rain. These stoic faces of theirs are a sham. His eyes scanning the crowd, Charles notes that none of them look the part of warriors, least of all him. Instead, they only need mortarboards and graduation gowns to betray that their most recent barracks were the dorm rooms overlooking idyllic quadrangles of Ivy League alma maters. They have the sloping shoulders and occasionally bespectacled eyes of intellectuals and idealists, motivated by the injustices they've read about in newspapers and seen on film reels in their dormitory's lounge. Their own country, after all, had yet to stand up to the tyranny overseas when they signed their contracts two months ago. But their faces are somber in the attempt to convey the look of the men that they hope to be. *We are the serious ones. The first. The bravest. The ones who will represent America as it should be.* But then, without warning, a nervous giggle will begin at the front of the line and travel all along, the joke always something juvenile, about the rain camouflaging those among them who would soon mess their trousers, or the crimson scent of a Harvard man's flatulence.

Charles smiles and crams his hands into his pockets, trying to imagine the familiar pattern of the chessboard. It is a welcome respite from the useless conjecture his mind makes about what will greet them in a week's time when they land in Bordeaux. He'd been taught to play chess on his father's onyx set and he remembers those long afternoons pleasantly, the fire dying down, his father's whiskey replenished regularly, the family dog sighing loudly in a dream. While at Harvard, Charles played in a bridge club as well as a Sunday afternoon chess bracket, but only once since coming home from college had he and his father played on the onyx set in the parlor. It had ended badly, with his father excusing himself a move before checkmate, claiming he was late for an appointment across town. Which was why, when he'd gone for his physical at the Rockefeller Institute, the notice posted by the Women's Auxiliary caught his eye. They were offering to match volunteers with civilians in a pen-pal arrangement. Charles took down the number and placed a call to a woman who agreed to search for a chess partner for him.

After the very first letter, however, Charles understood his opponent was hardly the kind of dutiful patriot he'd expected to volunteer for such an assignment. A journalist by trade, Mr. Sacha Dench of West Thirteenth Street made it clear in that first letter, which was mailed just weeks before Congress's war vote, that he was a pacifist and would work every day to prevent the United States from entering the war, that he found anyone who would volunteer to participate either daft or tragically misinformed, but also that he did not think personal sacrifice should go unnoticed, however foolish.

As Charles considers their current board and his opponent's

ruthlessness, he further understands that the endeavor may not be as charitable as he'd first expected. Mr. Dench has taken one of Charles's pawns in the third move of the game, their bishops facing one another and the next move of utter importance. Charles must be wary of the temptation to play too aggressively, putting his own pieces at risk in the next turn, which, he senses, is probably his opponent's strategy. A classic lure. But playing like this, without body language or eye contact, is a new challenge. And knowing that Mr. Dench thinks him either "daft" or "tragically misinformed" has shaken his confidence. He posted his latest move yesterday with the timidity of a boy, turning over all of his options in his mind once more before he had the nerve to seal the envelope.

Now, as the order comes that they will embark momentarily, he tries to reassure himself that he's made the right move. He wants to win. He wants to prove the guy wrong. About everything.

When they are thoroughly drenched and their duffels are carrying more water than supplies, the whistle sounds and they board the ship.

They stand on the deck, smoking, waiting. There are several women still on the docks, holding big black umbrellas and white linen handkerchiefs. For the love of their brothers or husbands, their betrothed or sons, they shake their linens. A stupid tradition, Charles thinks. Melodramatic; fruitless. But he also looks around, searching the deck for the men who are waving back, the men to whom those limp, white hankies are declarations of love, the pale quivering of passionate hearts.

His thoughts linger only briefly on his mother and father, the croquet party they'd planned for their weekend guests in the country, now ruined by the weather. The mood there will be black for many reasons, not just their bitter disappointment about his "foolish, crassly transparent rebellion." It's better that they're not here, he thinks, as he wonders what move Mr. Dench will make and how long it will take for it to find him in France.

The ship pulls away from the dock and it appears as though the island of Manhattan is the one being set afloat, being cast out to sea. Hard to tell that the ship is even moving. Soon enough, the horizon is blurred out by the storm and they seem to exist in a vast tunnel, ever darkening, ever deepening, only the black sea in sight.

Hensley Dench feels the train inside of her. Its wheels turn and its axles move deep in the dark places that no one can see. Its rhythm, its power, its forward motion. It is already the second day of their journey, the twenty-ninth hour: New York is so far away it is a dream. A dirty, shiny scrap of a place that she's made up in her girlish imagination. Now there is only this sky, a huge cistern of blue that clouds over in the afternoons, turning dark and ominous, like a tragic grand finale to each day. They sleep on their berths, she and her father, as the night sky unfolds itself, dumps huge buckets of rain and then returns in the morning, so blue and optimistic it hurts.

There are pieces of soldiers on this train. Photographs and letters tucked into breast pockets, hidden between carefully folded sweaters; tokens, marbles, flasks. Each passenger is either remotely or intimately connected with a boy bound for the war. Her father keeps a piece of one in his coat pocket. The curving black lines of Mr. Charles Reid's handwriting reveal that he is unwavering in his convictions. He wants to know if Mr. Dench is a believer and if he is, will he pray for him. Will he pray for the souls of the men who are blown back by guns that remain unseen?

And then, eventually, he reveals his next move. He will move his queen's pawn two. This is what her father's been waiting for. He sets up the chessboard like an altar, arranging the pieces exactly as they were when he made his last move, via post, ten days ago.

He places his inkwell beside the board and removes a piece of paper from his satchel. Hensley has her own paper in front of her, sketching dresses she no longer needs. A narrow velvet skirt, perfect for the theater, worn with a silk lampshade tunic and a single strand of long, perfectly black beads. Her own take on the Fortuny tea gown, made from crepe and pleated everywhere except on the front placket, where she'd inlay a silk ruffle. After a time, though, these drawings irk her. She is restless and distracted.

Hensley stands between cars and throws off pieces of the roll she saved from lunch. The bread tumbles quickly down into the ravine on one side of the tracks and it gives her a jolt of adrenaline. If she herself were a soldier, standing between cars on a train somewhere in Europe—Russia or Austria or France or Britain—she would think of following that bread crumb. Or more likely a cigarette tossed away in a masculine gesture of disinterest; useless, now vanquished. Cartwheeling herself off of the thundering, monotonous machine into nature's terrain where the worms and rodents and wolves and snakes could dismantle her without an audience, without leaving her stench to spread across crowded trenches, into, even, the letters back home.

When her father is asleep, Hensley will read his reply. She will lift Mr. Reid's letter to her face and try to smell something of a person whose life is not beholden to a parent. A life in which one's decisions are one's own. Then she will scan her father's black scrawl to see what he's told the boy about belief.

God is and always has been a substitute for true belief. For sacrificing and forsaking ego in the service of real & actual good. God feeds men's egos, giving them more self-importance than they deserve. If, in fact, there were a God who was almighty and all-knowing, this being would not tolerate humans speaking for him. The fact that religion requires belief above rationality renders it useless to me. God, it seems, is actually the antithesis of thought, which is what I hold sacred. But as I close my eyes and listen to the machinery beneath my feet, I ask for your body and soul to be safe. I know not of whom I ask this, but if my thoughts have any power outside of myself, let us call this God. Take no offense from an old man's heresy, please.

Be advised that just as you are embarking for Europe, my daughter and I are on our way west. Fortunes demand my relocation, at least temporarily, to Hillsboro, New Mexico. You may write to me there, care of the Ready Pay mine. My next move is my queen's knight to QB4.

Even for a desperate man, who fears his own eyes will be a soft, easy meal for shit-colored rats as soon as the right bullet finds him, Hensley's father will not lie. Hensley cannot help being both ashamed and awed by his conviction as she reads. She will have empathy for Mr. Reid because she knows her own eagerness to hear words of comfort from her father. Her own efforts to evoke reassurances, even on this trip, even as they boarded the train in Pennsylvania Station, even as they entered the dark tunnel beneath the Hudson and saw the skyline recede as they emerged, have failed. How she has longed for words of encouragement from her father. She knows nothing more of their destination than what he's told Mr.

Reid. Her idea of New Mexico comes only from the Winnetou novels her brother loved as a child. But surely, she reasons, as she stares at her father's script, even if they are living in tents among bison and mustangs, it will be better than walking every day past the school, its wide double doors framing the scene of her heartbreak.

As she reads her father's letter, she will not be able to stop herself from scribbling her own empty words of sunny optimism, tucked into her father's wide margins. *You will come home soon, stronger and wiser. You're fighting for all of us. Your pen pal is a rabid pacifist with a dead wife, an estranged son, and a deviant daughter; pay him no attention. What you must do is believe with all your heart that you can come home and when you do, all the horror that surrounds you now will recede into a past that you can leave behind as simply as a train leaves a depot.*

As she lets the air whip at her cheeks, she thinks of what her brother has told her he knows of the atrocities at the front. Silent gas attacks that leave the trenches full of blinded, gasping soldiers; conditions so wet and filthy that boys' feet begin to rot inside of their boots; engorged French rats who scurry at night across sleeping soldiers' hands. She imagines what those creatures must think of their sudden change of fortune. What tremendous luck! Humanity's brutality like a lottery for these rodents, who, for generations, scrounge only nuts and rotten fruit, the occasional dead lizard or fallen baby bird, and now this: a bounty so outrageous, so warm and fresh, so plentiful and gorgeous it could make even a rat believe in God.

The conductor finds her in between cars, half a dinner roll becoming sticky in her palm.

"Are you ill, miss?" he shouts above the noise of the train.

She shakes her head. "Just taking some air."

"Passengers should remain inside one of the cars. Can I help you back to your berth? Would you care for some seltzer from the dining car?"

Hensley nods again. He extends his arm, waiting for her to take it. The wind is at her back, throwing her hair into her face, where it clings to her lips. She pictures the glass, the train's silhouette etched into it, the bubbles from the seltzer fizzing over the rim.

She turns away from the conductor, putting her face into the wind, shutting her eyes, and letting the world go black. She feels him move closer to her. He is worried. Is her heartache so apparent that he thinks she might actually jump? That he might have to watch her tumble down the embankment at dreadful angles and terrible speed, her skirt ripping, her face aghast? And the momentum of the train a near impossible thing to stop, here in the middle of, where? Kansas? Illinois? To have to jog through the cars—his brow sweating, his heart galloping, his fingers numb—all the way to the engineer so that they can heave the heavy metal wheels to a stop and send out the crew to reclaim her body.

The passengers would wonder what had happened. Indignant, they'd complain about delays and incompetence. Then a rumor would spread quickly from car to car. Their faces would press against the glass, their hearts both eager and afraid. A glimpse of dark color in the grass would elicit small gasps from every woman. But they'd all disembark at their final destinations with a story to tell, an unanswered question, and the relief that it was not them, or one of their own.

Hensley opens her eyes and the conductor's hand is on her shoulder. "Miss," he says again, his voice now close to her ear. She opens her fingers and lets the roll go. She turns her face toward his.

"I just needed the air." The warmth of his hand makes her throat feel tight, her skin hot.

He smiles. She threads her arm through his and he yanks hard on the lever to open the door. "Thank you," she says, as he ushers her through the train car, like a groom retreating from the altar, newly married. When they've reached her place, he lets her go.

A waiter brings the seltzer to her. She has pulled her feet out of her shoes and tucked them underneath her. Holding the glass near her face, she lets the bubbles jump and cling to her nose and chin. Hensley closes her eyes, tired. She thinks of her school friends, choosing bathing costumes and readying their trunks for summer travel. Swim caps and unsanctioned novels stuffed into little hollows between skirts and shoes. To the shore, to the lake, to anyplace where there are waves and ice cream and umbrellas. She thinks of Lowe, who is surely already in Maine, already riding his bike barefooted, unashamed of his civilian status. Spreading blankets for some other girl under ancient branches and handing her a peach, a handkerchief, a flask.

"Brooding?" her father says.

She does not open her eyes. "Emphatically."

She feels him lean across her and open the window, filling their area with the noise and heat of the prairie rushing by outside. She tastes grass and dirt and metal in the back of her throat and brings the water to her lips to wash it away, but it lingers.

"I prefer it closed," she says.

Her father sighs. She can tell he has already settled back in front of the chessboard, trying to predict the future. Before he's even handed the letter off to be posted at the next stop, he's already imagining all the possible moves the boy on his way to the front has open to him, moves he may never get to make.

He stands anyway and closes the window for her.

Hensley thinks of the letters Lowell had said they would write to each other. They were backstage, before the final curtain. His breath warmed her ear even as he said nothing. She'd turned her face to his, smelling the pomade from his hair. *You will write, won't you? When I'm in New Mexico?* She'd understood the way his eyes narrowed, the way they seemed to swallow her own words as an affirmative answer.

That was before. She knew better than to expect a letter now. But, still, she hoped.

What might she say in reply, if he did write?

Dear Lowe—she imagines the letters on the page—*I want to throw myself from the train because of you. I would have given up Wellesley for you. I ought to have known how easily you slid out of your trousers. What spell was I under? Whatever it was has shattered. With kind regards, Hensley.*

And yet, she wonders, as she finishes this composition, is she really so changed? If he walked into this car right now and sat himself beside her, recited Shakespeare or Wordsworth or Tennyson, how many miles would pass before she would allow him to slide his hand beneath her skirts, while she smiled at his audacity and gripped the armrests a little bit tighter? What despicable loneliness this train has churned in her! Certainly his hands should never be trusted again. Knowing that his words are duplicitous, his body opportunistic, his heart—

What heart? And why should she ascribe feelings to his heart? The heart is a muscle that moves blood through the body. That is all. First-year biology. Has she not more sophistication than that? She pouts at her own reflection in the train's window. As much as she loathes the caricature she's become, she cannot change it. What's passed between them is over. And yet. What does she know, really, of the rhythms of courtship? Perhaps she has it all wrong. Perhaps what has happened, though shameful, is not entirely unique. If the heart is simply a muscle, then what is her desire?

No matter that, she's here, on this train. The miles between them growing with each turn of the wheel. Her new life waiting for her somewhere in the middle of nowhere.

Dear Future, she writes in her head, imagining the strokes of her pen as though it is moving across sand, illuminated every so often by a large searchlight. *When I see you, I may not want you, though you've been waiting there, pulsing so faithfully. Please help me to want you. Dress yourself up or offer warm soup or a long-lost friend.*

A surprising tear escapes, unannounced, as she imagines Lowe coming to find her. Remorseful and contrite, his arms holding her tight, rocking her along with the rhythm of the train.

Despite her best efforts, she's still just a girl whose heart has been broken.

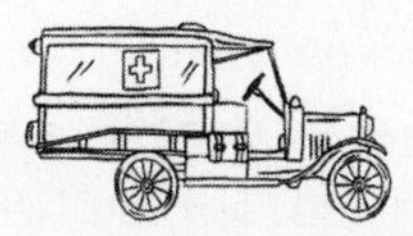

The ship docks in Bordeaux just after dawn and Charles admires the way the sun glints off the metal roofs along the dock. They board a train to Paris, all of them eager to see the first glimpse of the Eiffel Tower. There is a dinner cruise along the Seine and an outing to a club where an American jazz band plays horns that make them all glad to be alive. The next day, they are driven to May-en-Multien outside of Paris, where they will be housed for the next several weeks, given basic training in triage and driving. Their cots are established on the top floor of a picturesque farmhouse. Almost immediately, they are introduced to the fleet of Fords they will be driving. There is some fuss made over the new American volunteers by the staff. The matron who cooks for them greets them that first morning and each successive one by crooning, *"Les Americains! Hooray. Les Americains!"* Her happiness and gratitude cheer them mightily. The thick pork sausage and jam-filled pastries are as welcome a breakfast as Charles has ever had. He cannot help but feel buoyed by her enthusiasm. As she pours more coffee, he smiles at her and nods. It is just the welcome for which they'd hoped.

Charles isn't as boisterous as some of the others, but still, he wants to believe that America will turn the war. Just before he left

New York at the end of May, Congress passed the Selective Service Act and there will be American soldiers boarding ships every day now. His own presence, his wits and efforts, he tells himself, will certainly make an important difference. Isn't that what his privilege demands of him? Not more profits or more property, but a lasting impact upon the world. It seems to him that his parents regarded his education as simply a pastime until he accepted his ultimate occupation of overseeing the family fortune. In fact, when he announced that he was studying science at Harvard in order to prepare for medical school, his father laughed. "Study whatever you want, Charlie. It doesn't matter one bit."

Charles's grandfather had arrived on Ellis Island from Scotland just before the Civil War began and used his life savings to buy twelve sewing machines. Everyone thought he was crazy, but in a small room near the water in Brooklyn, those machines stuttered along day and night beneath the nimble, aching fingers of Scottish immigrants to produce the textiles required by the regiments of the North. Soon he had built an entire building in which he would oversee the largest textile operation the North had ever seen.

Under Charles's father's stewardship, the company had grown and diversified into steel and oil. There were ships in the harbor that sailed only for him. As soon as Charles turned twenty-one, his father had been eager to train him in the art of being a baron. Medicine was a dirty, humble profession.

When Charles first sits behind the wheel of the training ambulance and drives it across the empty field covered in early morning dew, he hears his father's refrain in his ears. *It doesn't matter one bit.* He looks in the rearview mirror at the tracks the truck is leaving behind it, two straight lines shaded and flat. The world bursts with all varieties of color on this summer day. Charles turns his gaze to the horizon, a perfect contrast between deep blue and green. As he picks up speed, the fellow sitting next to him straightens his back and puts a hand on the dash. "Easy, man," he says. "It's not an airplane." But Charles can't resist the urge to push the engine to its limits, to see his effect on this machine. The steering wheel beneath his fingers vibrates its own warning. He heeds nothing but the dark impetus in his gut for a palpable effect of his will, even if it means destruction. The groan of the engine thrills him and the heat coming from the floorboards makes his foot even more intent on its mission. He grips the wheel and narrows his eyes and the ambulance blows past the end of the training track.

Beside him, Rogerson braces himself more severely between the dashboard and the passenger's seat. "Whoa, Reid. Are you out of your mind? This is fucking idiocy."

Charles hears the panic in Rogerson's voice, but he feels completely in control and ignores his plea. Their speed seems an antidote to the doubt that descended upon him in the darkened room last night. Charles wants to be fearless and this is the first time he's felt so.

Just short of the lake at the edge of the farm, Charles removes his foot from the gas and transfers it, with just as much conviction, to the brake. The truck hisses and whines and stops with a sudden, violent lurch. Smoke escapes from the hood, matching the steam coming off the water in front of them. Charles lets his grip loosen and his forehead fall against the wheel.

"Okay," he finally says to Rogerson and himself, as he raises his head. "Okay."

"Really?" Rogerson asks, his voice rising with anger. He reaches across the seat and grips Charles's jaw in his hand. His fingers dig into the meaty corners, leaving Charles immobilized. He cannot even complain.

"What the hell were you thinking? Are you a total lunatic? I didn't come here to be killed in a lousy motorcar by some reckless rich kid."

Charles can't answer. He tries to swallow the saliva gathering in the back of his throat. The tendons in his jaw throb with pain. He shakes his head. With no effect, he pulls at Rogerson's arm with both of his hands. Rogerson gives him a deep, final squeeze and then lets go.

Charles gasps, opening and shutting his jaw slowly, letting the saliva drip out of his open mouth and dampen his trousers.

"Never again," Rogerson says, quietly. "You got it? Never again."

Charles nods, but as the floorboards continue to heat the soles of his boots, he smiles. "I might've taken us for a swim."

"More likely a dive," Rogerson says, his anger fading slightly.

Charles laughs, his hands sore from the exertion. When he was a boy, his father's overly firm grip used to leave his hand aching and lame. He can't remember when he'd outgrown the pain, but when his father shook his hand last, on the evening before he left America, he felt nothing.

"Shall I turn it around?" Charles asks, blowing into his palms.

"You better. Whatever damage has been done is your take, not mine. You might owe the Crown a new truck."

Charles nods, replacing his foot on the gas and letting the wheels move slowly across the thick grass.

"The King George has a lot more left in it than you think," Charles says, christening their vehicle as it trudges back toward the main building, the kitchen chimney smoking cheerily and the royal blue shutters welcoming them back to the hued world.

They've changed trains in Chicago. A new day begun on a new train. Hensley's father has his nose buried in the morning's newspapers, a pot of tea on the table between them. As the buoyant, golden fields of grain blur into a single, endless rectangle against the Midwestern sky, Hensley closes her eyes. Neither geography nor topography captures her imagination. Very little can prevent her from filling the endless hours with thoughts of the recent past.

She remembers the day she met Lowe with searing precision. It was a Thursday. Tryouts were to be held at the school at five o'clock. The senior play was the culmination of every year, written and performed by the girls of the graduating class. At four thirty, her father came home from his job at the *Times* as he did every Thursday, drew the curtains, pulled the chessboard from its homemade felt envelope, and placed it on the mahogany dining table. From a separate felt bag that her mother had also sewn for him one Christmas before she died, he pulled the dull black and white pieces. He arranged them mindlessly on the board and asked Hensley if she would please fetch the sack of walnuts he'd bought for the occasion. She went to the kitchen and removed the sterling nutcracker that her parents had received as a wedding gift some twenty years before and noted how tarnished it was. Her mother would not approve. Sighing, she wrapped her hand around it and found the bag of walnuts in her father's briefcase. Placing both on the dining room table, she kissed her father's cheek as he set the black queen in her place, and bid him good luck.

Smiling at her briefly, he took his voice to a faux-formal tone and said, "Thank you, daughter, but there is no such thing in chess."

Smiling, she said, "Then, think well, Father."

"And you? Will your activity require luck?"

Hensley thought for a moment, wondering if any other girl was subjected to such a line of questioning. "It's an audition, Daddy. Yes. I will need a good deal of luck. For it is not an objective endeavor, like your game. The casting of parts is a subjective decision made by the director, of whom I know absolutely nothing. So the soliloquy I've prepared may be one that he detests. It may be that his poor heart has been broken and he cannot stand Tennyson."

"Which one?"

"'If I were loved, as I desire to be.'"

Her father nodded as he closed his eyes. "'What is there in the great sphere of the earth / And range of evil between death and birth, / That I should fear,—if I were loved by thee?'"

"Of course you know it."

"Why 'of course'?"

"Because you know everything, Daddy. You probably already know whether or not I'll get the part."

He looked amused. "Yes, in fact, I do. With that poem, I've never known anyone to be rejected."

Hensley raised her eyebrows. "Really? Do tell," she said as she pulled on her gloves.

"It was one of your mother's favorites. One of *our* favorites."

Hensley nodded. She'd known this, of course. It had been her mother who'd first recited it for her when she was just a girl. But she'd wondered if her father remembered. Now she knew.

"So, wish me luck," she said, putting on her hat.

"I will only wish that the director recognizes the bounty of talent you possess."

"I should be back by seven. Marie and I will walk together."

He nodded, satisfied with this exchange. "But, please, do be quiet as you enter."

She knew his opponent, Mr. Wern, would arrive within the half hour, and after a limited conversation, the apartment would become a hushed sanctuary. The sewing machine, the guitar, the sound of her feet crossing the floor were all considered too loud. A chess player's concentration was a sacred thing, perhaps the only sacred thing in the world.

And who was she to deny him this respite from his daily work, which increasingly produced a furrowed brow, fraught words, and tense coughs? Her father didn't trust Wilson, or the rhetoric that had become his foreign policy. He was worried that it was only a matter of time before the United States joined the butchery overseas.

She had not always been so understanding of his habits. When she was eleven and twelve and thirteen, Hensley had spent most of the time sullen and angry at his archaic inclinations. She would slam doors to accentuate her silent voice. Stomp her feet when he addressed her as "daughter." She missed her mother and wanted an embrace. A smile. Warmth without humor. Her brother, away at boarding school, had been no help at all. If anything, on his visits home, he highlighted her isolation by going out every night with his own friends.

On her fourteenth birthday, her father had looked at her earnestly. "Is it a happy birthday?" he'd asked.

She did not reply. She wanted to scream at him. To ask him why he couldn't just wish her a happy birthday the way he was supposed to. She wanted to tell him she'd never had a happy birthday, not since Mother died, and that he was a poor, poor substitute. Instead, she was silent. He walked across the living room to the front closet and pulled a large, clumsily wrapped package from it. "See if this makes it a happy birthday." He carried the parcel across the room and placed it on the low table in front of the sofa.

Hensley crossed the room, her heeled shoes making loud punctuation marks. "What is it?" she asked, standing beside him.

"Why, I do believe it is a gift." He smiled and sat on the sofa.

"What type?" she replied, unwilling to be placated so easily.

"Are there types? Tell me the categories and I will attempt to classify it."

Hensley stomped her foot. But she caught her reflection in the antique glass beside the fireplace and suddenly, on the occasion of her fourteenth birthday, her juvenile foot stomping looked either ill-mannered or comical. She turned directly to comedy.

"One: useful but boring. Two: entertaining but useless. Three: perfect."

Her father's face betrayed no acknowledgment of her sudden transformation. "Perhaps the receiver of the gift must apply the category. For it depends, completely, on her. That is the risk of gift giving."

"True." Hensley sat gingerly on the sofa beside her father. His beard and his eyebrows had gone white and she couldn't say when this had happened.

He placed a hand lightly on her back. "Go on," he said. "Let's see how I've fared."

The paper was brown and thick and there was a single purple ribbon coiled into a circle and placed on top. She removed this, smoothing it into her lap. When she pulled off the paper, there was a gorgeous black sewing machine. With a formidable hand crank and gleaming metal components. Hensley touched the crank with her fingers. It felt cool and heavy.

"Daddy," she said. "It's perfect."

"Aha. Type number three. I couldn't be happier."

"Where did you find it?"

"A little storefront on Broadway. Your mother used to tell me of walking by and admiring their machines." He took off his glasses and cleaned the lenses with his handkerchief.

The room grew quiet. Noise from the street below filled their silence. Shouts from a newsie selling the evening paper, vendors' wheels cutting loudly into the cobblestones, engines and horns navigating traffic.

"So, a happy birthday, Hennie?" her father asked, standing and replacing his glasses on his nose.

"It is. Thank you."

"You're quite welcome. Now, let the sewing begin," he said and she smiled at him.

"On an empty stomach?" Hensley asked and her father bowed his head.

"Such cruelty you endure. Shame. Shall we go out for dinner, the first of your fifteenth year?"

Hensley stomped her foot again. She liked the way it felt now, like a grown woman imitating her long-gone childhood self. "To Polly's."

He stomped his own foot, mimicking her. "At once."

Since then, Hensley had used the Willcox & Gibbs every day,

at once losing and finding herself in the cutting, measuring, pinning, pulling, constructing of clothes. And how remarkably different their relationship had become, each of them enjoying the other's idiosyncrasies with less judgment.

The night she remembers now, as the train rocks her head back and forth, she wore clothes of her own design, sewn on the Willcox & Gibbs: a black skirt cut close at her hips and flaring in thick pleats around her calves and a linen dress shirt of her father's refashioned into a pin-tucked blouse that hung in a jaunty, uneven hem around her waist. She wrapped herself into one of her mother's wool coats adorned with a tuft of fur she'd removed from a sweater she'd outgrown. She found her umbrella and left her father to his game. He said the same thing he said each time she left the apartment: "Be good, Hennie."

For a man who spent his days searching for specificity, it was a perfectly obtuse instruction. She hardly even heard it anymore. Though she never intended to be anything but.

Standing on the stage, one by one, each girl recited her monologue while the others waited in the cold passageway outside. Under the bright lights, it was nearly impossible to make out the face of the director, but the gossip in the hall was that he was young and handsome. A relative of one of the school's trustees with London stage experience.

When Hensley finished her soliloquy, he said merely, "Well done. I suppose Tennyson is a favorite of every starry-eyed seventeen-year-old girl."

Hensley blushed brightly. "Oh. I'm sorry. Has there been an awful lot of it today?"

The theater was quiet. For a moment she thought he hadn't heard her. Then, with his deep, articulated voice, he said, "Only yours."

The final cast list contained no surprises. Hensley shrugged as she read over the names. Her own disappointment at not seeing her own was lessened almost immediately by the image of Lily Benton dressed as a man, her golden curls slicked back and tucked beneath a top hat. It was a girls' school, after all, and since the play had been penned by one of their own, it was, inevitably, a romance, and the semblance of men would be required.

Despite her fair complexion and slim figure, Hensley would be relegated to being a stagehand, producing the program, or acting as an usher. Her friend Marie, who was soft-spoken and hadn't even wanted to audition for a speaking role, was cast as the disapproving grandmother. She was mortified. "Please come with me. I've got to get out of it. Maybe he'll let us switch places. You're a much better choice anyway."

Hensley acquiesced. And it was then that she was first able to properly assess Lowell Teagan.

He entered the theater wearing a black hat and a beautiful black overcoat, cut slim and flattering for his tall frame. He walked past Hensley and she looked down at her feet, ashamed of the way she wanted to reach out and touch his coat just to feel it. She raised her eyes after he passed, studying his back.

Suddenly he stopped and turned and looked directly at her as though he could read her mind. "Hensley?" he asked and walked back toward her. He lifted his hat off his head. "I hardly recognized you without that dreamy look in your eye."

Hensley felt herself capable of nothing but blushing hotly when he spoke to her. His face was pale and accentuated with straight black eyebrows and a thick crop of black hair. His amber eyes darted energetically about as he spoke, and then they settled, unnervingly, upon her as he spoke the last word of his sentence.

"And Marie, is it? Our dear Granny. What can I do for you girls?"

With a slight nudge from Hensley, Marie asked, politely, if he might assign the Old Granny to Hensley. As she spoke, Hensley watched Lowell's eyes move quickly around the theater and then, when Marie was silent, he looked again at Hensley.

"You want to be the Old Granny?"

Hensley mumbled. "I'm amenable to anything."

"Yes, well, though that is a nice quality for a lapdog, it will not do for an actress. Marie remains our Granny. But you, Hensley, have a talent you did not share at the audition."

Hensley, with newly permanent crimson cheeks, did not reply.

"You sew, I'm told. You will be our costume designer. I will need to consult with you before tomorrow's rehearsal. Come here directly after class. Thank you, ladies," he said and fixed his eyes toward the stage, upon which he leaped moments later, throwing his hat into the empty front row.

She decided she hated him. Anybody who could make her so perpetually flush irked her. Even as she sewed a new velvet band for her hair that night, she fumed at his condescending attitude. She intended to walk into the theater at the appointed time the next afternoon and stonewall him and his larger-than-life ego.

And she had, in fact, stood in the aisle with her hands straight at her sides, her mother's owl brooch pinned to her coat, and told him that if he wanted her talent, she would require total creative control. He must give her final say on all designs. She would not answer to any of the cast, nor to him.

He was sitting with his feet propped up against the row of seats in front of him. He held her gaze and she promised herself, no matter how rude his reply, she would not blush.

He let the noise from the hallway, the afterschool banter, fill the space between them. When he finally spoke, he said only, "Splendid."

Hensley had been prepared to argue, or to turn and walk away without allowing him to have the final word. Instead, she smiled.

"Really?" she said.

His eyes traveled from her face, across her torso, and ever so subtly to the skirt that hung tightly around her hips and fell into a puddle of pleats at the floor. "I'd be a fool to decline," he said finally and, despite her best efforts, she blushed. "You are obviously the most fashionable girl here, or in half of Manhattan, for that matter. Did you make these clothes you're wearing?" he asked, motioning to the full expanse of her body with his long-fingered hand.

Hensley nodded. She felt slightly hollow, as though with that motion of his hand he had rearranged her most essential internal parts, making space, creating turmoil. "Made or adapted," she said quietly, unable to conjure the typical force of her voice. "Sometimes I use my father's shirts or some of my mother's things that are still in the closets."

He seemed to be studying the seams of her blouse and she was afraid he would notice a place where they were not quite perfect. "We will need all the pieces for final alterations at least a week before the first dress rehearsal. This is no small task," he said, returning his gaze to her eyes.

Hensley nodded. “Thank you,” she said. As she turned to walk away, her body strangely weightless, he spoke again.

“You could have played Old Granny, or any other part in this play, for that matter.” He put his feet on the floor and stood, walked directly toward her, and then turned sharply toward the stage, his hand just grazing her shoulder as he passed. “That’s the problem,” he continued, addressing the stage, his voice nearly swallowed by its great expanse. Hensley moved closer, to be sure to hear him. But, without warning, he turned back and was suddenly just inches away from her. “I find it’s never good politics, especially in a school like this, to let the obvious star outshine the rest of the players. At its best, theater is an ensemble. That is the lesson I’m charged with teaching. I hope there are no hurt feelings?” His green eyes, which so often looked gold, were studying her own.

Hensley shook her head. “No. Not at all,” she said and implored her feet to carry her out the door.

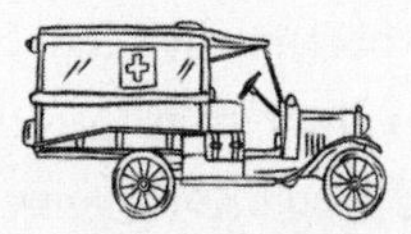

Candles adorn each long table, feigning a kind of elegance in the small mess hall. As it melts, the wax smells of the onions they are stored with in the kitchen. After dinner, Charles smokes and studies the chessboard in his mind, occasionally drawing it on his napkin when he must. At first, he longed for an actual board, one of many everyday items he now cherished in its absence. Like an extra pair of socks, soft bread, books, cold beer, chocolate. But now, he is grateful for the utter concentration required to conjure the entire board in his mind. The day's noise and smoke and brutality are forced into a less prominent place, where they continue to rattle and hum, but do not take over him completely—a respite.

They had been so eager to be assigned to their posts, to be in the thick of it. He grimaces when he thinks of that anticipation of just a month ago. Had they known how life would become a dark, narrow hole in which they would sleep less than they ever thought possible, hardly ever see a horizon without smoke or fire corroding its edges, eat turnips and potatoes that have been boiled into a bitter white mash at nearly every meal, they might have enjoyed even more those empty days that began with overly salted sausage and sweet jam, were filled with long walks across tangled, abandoned vines and beneath thick groves of apple trees, and ended with cognac, a piece of Toblerone, and the BBC on the wireless.

When Charles wrote to his parents, he told them that he and Rogerson, his closest friend there, would both be assigned to Casualty Clearing Station #13 on the western front. Their location probably matters more to his parents than it does to Charles. As far as he can tell, the soldiers who climb over the edge of the trenches at the front, those who he and Rogerson intercept from relay posts and advanced dressing stations and carry into their own resuss or preop tents, don't care what day it is or what country they're in.

The officers at the front wait to hand out the daily post until dusk. Since the nights are usually relatively quiet, each front exhausted and requiring replenishment, whoever has survived the day has the possibility of a letter to read by the light of his own cigarette. In solidarity, the CCS #13 abides by the same schedule.

"Geese are early flying north this year," Rogerson reports as he folds his mother's letter and hands it to Charles. He's left his mother and younger sister on their family's farm, forced to hire itinerant laborers in his absence. His father was French—his mother never questioned his decision to enlist. "She baked an apple cake and took it to the neighbor whose chicks our own hound ate in the night. I say send *us* the damn apple cake."

The next morning on the drive between CCS #13 and the relay post eighteen kilometers closer to the front, Charles and Rogerson take turns guessing the response the Rogersons' neighbor would have had to the conciliatory pie.

"I'd offer you some fresh eggs, but..."

Rogerson guffaws loudly, his eyes scanning the horizon for bombers. "Yeah, thanks. Pie smells great. Can it be scrambled? Poached?"

Charles puts his boot on the dash. He is laughing so hard it hurts. The two of them have quickly, quietly realized how much funnier everything can be if you think you might die within the hour.

They pass a green field yet to be destroyed by mines. There are yellow daffodils and blue-breasted birds sitting along the wooden fence, oblivious to the carnage just kilometers away.

When they reach their destination, there are three soldiers leaning against the brick wall of the ruined house that is the relay post. They each hold a muddied handkerchief across their nose and mouth.

Before they've even stopped the truck, one of the men has his hand on the hood. They are Brits.

"Hey," he says from behind the cloth, his eyes wild with panic. "We pissed on 'em. Will we be fine, then? It was gas. We got caught in the latrine at the reserve trench without our masks. What do we do? I'm bloody thirsty."

Rogerson takes the soldier by the arm and escorts him to the back of the King George. Charles follows his lead and grabs the other two soldiers, their handkerchiefs smelling of piss, even though he knows that this is only a short-term remedy to ease the symptoms. The effects of the chlorine gas will asphyxiate them by morning. Until then, they will occupy three beds in their resuss tent, begging for mercy.

Charles hasn't seen it before, but they were warned at Basic that they should never give them water, nor cut off their clothes without donning their own gas mask. These men will feel that an iron ring has been cinched around their necks and is being slowly tightened, hour after hour, until their last breath.

Charles puts the truck in gear and turns it around. They'll have to return later for the rest of the wounded. As a precaution, Rogerson hands Charles a gas mask from the box between them and attaches one to his own mouth. There is probably enough residual gas in the space between the soldiers' clothes and their bodies to kill another man.

Charles affixes the mask and breathes deeply, biting on the valve. It smells of hot plastic and gym socks.

Rogerson turns around in order to address the boys sitting side by side on the floor between the racks of stretchers. He pulls his mask aside for a moment and speaks loudly. "You're gonna be fine. We've got the best docs back at Number Thirteen. You'll see. First-rate French doctors."

Charles cannot see their faces, but he hears one of their panicked voices reply, "I feel like I can't breathe. I can't bloody breathe."

Charles nods. "Yes, you can, brother. Just relax. It's important to be calm. Your lungs are muscles, too. You don't want to strain them. So just take it easy. Nice and slow."

This seems to satiate them for a while. The truck is silent save for their occasional coughing. The ground rumbles behind them, the shrieks of incoming shells wailing in the distance.

Just as they are passing the same wooden fence with the daffodils and the birds, one of the soldiers says, from behind his kerchief, "At last we're not back there getting hammered. Probably a lucky break, this gas. You heard him. They got good docs, they do."

Rogerson bangs his fist hard against the dash and Charles swerves slightly, nearly sideswiping the fence. The birds lift, en masse, in front of the truck, their wings flapping a sharp rebuke to this disturbance.

"Fucking bastards," Rogerson says, glaring out at the road ahead of them.

Charles concentrates on driving. He suddenly wishes that he hadn't followed Rogerson's lead and loaded these soldiers into the truck without even examining the others at the relay post. Their own triage skills are limited. But if he hopes to be any good here at all, he cannot be sentimental. Practicality must overwhelm any sense of emotion. There may have been boys there that could be saved. And they've just driven off, leaving them to suffer through another attack before being evacuated.

When Charles pulls the truck in front of resuss, Dr. Foulsom is standing outside, smoking. He approaches the vehicle, his arms outstretched, ready to assess their patients. "What have you?"

"Hey, Doc, stand back," Charles says, pulling his mask away from his face as he puts his boots in the dirt. "We've got gassed boys. I'll remove their clothes, get 'em gowns. Give 'em a bed in resuss?"

Dr. Foulsom throws his cigarette into the dirt. "*Merde*, Reid. Why are you bringing them to us? We cannot do a thing for them. Not even morphine. *Rien.* We're running too low. Leave them at the front where their *amis* can help them die. Take them back and bring me the bleeding. *Ils meurent.*"

From beneath his gas mask, Rogerson spits in the dirt. "What kind of a doctor are you?" he begins, but Charles, who is standing behind Rogerson, his foot resting on the truck's tire, interrupts. "Sir," Charles begins, but Rogerson claps his thick hand against Charles's shoulder.

"Why don't you just take your pistol and shoot them?" he says, pulling off his gas mask and throwing it to the ground, recklessly close to Foulsom. "That's about what you've done. Leave 'em at the front? Our job is to clear out the wounded."

"No, Rogerson," Foulsom says, pushing the gas mask away from him with his boot. "Your job is to evacuate those who have the best chance to survive. These boys have no chance. Quite honestly, a bullet would be a mercy to them."

By now the three boys have climbed out of the back of the ambulance and, their mouths still covered by their kerchiefs, they stand, listening.

"What about the docs? The best, you said," one of them—the red-headed one with a copious amount of freckles—says, without recognizing Foulsom's status. Dressed in army-issued pants and a graying T-shirt, Foulsom looks like some private just out of the latrine. The docs are hardly ever in uniform. Too much blood.

The redhead begins coughing, a short, wet little sound that is not alarming except for the way his eyes bulge, panicked.

Charles lays his hand on the boy's shoulder, while his friends look frantically from Rogerson to Foulsom.

A sister walking from the supply tent, her arms full of bandages, hesitates near Foulsom. Quietly, she says something in French to him before disappearing into resuss.

Momentarily, she returns with three pairs of salvaged trousers folded neatly in her arms. She hands them to Charles in silence.

"Get them changed," Foulsom says, before he grinds the cigarette butt into the dirt beneath his boot. Then he turns and crosses the small yard connecting the group of medical tents.

The resuss tent has six beds, all of them fitted with heaters and transfusion packs. It's where they attempt to stabilize the most severely wounded for surgery. For the next twelve hours, however, it is where the gassed boys lie, their skin ever paler and their coughs producing pieces of their own burned lungs in small clumps of charred red tissue that the sisters pluck from their bedsheets and carry away in their small, gloved hands.

At noon, the train stops in El Paso, where Hensley and her father, along with a dozen other passengers, disembark. It has been nearly a week on the train. The sun shines directly onto the platform, turning its concrete a bright and blinding white. Hensley pulls the brim of her hat down, shading her eyes. Their journey is not over, but they will travel the next two hundred miles by automobile. Hensley stands still, grateful for the cessation of movement, the solid ground beneath her feet. She never thought it would end, the churning, chugging, aching motion of the train. As she stands there, she is similarly amazed by the way the air is so hot and dry, unlike anything she's ever felt before. Her skin seems to contract and shrink around her jawbone and her knuckles. Hensley leaves her father on the platform with the porter, who is transferring all of their belongings to a trolley, while she goes inside to find the restroom. The station is brand-new and reassuring. It is surprisingly cool. Hensley likes the way her feet sound as they smack the stone floor.

The bathroom is large, with three sinks, three divided toilets, and pretty blue tile on the walls. As Hensley enters, a young girl emerges from one of the toilets, her black hair like a blanket over her head. Her skin is the color of their mahogany dining table, which they left in New York. Her face, too, is as smooth and expressionless as the wood. She is dressed in brown jodhpurs, like the boys wear in New York, and leather ankle boots and a tan jacket. Hensley forces a smile, but the girl bundles her hair beneath a large straw hat, turns her eyes to the floor, and leaves without a word.

Hensley does her business, wipes her face with a towel, studies it for changes. Shouldn't she already be a different person, in such a strange and faraway place? But the same pallor and blue eyes stare back at her in the glass.

When she finds her father in the station, he is in animated conversation with the girl from the bathroom. The girl with skin like dark wood.

"Hensley," he says, extending his arm. "This is Humberto Romero. He works for the mine. He's going to drive us to Hillsboro."

Hensley frowns. "Humberto?" she says. "But..."

His eyes harden. There is no acknowledgment that they were in the same women's restroom moments earlier. Hensley turns her head to see the door, to make certain she hadn't accidentally been in the men's bathroom. Perhaps she is confused. Perhaps this dry heat has affected her eyesight.

Humberto reaches out his hand and shakes hers, gripping it harder than necessary. "Welcome."

Hensley looks closely at this face, its eyebrows gracefully arched, its lips smooth and full. Humberto could easily be a girl of profound beauty, but his eyes are so dark and fierce and her grip so strong that Hensley says only, "Thank you," and follows her father and Humberto to the truck parked in the lot behind the station.

* * *

They sit in a row on the bench seat, her father sandwiched between them. Humberto handles the truck confidently on the paved roads of El Paso and soon enough they are traveling a well-groomed dirt road, supposedly headed northwest. Her father doesn't say much, but he leans forward, his hands on his knees, as though in a theater, afraid to miss a single line of dialogue.

"This is New Mexico," Humberto says eventually, lifting a hand from the wheel and motioning to the land in front of them, though there is no obvious change in the scenery.

Her father echoes Humberto's words, in case Hensley has not heard. "New Mexico," he says, gesturing out Hensley's window.

"Got it." Hensley inventories the terrain: scrub, scrub, rock, tree, dirt, scrub. She wonders how anyone could ever locate herself in such a never-ending, wide-open landscape. There is no uptown, downtown; no east river, west river. No storefronts or street signs. No people. Not a single, wretched person is on the road with them. She sees a rabbit in the scant shade of a scraggly bush, watching their truck pass. Her face brightens. There are squirrels in Central Park and rats in the subway tunnels, but she's never seen a rabbit—the way its front paws hang in front of its chest in prayer. The constantly twitching nose. The oversized teeth and ears.

"Rabbit," Hensley says, pointing out the window.

Humberto laughs a high-pitched giggle. "What? Never seen one?"

Hensley looks at her father. Surely, he, too, can hear this girlish laughter.

He only smiles and says, "Rabbits are not the main inhabitants of Manhattan, I'm afraid. The wildlife there is mainly pickpockets and politicians."

Hensley looks back at the small creature under the bush. She finds herself composing a letter to it: *Dear Little Rabbit under the Bush, You are not as dull as they think you are. You are the first living thing in New Mexico to make me smile. Aptly grateful, Hensley Dench.*

She looks at Humberto's slender brown hands holding onto the steering wheel. Hensley would like to announce that she's just composed a letter to the rabbit under the bush. That she already cares more for that rabbit than she does for anyone else she's met in this vast, dry place. Especially more than she cares for that pretty girl with the long shiny hair in the ladies' restroom in the El Paso train station. The girl who wouldn't smile at Hensley. The same girl who Hensley is sure just laughed at her for noticing a plain brown rabbit along the side of the road.

If she had the courage, Hensley would sabotage this fool's errand; return to New York and let New Mexico remain a faraway, irrelevant place. Go back to the city that was her home. Tell her father to write whatever the *Times* said he had to write. The war will go on, whether or not Sacha Dench approves. Whether or not newspapers take their orders from the Committee on Public Information.

She looks at her father's eager face, the wrinkles around his eyes speckled with dirt. What would her mother think of their exodus? Hensley closes her eyes, an ache in the back of her throat. The agony of this loss courts her, showing up just often enough so that she does not forget. Her mother's face is suddenly so close she can touch it, but then it is gone and Hensley has a glimpse of her father's heartbreak. The awful train that has carried them away from New York, like the black death that carried her mother away. Leaving them in an unknown, empty place where nothing makes sense and neither of them feel whole.

Back in the heat of July last year, there had been a series of explosions in the middle of the night when the artillery factory on Black Tom Island blew up. Her father had roused her from her bed, leading her into the street with the other neighbors, where they stood shoulder to shoulder, watching the skyline burst and burn. Later, investigators discovered that the fire was set by German saboteurs, but at the time, her father was hopeful that such a display of violence, whatever its cause, would be a warning to Americans that entering the war would be a grave mistake. A few children in their mothers' arms started to cry, but were soon distracted by the exhilaration of being in the middle of the street in the middle of the night and began games of chase while the adults carried on rowdy conversations amid the fireworks. Nobody knew what had happened, but the blasts soon grew louder and a window shattered on Broadway and this ended the strange block party as people hurried inside, afraid of what might happen next.

Her father stayed up nearly all night writing a preemptive editorial, trying to turn this brilliant spectacle into a symbol of the destruction that American artillery would cause overseas. He hoped the event would quell the nation's warmongers, whose voices were growing louder each day. Hensley had curled up on the couch near his desk, shivering beneath a blanket, though the midsummer heat was palpable all night. She dozed on and off, listening to the scratch of his pen against paper. Finally, as the room ever so slightly brightened, he'd noticed her crumpled figure.

"Hennie?" he said, placing a warm hand against her brow. "You must get some sleep, child. I thought you'd gone to bed."

"Daddy," she said from a place between wakefulness and sleep, "why must you work so much?"

He stood above her, his hands deep in his pockets. He walked away from her, toward the fireplace. Then he turned and, as though speaking to a room full of colleagues, said, "The disagreements between rich and powerful men should remain just that. But an entire generation of young men is bearing the burden of royal tempers and old grudges. It is immorality of the worst kind. Those with plenty turning their countries into slaughterhouses for the sake of what, I ask?"

"Is that what you've written?" Hensley asked, sitting up.

"Partly. I won't bore you with the rest. But it is the only thing I can do. That is why I do it. I must. It is not a choice. It just is."

Hensley watched his face, the corners of his mouth twitching with emotion.

"But if our participation would quicken the end..." she began, echoing what she'd heard from classmates and teachers.

He turned away from her and pounded the mantel, making the mirror beside it tremble. "Where is the absolutism of religion now? Morality is not negotiable, Hensley. Unleashing a war machine in order to end a war? An absurd Olympics of semantic excuses. Ludicrous."

Hensley threw the blanket off. "Meanwhile, the slaughter continues," she said, "while we stand on our very firm moral ground."

Had she known that less than a year later she would be lost in her own sea of moral ambiguity, she might have paid closer attention to her father's certainty. Wrong is wrong.

Because the first time that Lowell Teagan met her at the theater to look at her sketches and placed his hand on the curve of her waist to inquire about the placement of a seam, she knew it was wrong. They were not family and they were not betrothed. But even more than that, his touch was not demonstrative or inquisitive. It was authoritative. He was begging her to question his authority, to doubt his own morality, but she did not. Instead, she took his hand in her own and placed it slightly lower, just where her hip bone flowered, and correctly showed him where the pleat would begin. In this way, she became a living mannequin they each manipulated, displaying the way a fabric would drape or taper on her own figure.

The other girls might have been jealous of this time he spent with her, backstage, placing his own pencil marks on her paper and plying a straight pin from her mouth, his fingers grazing her lips, lingering slightly on her delicate chin, because nearly every girl in the play had developed a wild crush. But he saw the players every day for rehearsals, his attention captivated by each of the girl's efforts to become her character, to inhabit the skin of a wholly imagined person. His entreaties both terrified and thrilled them. "Nobody wants to see *you* onstage, Miss Coe. How disappointing. You must *become* Mr. Johnstone completely. Dispose of all your boring, girlish teenage gestures. I do not want to see you place your hands on your hips while you are on that stage. Get inside Mr. Johnstone. This is your chance, don't you see? You are allowed to step inside of him, feel his skin, taste his food, *move* his body. There are not many opportunities in life for that kind of intimacy."

All the girls hung on his words, longed for his gaze, shrank from his questions. But none of them had felt the weight of his hand on her hip nor the heat of his exhale on her neck, except Hensley. For this she was both ashamed and elated. In the wake of her father's moral absolutism, she was utterly confused.

The first time he kissed her, it seemed like a foregone conclusion. As though, perhaps, they were both just occupying the same space and their lips had no choice but to touch. It was merely an extension of their work together. He did not place his hands on her, nor try to extend the contact. He simply smiled, which was rare, exposing his one physical flaw—undersized teeth. They appeared shrunken, immature, as though he were still waiting for his adult teeth to arrive. Hensley swallowed hard, trying to decipher the tingling that had begun in her lips but was now traveling across her chest. Was it fear or longing?

Before she left the theater that night, he placed a hand on her elbow and said only, "Your talent takes my breath away, Hensley. It is difficult for me to contain my admiration. Please forgive me."

Hensley merely blushed and let him slide her coat onto her shoulders.

Walking home with Marie, she smiled the whole way. "What, you, too?" Marie asked as they crossed Broadway.

"What?"

"You've gone 'round the moon for him, too? We're such a bunch of sillies. Of course, since I've *become* Old Granny, he's not that keen on me."

Hensley laughed but she wondered about the other girls. They did all adore him. He was undeniably the most interesting man she'd ever met. Of course, she hadn't met many men except her brother's Columbia chums, who were the epitome of dull. But she thought of Sara Coe and Lily Benton, with their perfect, shiny hair and melodious voices. It was she, not they, whom he had kissed. It was she, not they, whom he found irresistible. She didn't dare tell Marie that Mr. Teagan had kissed her. But she wondered, as Marie walked beside her in the fading spring daylight, if that kiss would be the beginning of their love story.

As she and Marie parted ways and she turned onto her block, her lighthearted mood shifted. A newsie called out the headline, "Wilson to ask Congress to declare war!" She could see from the street below that the light in the apartment was lit. Her father would be writing, the sound of his ink stretched across an unending stack of paper.

"Daddy," Hensley said as she took off her hat. He was not writing. He was sitting on the sofa, his spectacles in his hands. She sat beside him and leaned her head against his shoulder. "I saw the headline."

Her father placed his hand on hers. "I remain appalled but hardly surprised. It's been a long time coming."

"But aren't you going to keep writing? I mean, surely you can't just give up. You have to speak your mind."

He smiled, then wiped at his eyes, which looked tired. He looked at her anew, as though he hadn't done so in years. "You are turning into a lady. Right here before my eyes. How are the costumes coming?"

"Fine, just fine. I met with the director tonight. Lowell Teagan. He really likes my ideas. I've a veritable closet of clothes to sew, however."

Her father nodded. "Of course. Splendid."

"Daddy? Maybe we should go out for dinner. A little distraction this evening might be nice."

He shook his head. "I've had a slight setback at the paper, Hensley. I've been taken off editorial completely. They are putting a noose around my neck. Just about the only thing I can write about is the weather. And the worst part is that they assume it has something to do with my heritage."

"That you sympathize with Germany?"

He stood. "Well, I do. I sympathize with the whole world. But I believe in peace, Hensley. Not one country or another."

"Well, just tell them," Hensley said.

"I've written nearly ten thousand words this month alone, Hensley. They are not listening. Nobody is."

At that moment, Hensley wanted more than ever to be back in the theater, behind the dusty red curtain, with the scents of chalk and wood polish and Mr. Teagan's hands manipulating her body with utter confidence.

"Well, I don't know, Daddy. I suppose you'll have to write about the weather, then."

His face conveyed the kind of darkening that a rain cloud does to a blue summer sky. "Like bloody hell I will," he said. "In fact, the idea of writing about absolutely anything else is rubbish. I'd rather dig ditches than pretend this doesn't matter—that every ounce of ink in New York shouldn't be spent on it."

"You would tell me, if I happened to be the one speaking in such hyperbole, that dramatics are not a sound debate tool."

Her father started to speak and then did not. He replaced his glasses and looked back at the papers on his desk. He nodded. "There is no turning back. Wilson will get his vote and our boys will be sent away before summer."

"Harold?" Hensley said, thinking of her brother, the freckles that stretched across his cheeks and rimmed the tops of his ears.

Her father shrugged. "Perhaps."

Hensley reached into her sleeve for a handkerchief she'd tucked there and wiped her eyes. Her father glanced at her gesture and then looked away. "If not your brother, somebody else's brother. They do not recruit soldiers from some reserve of the unloved and unattached."

In her mind, Hensley imagined an emporium, like the large fabric store she liked to browse on Forty-second Street, filled entirely with lonely, solitary men holding their lunch pails, waiting to be given a uniform and a weapon.

"I don't want Harold to go."

"That will be up to him, Hensley. Or the Congress."

"Well, you'll have to tell him he can't."

"Your brother has never taken my instruction well, Hennie."

"And what about us? What will you do?"

"I am looking into other ventures. Your mother's cousin, Thomas Wright, has asked me to look after a mining interest of his."

Hensley didn't hear anything more he said. Would Mr. Teagan sign up? she wondered. Would his long fingers and piercing eyes soon be in France or Belgium? Would every good and strong boy be sleeping in the trenches far, far away?

"I'd better get to work," she said, standing and holding her sketches close to her chest. "I'm sorry, Daddy. About Wilson and the paper and all of it."

He nodded but was already sitting at his desk again, dipping his pen into the inkwell.

Hensley stood in her room in front of the glass, examining herself. She liked the way her bosom looked in the tunic and the way her newly bobbed hair just skimmed her jawbone. Her nose was too long and her eyes a little too wide, but altogether, she thought she was a striking girl, whose refinement was underappreciated by boys her own age, who only thought about whiskey and sports. She looked closely at her lips, startled that they'd been so recently touched by Mr. Teagan's. But she also decided, as she moved her own finger across their soft expanse, that there was no better use for them. There in front of her own reflection, she became grateful for his audacity, enamored of his disregard for politesse, and terrified that he would be lost to the war.

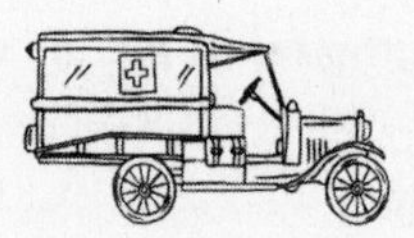

When Charles's post is handed to him, the envelope from Mr. Dench is markedly different. Drawn on the back of this envelope is a small green tree with a little owl peering out of its branches. In a speech bubble, it says, "Hoot." This is unlike anything Mr. Dench has ever done before. Charles wonders momentarily if the censors have added it. But it is too whimsical and delightful for that. Slowly, he pulls at the paper, careful to preserve the strange little drawing.

In the margins of Mr. Dench's reply, there are faint scribbles in a hand he does not recognize. For some reason, this small act of mystery sends a jolt of life down Charles's spine. It is unexpected, refreshing, wholly strange. It jars him from his hardened, protective armor of practicality.

Mr. Dench's daughter has pirated his reply and placed her own mark upon it. Her ink across the thin onionskin paper seems to wink at him with its audacity. Quickly, before Rogerson has finished reading his own dispatch from his mother, Charles shoves the letter into his jacket pocket. He is afraid, already, of discovering that it's a mirage—something the monotony of war has constructed in his mind. But he knows his own mind. This could not be his own invention. It is outside his idea of what is possible.

Usually, the two of them share all correspondence. It is one of the small rituals they've settled upon without speaking of it. But this night, Charles doesn't take the letter from Rogerson. "Keep it, man. I've got nothing. Mr. Dench botched it. Sent an empty envelope."

Rogerson looks at him hard. He and his mother and sister live on a vast farm in Minnesota along the Canadian border. Their isolation has bred an instinctual skepticism. "You two having a love affair?" He punches him gently on the shoulder. "I saw you reading something, chap. Hand it over."

Charles shakes his head. He makes no move to retrieve the letter from his jacket. He wants to study it on his own, to read again the delicately curved, feminine lettering.

"Come on, Reid. Even better if he's declaring his love for you. It's almost like being in the theater. High drama." Rogerson pulls at Charles's jacket.

Charles swats his hand away. "It's not like that. It's just . . . I need to read it again myself. You know, figure out my next move. I don't want the bastard to win this one."

Rogerson pulls a cigarette from his own jacket. He lights it and blows the smoke toward Charles's face. "I got moves, too. We can figure it out together."

Charles shakes his head and fiddles with the salt and pepper. Rogerson places his lit cigarette on the table in front of him. Charles knows what might be next, but he keeps his eyes on the small black char Rogerson's cigarette is burning into the tabletop.

Rogerson wraps his strong hand around Charles's wrist and, in one motion, sweeps it around to the middle of Charles's back. A hot ache is born in his shoulder and a shard of pain travels all the way down his back into his hips. With his free hand, he pulls his jacket together. Their struggle is a simple test of strength, and they both know what the outcome will be. Rogerson pulls hard against Charles's grip, and an army green button from his jacket flies across the table, landing soundlessly on the straw-covered ground. Rogerson shoves his hand inside Charles's coat, while Charles tries to grasp his jaw the way Rogerson gripped him back in May-en-Multien. His hand is no match for Rogerson's wide, square jaw, though. As his fingers dig into the sharp bristles of his whiskers, they merely pucker Rogerson's mouth into an ugly, wet pouch. Rogerson easily pulls the envelope out of the place close to Charles's chest, its sweet little drawing still preserved just below the open slit.

Rogerson releases Charles's arm from his grip and pushes his hand away from his face, wiping his drool across his sleeve. Charles is defeated and chagrined. Rogerson retrieves his cigarette, inhaling deeply as he studies the owl.

His eyebrows rise. "I was kidding, chap. But has he actually fallen in love with you? Dim the lights. This is getting good."

Charles massages his shoulder as he watches Rogerson take in the letter. His cigarette has burned down to the filter and is still a small orange stub between his yellowed fingers.

Finally, he speaks, quietly. "She's lovely, chap. I can almost see her, hear her voice. A pixie of a thing, eh? Probably blond, with smart clothes and a musical laugh." His face is relaxed, transported, as Charles has never seen it before. There is a silence as he refolds the letter and gently slides it toward Charles. Charles does not disagree. He replaces the letter in his jacket pocket.

The cigarette butt sizzles as Rogerson flicks it into his cup of water. "Not my type," he says abruptly and excuses himself. Then, pausing momentarily in front of the door, he turns and the fierceness has returned to his face. "I like 'em big and hairy and illiterate," he says, before pushing open the door and letting it slam hard behind him.

Through the night, as he does every night, Charles smokes. He lies on his cot, reading the letter over and over until he has memorized all of her lines. Even when he's folded the letter and placed it on his chest, hoping for sleep, he recites her words, seeing in his mind the way they look on the page. He imagines her hand, her fingers, the same black ink here on this paper perhaps staining her fingertips. He tries to imagine the rest of her; he wonders what it is she's done to label herself *deviant.*

He's spent the last six hours wishing for silence but now that it's come, he does not feel the relief he thought he would. The latest crop of gassed boys—their continued violation of protocol—have died, each having had the chance to dictate letters home through one of the merciful, fearless nuns. This bit, an opportunity for a last word, is why they continue to defy Foulsom. Charles has made a ritual of standing in the doorway after dinner, listening, as a tow-headed soldier, between coughs, entreats his younger brother to take care of their mother, to keep his hands off his girl, and to think of him when he can.

As always, as punishment, Foulsom will see to it that it is he and Rogerson who drive the boys' bodies up to Base Hospital #8 at dawn, where there is a morgue and crematorium. Charles can't help but remember the way the first boys stood outside the relay post, their handkerchiefs held to their faces as if in response to a spring allergy. But, without their knowledge, their bodies had already begun decomposing; their lungs were already stinging from the burn of chlorine gas. There was nothing to be done. They watched their own deaths, feeling the clots of burned tissue against their tongues, gasping for an ever-diminishing supply of breaths. Now Charles wonders at the matter-of-fact nature of all this horror. As he lies here, listening to the quiet, imagining the weight of the body bags that he will lift come morning, he notices that panic no longer hovers around him. The boys' flesh is now worthless, just waste to dispose of. A job to do. A part of what must be done. The thin line between living and dying that seems to be fading more quickly each day.

He cannot stand the quiet any longer. He pulls on his pants and walks out, past the medical tents and into the field behind them. There is a long-abandoned barn, its charming shape lost in the darkness, but its white gables like the dim, slow arcs of shooting stars. The letter is still in his hand and he places it against his chest and runs hard and fast into the night so that the paper holds there, stuck to him by the force of air. He runs until his lungs burn and his legs ache. Then he falls onto the cool dirt, looking up at the stars. The perspiration on his chest has glued the letter to him.

He watches his chest heave, working to keep him alive. The sound of his breath is like a secret code, revealing the meaning of his survival. But it remains undecipherable to his ears. He imagines those hands, those words. They are now his own. *What you must do is believe with all your heart that you can come home and when you do, all the horror that surrounds you now will recede into a past that you can leave behind as simply as a train leaves a depot.* He wishes she were here beside him, listening to his breath, because for some reason, he is sure that she would be able to decipher this code. He is sure that she could place her hands upon him and tell him something true. But this is yet another fantasy. He is getting so good at living without. Beneath him, the dirt has dried in hard crags after the most recent rain and it digs into his shoulder blades. He sits up.

Walking back to his tent, he folds the slightly damp letter and holds it between his fingers, letting it swing and crinkle in the midnight breeze. These letters from Mr. Dench are never short on political commentary. Charles suspects that for Mr. Dench, winning the chess game would be tantamount to winning the argument about the war. He is a hell of a chess player, and a thinker, and the challenge of beating him just once has kept Charles's interest. But Charles cares less about beating him now than he did. All theoretical arguments about the war are laughable. To be here is to know that the only one who's right is the one who wins. He cannot prove to anyone the correctness of his choice to join this bloody war. He no longer cares if it was right or wrong. He does care, however, about cultivating another missive from Mr. Dench's enigmatic daughter.

The other letters that have arrived for him now matter very little, including those from his mother, who writes weekly, dutifully describing her appointments, the weather, and the week's menu. Her anxiety is palpable and unwelcome. She alludes to his father's hope that, if nothing else, this "stint" will rid Charles of his medical aspirations. She marvels at the number of girls who have cut their hair short and recounts the dreary task of choosing a new fabric for the furniture beside the pool in the country. At least she supplies endless fodder for the banter he and Rogerson engage in during their runs. Even his correspondence with a couple of friends from college, an uncle in San Francisco, and a girl he once courted in Boston have lost their appeal.

The only images he wants in his mind are the chessboard; the room in which it exists; and the girl who sits watching it. Who is she? Where does she sit while her father writes to him? What do her hands look like? Does she touch the pieces on the board, tempted to rearrange them just as she's rearranged his thoughts?

Charles returns to camp no longer intent on playing a perfect game of chess. His next move suddenly matters very little. Mr. Dench has brought out his king's knight to intimidate him. Charles will still take the king's pawn. He will not spend any more time trying to forecast Mr. Dench's next three moves. He will only imagine the way the white pawn might look in that room, removed from the board and cast aside, perhaps just beside his own letter. And he will imagine that if nothing else, it might elicit more marginalia from Mr. Dench's daughter. In fact, if Mr. Dench's next letter arrives without any trace of her, it will be worse than a bad trouncing.

He cannot inquire directly about Mr. Dench's daughter, as this may jeopardize their continued correspondence. Instead, he will simply ask about their new address. Or perhaps he will hope she's as astute as she seems and understand a hidden message. Perhaps he will wonder if the species of owl in New Mexico is as interesting as he's heard. *I've always admired the daring and wisdom of those birds, their round, echoing hoots making even the darkest night less lonely.*

To the south, Hensley sees cascading gradations of brown that stretch to the far-off horizon. To the north, a distant mountain range stands blue and solemn.

"There she is."

"Two weeks I've been here," Hensley says, wiping the sweat from the back of her neck with her father's handkerchief. "And I still don't see anything but brown."

Berto laughs with the high feminine cadence that Hensley cannot believe her father hasn't yet noticed.

"The mine, Hennie," her father had said to her when Berto first pointed out the scar in the land. "The Ready Pay."

They'd been riding for hours when suddenly Berto had brought the truck to a stop right where the drop-offs on either side seemed the steepest. Now she is on horseback, and the drop seems even less forgiving.

"That's the mine? The one that's going to save us?"

Her father had stiffened his back. "Salvation, Hennie? What a quaint concept—one I thought I'd succeeded in educating out of you."

The mere memory of it makes Hensley's forehead burn from

the hot prickles of her father's reproach. Now, fingering the braided leather of the reins, she stares at her own hands, still pale and gaunt, folded in her lap like two dead swans. *This is just the way my hands looked in New York,* she tells herself. *I could be sitting in a subway car or in a taxicab. On my way to a luncheon or an afternoon in the park.* She concentrates only on keeping her hands utterly still, as though their inaction can disguise her distress.

Her mind floods with this small task and, still, a tear escapes and falls onto her skirt. This drop, this nothing, this small bit of herself becomes a dark circle on the fabric. An imprint of her present self in this place she can't comprehend.

Certainly Harold has given her no reason to expect that this pacifist demonstration of their father's is reasonable. But she also knows he is not objective. With two years of law school completed, he serves as a lawyer in an office at the Naval Yard in Brooklyn, helping to write the legal justifications for the war their father deems unjust. This has left relations chilly between the elder and younger Mr. Dench.

The day before they left, Harold came to the apartment in his uniform while she was packing flatware into boxes. Hensley clung to him, immediately ashamed of her tears, surprised by her own emotion. Her father had sprung the news on her just the night before, giving her only two days to prepare for their departure.

"Oh, Harry," she said, wiping at her face.

"He's crazy," her brother said, offering her his handkerchief.

Hensley stepped away, shaking her head. "They fired him."

"He knew they would."

"That doesn't make it right."

"Don't be a simpleton. We're at war, Hen. He's reckless."

Hensley couldn't help smiling. "Daddy?"

"Doesn't New Mexico sound a little reckless to you, Hen? What the hell does he expect you to do? Marry a miner, pan for gold in the dirt?"

"Good God, Harold, it's just for the summer. We'll be back and I'll go to Wellesley in the fall." She wished she could confide in him, confess her confusion, her own anguish about Mr. Teagan, but she didn't.

"Is that what he's told you?"

"Why not?" She turned her back on him, resuming her chore.

"You think the *Times* will rehire a German American pacifist in three months' time? The war will only get hotter, Hennie. If you go, you should be prepared to stay." Harold put his hand on hers. She pulled it away.

She couldn't bear his self-righteousness anymore. "Fine. Then stay I will. There. Happy? You are always right about everything from the very beginning, Harry. The rest of us must do a bit of floundering."

Now, over four weeks later, she lifts her eyes from her lap as she hears Berto call back to her.

"Shall we go on?" he says from ahead. They are both sitting astride their horses, Hensley having declined a sidesaddle out of some attempt to garner a confession. "I won't use one if you don't," she said to Berto as he stood in front of the pen, a sidesaddle over his arm.

He raised his eyebrows, without a trace of guilt or recognition. "Huh. So you are a suffragette?"

"Of course. Aren't you?"

"I am a Mexican."

"Yes, but don't you think women should have the right to vote? All women, everywhere?"

"I'm tired of fighting for anything."

So they both saddled up and luckily Hensley was wearing a skirt she'd made upon their arrival: loose, pale gray linen with a longer hem than usual, because she'd abandoned her heels in favor of daytime boots, and a matching jacket that she draped across the back of her saddle an hour ago. Straddling this saddle would have been impossible in a hobble skirt and heels. Really, fashion in Hillsboro is somewhat of an oxymoron.

Their horses clop forward and Berto lifts his hat ever so slightly to cool his forehead. Hensley sees the thicket of black hair that's been dragged up from the nape of his neck and hidden away. This secret, like her own, sends a jolt of danger up the back of Hensley's spine.

As the large brown horse named Thunder shifts beneath her, Hensley wonders if she will ever have a post from Lowell. Has he already forgotten her? Or has the dialogue of some new play taken residence in his head and supplanted her entirely?

Two hawks circle high above, and then, with sudden, startling velocity, they dive. She and Berto both pull on their reins, searching the ground for the birds' prey. Each hawk gently touches a mound of rocks, one on either side of them, and pulls away with a lizard dangling from its talons.

"That's amazing," Hensley says, impressed by the efficiency of their hunt.

"Redtails are good hunters. In Mexico, I saw one grab a puppy."

Hensley gasps. "How awful. I never want to see that."

"I've seen worse," he says, nudging the heels of his boots into the horse's side. "You think you could manage the ride home by yourself? I've got an errand."

How? she wonders. And where is home and how to get there? How to undo this terrible journey, to follow the faint line of their migration all the way back to New York. Is it possible? Or has her past vanished? Is there nothing behind her but a black hole?

Of course she knows that Berto means the "home" that her father claimed as theirs in the superintendent's house they moved into when they arrived. Home; a new beginning; a revolutionary new life, he said. There are snakes and hawks and, for all she knows, Pancho Villa lurking somewhere nearby, but sitting astride Thunder in her white cotton shirt, she feels nearly revolutionary herself. Is this what it takes? she asks herself. Is it the kind of hopelessness she feels that incubates insurrection?

Berto brings his horse back toward her. "It's okay? Here, you should take my pistol."

Hensley shakes her head. "I've never even held a gun. I'll be fine. It's not far. Thank you."

Berto shrugs and then repositions the gun in his holster. "Suit yourself," he says, touching his hat before he gallops away. The dust in his wake seems to hang in the dry air, settling slowly back onto the road that looks more like a dried-up riverbed than a way home. Pressing her heels into Thunder's ribs, she lets the horse navigate the terrain as she traverses the memory of her last week in New York.

As opening night approached, Hensley attended all the rehearsals, grabbing girls when they were offstage for a quick fitting or adjustment. When the other girls left, exhausted from standing under the hot lights for hours, with homework awaiting, Hensley lingered, taking time to pin each costume with her notes, folding the garments carefully to fit into her satchel.

Then, as had become their routine, Mr. Teagan fixed her a cup of sweet, milky coffee he'd brewed in the kettle in the teachers' lounge. They would sit in the red velvet house seats discussing his frustrations with the blocking, or the idea for her English thesis paper, or his family's summer house in Maine and how he'd love to show her the shoreline there, eat crabs from the stalls near the dock, and ride bikes to a perfect picnic spot beneath a summer moon. The way he spoke, it was as though their lives were already entwined. He would sometimes reach for her hand and bring it to his lips, holding it gently as his breath warmed her. Letting her fingers feel the power of his words, he'd recite a line from Tennyson. "'All the inner, all the outer world of pain, / Clear Love would pierce and cleave, if thou wert mine...'"

He placed one hand upon her ankle, letting its heat settle into her. Then, as though tracing an unknown path, he pulled his fingers ever northward, lingering on the back of her knee, its pale, hidden crease. He laid his hand with a gentle force upon her groin, sliding the linen of her undergarment against her. Hensley felt struck, paralyzed, as she looked up at the rafters, the ropes connected to the curtain, and the backdrops hanging so far above. As though she had become a spectator of this play, an observer who simultaneously longed for the girl below to rebuke him and hoped she didn't. She doubted everything but the truth of the performance; like the best theater, she forgot that it was all orchestrated, arranged. She believed his performance, his certainty that she could relieve his suffering with just one look, could assuage his temper if only he had her lips upon his, could look forward without despair if he knew she were his. And his voice, as he seemed to unfold her, admiring each piece of her as he did, was utterly irresistible.

As she walked home alone, the sun just setting over the Hudson, she reassured herself that nothing had been lost. He would not, he assured her, ruin her. He knew how to protect her, how to keep her pure. When he bid her good-bye, the headmistress watching over them as they exited the school building, he merely shook her gloved hand as though there was absolutely nothing between them. Was this, she wondered, the secret of adult life? Was coupling not a sacred mystery at all, but rather tucked into nearly every corner, as ordinary as a cigarette case or bus fare?

When she entered the apartment, her father was stretched out on the couch, his fingers drumming gently upon his chest.

"Good rehearsal?" he asked quietly.

She dropped her satchel and removed her hat and gloves. "Hectic," she replied, blushing, afraid the desire had not yet faded from her eyes. "But Mr. Teagan is utterly brilliant. It will all come off."

Her father sat up. "Do you have someone to talk to, Hensley?"

"What do you mean?"

"About your life. About what is happening in your life? I'm not much good at girl talk. Your mother would want you to have that."

Hensley felt perspiration forming around her hairline. What could he possibly know? She removed her coat. "Nothing's happening. Why would you say such a thing?"

"I am not accusing you of anything, my dear. But I know—I've been told—that girls can often let their hearts precede their heads."

"Really? Is that what you've heard? Well, I've been told over and over that men often let their guns precede their heads. I don't believe one gender has the monopoly on irrationality."

"Touché, Hennie." He massaged his temples, as though easing some deep, ancient pain. "I only know how often I yearn for your mother's wisdom. I'm sure you do, too."

Hensley nodded. Her father stood up and, before settling himself behind his desk, he placed a strong hand on her arm, giving her a quick squeeze.

She swallowed hard in order to clear the regret and the guilt that had gathered in the back of her throat.

"I will make a carrot soup. There is always wisdom in that," she said brightly, wondering when she'd become such a good actress.

At the final dress rehearsal before opening night, Hensley had a thousand final alterations to make and Mr. Teagan stayed with her, pacing behind her as she worked.

"Nervous?" she asked, threading her needle.

He grabbed her shoulders, held her face close to his. "I've done it. I've enlisted. I will ship out this summer."

"What? I thought..."

"I was compelled. I thought about you, how perfect you are, and I want to protect that. I want to give my life to the fight, Hennie."

"Lowe, my God. Are you sure?"

"It's done. Oh, Hensley, my love. It didn't feel real until I cast my eyes upon you this afternoon. Now, I understand what I will lose. What grief I've brought upon myself!"

His eyes seemed about to flood with tears. Hensley wrapped her arms around him. "You will not lose anything. You will be fine."

He pressed his lips against hers, the warmth of his tongue cajoling hers. He was excited, unbuttoning her blouse with a fierceness that startled her.

"Lowell," she said, pulling away. "Mr. Teagan, I have loads of work to do. Tomorrow is the opening and there are a thousand seams to sew. Perhaps I should take all of this home with me."

"And leave me? When I am most vulnerable?" He walked to the

center of the stage, his footsteps echoing across the theater. Beneath the dimmed lights, he spoke. "This," he said as he gestured to his heart, "does not make excuses, Hensley. I've made my home beneath your skin, in the place where your breath begins and your pulse throbs. You cannot deny me now. I may never return."

He walked back across the stage, breathless, his shirt open. "Let me show you what it is to truly be inside another. To live in the deepest part of ourselves."

Hensley was trembling at the audacity of his suggestion. But she was also terrified of his death. There were already tears forming as he led her to the stable that the prop department had constructed with cardboard and straw. A papier-mâché horse stood watch as she allowed Mr. Teagan what she believed was his heart's greatest desire.

It is nearly noon and the house cats are basking in the summer sun that drenches the small courtyard behind the house when Hensley ties Thunder to a post nearby. They are somehow oblivious to the tin of smoked trout Hensley opens, anticipating her father's return for lunch. She plates the fish, pulls a handful of crackers from the barrel, and apportions some of the deep red raspberries she collected yesterday from the riverbank into a small bowl.

Hensley pushes the screen door open. The cats, Isaac and Newton, blink in acknowledgment. Hensley drags her fingers across Newton's gray head, his fur hot and dry. The cats were here when they arrived last month, though nameless. They mewed loudly the first few days, staking their claim to the patches of sunlight that warmed the wood floors and the muslin-covered settee that stood before the fireplace, placing dead mice upon the hearth and at their bedsides. They also tumbled and played against each other with such alacrity that her father thought they were a perfect embodiment of Newton's Third Law of Motion. Their antics are a welcome diversion for Hensley, but their indifference reminds her again and again that they belong to the house, not to her.

Her father likes to call this small patch of unmortared bricks their terrace. But it is really just a blank space between exterior walls. It is also where they've stacked several wooden crates in which their belongings were packed. Hensley leans against this stack and looks to the land beyond their house. The absence of buildings, bridges, motorcars, fireplugs is still disorienting. The blue sky haunts her with its immensity; its constant, aching presence. Hensley sometimes winces when she walks outside, afraid of the way the landscape shrinks her. She has never felt so small and inconsequential.

The mound of dirt behind their house slowly rises, becoming a steep hill just one hundred yards away. There are several structures, one just a pile of logs hammered together with a tarp thrown over the top, that look down upon the back of Hensley and her father's house.

Berto's house is at the top of the ridge, with a view over the town and beyond. He shares the place with his sister, but Hensley has only seen the girl once, in the twilight, smoking a cigarette, her long dark hair falling in front of her face. Hensley waved, but the girl threw the cigarette to the ground and stepped on it, extinguishing its glow. Then she went inside and let the screen door fall closed behind her so that it echoed down the hill.

Their own house faces the main street, which is but a wide dirt boulevard lined with large cottonwood trees. A wooden sidewalk runs the length of each side, echoing the vibrations and noise of the town's commerce all the way to their front porch. It is the only piece of life here that reminds her of a city and she loves to listen to the wooden slats clicking and groaning as people go about their day. At noon and at sundown, she can hear her father's footsteps coming home, the notes of his distinctive stride carried to her through the thick adobe walls.

There are plenty of storefronts lining the wooden sidewalk—even a Chinese food restaurant and a dry goods store with several bolts of decent linen. But Hensley doesn't want to go out again, she doesn't want to acclimate. Nothing feels real here. Or, perhaps, "here" has very little to do with it. She touches the desk, the doorknob, saying the words to herself, or sometimes aloud, just to remember the existence of concrete, actual objects.

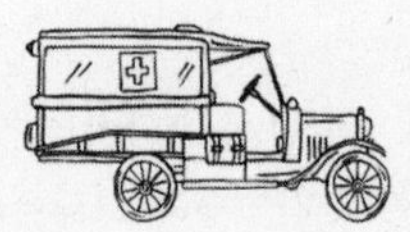

Charles leans so far forward, his chin nearly rests on the wheel. The use of headlights is strictly prohibited so close to the front. Nobody's eyesight is good enough for this, he thinks just before the road is illuminated and then decimated by a barrage of light. He stands on the brake and turns the wheel into the darkness. His chin hits the steering wheel and bounces off with a surprising smack as his molars slam together and ring in his head. The truck hangs on two wheels before jamming to a hard stop against some unknown obstacle. An inordinate amount of wet, slick blood drips into his lap.

He cuts the engine and grabs for his helmet, holding it over his head, waiting for another shell. The fear that makes his hands tremble turns his thoughts fatalistic. As he huddles there in utter darkness, already bleeding, he imagines the disappointment his father will feel at his death. How irked he will be that the fortune will have to transfer to his second cousin.

But the singe of smoke in the air is all that follows. And then, just beside the King George, there is an awful, deep howling. He must investigate; he must respond, damn it. As Charles reaches for the torch, he hopes this dim light will not get him killed. It appears that he is smack up against a tree, its deeply wrinkled bark almost an outgrowth of the truck's green metal. The incongruity of the two objects is momentarily disorienting. It is a blooming tree, with white flowers that are falling around him like a winter blizzard. The shrieking continues and Charles steps out of the truck, surmising that he's inadvertently come upon a field of wounded. Using the torch, though, he sees nothing but grass. No bloodied bodies, no pits emanating smoke and rot, no destruction at all.

He follows the sound with his light and is startled to see a horse, its nostrils flared, its eyes alight with panic. The horse bares its awkward, yellowed teeth, bellowing another horrible complaint. "Damn," he says quietly, wishing he hadn't bothered to get out of the truck. Wishing he'd just backed away from the tree and driven on into the darkness. But now he has no choice. Charles moves toward the animal and it quivers. It is standing on three legs, the fourth nowhere in sight. A bulging, inside-out wound is throbbing and oozing, its parts hanging in the space where there was once a leg.

"Oh, hell," Charles says, pressing his sleeve against his own chin. "What's happened to you, huh?"

The animal tries to move, to rush at Charles, but it stumbles and falls, crushing its own entrails beneath its body. It howls a terrifying protest and Charles holds both his hands out in front of him, hoping to calm or quiet the beast.

Charles realizes immediately that there is nothing to be done. He kneels on the ground and the horse continues to fight, thrusting its good legs in desperate, painful attempts to right itself.

Charles places one hand against the beast's face, wishing its terrible moaning would cease. The flanks of its jaw are soft and significant like Charles's favorite childhood Labrador, Tux. He strokes the horse gently with his fingertips, remembering how when he was a boy, he'd often sneak Tux to his bedroom, allowing the dog to sleep on his bed. Tux's heavy body near his feet was a constant, unspoken reassurance and when he awoke with the dog's soft, graceful profile having inched ever closer to his own, he felt adored. His mother and father didn't approve and both he and Tux were scolded when Charles appeared for breakfast with Tux's blond hairs clinging to his navy uniform jacket.

Charles tries to soothe the horse, speaking the reassurances that come without thought, the blood from his own gash dripping onto the suedelike muzzle of the dying beast.

Its eyes are black and knowing; its lashes as thick and pretty as any girl's. Charles lets the horse see the pistol cradled in his other hand.

"You've fought as hard as any of them," Charles says, sensing that the horse is grateful for the vibrations of his voice. He still whines with each labored breath, but he no longer screams. Charles thinks of all the carts that this creature has pulled across long distances, its regal silhouette providing comfort where there is none.

Charles presses the chamber firmly against the horse's forehead as his other hand rests upon the animal's hot, slick jaw. When his Labrador had developed a tender lump under one ear and he was unable to control his bowels, Charles's father put him on a lead and took him somewhere across the river. Charles never saw Tux again. His mother brought him the dog's collar that night as he cried beneath his quilt. She placed the faded leather strap upon his dresser. Then, with her hand on Charles's forehead, she shushed him. "Suffering is for little boys and the mothers who love them and hate to see them cry. It is not for animals." Charles can hear his mother's voice even now as he turns his face away and squeezes the trigger. The sound of the gun cracks and the bullet pushes hard against the horse's head, yanking it away from Charles, leaving it inches away from his hands.

Charles suddenly remembers the words from the margin of Mr. Dench's letter. *The horror that surrounds you now will recede into a past that you can leave behind.* Does this girl have any idea what it means when she writes the word *horror*? Can she possibly know what it might mean to him if she were to recognize his hidden message? Can she possibly imagine that he is thinking of her now, without even knowing her? Thinking of her words just after he's fired his pistol into this poor horse's head?

"I'm sorry," he says as the blood soundlessly leaks out, soaking through his pants where he kneels. He turns away from the horse and walks back to the truck and replaces the gun in its holster. Wiping his face, wincing at the throbbing he's just noticed beneath his chin, he backs the King George away from the tree. The engine whistles slightly, a wisp of smoke escaping from the hood. He ignores it and drives on up the darkened hill to where he fears men have already died on account of his delay.

Though he continues to aid Charles in his fool's mission to provide beds for the gassed soldiers from which they may dictate their last words, against the prohibitions of the doctors, Rogerson is loath to load any casualty who can talk. Also, he has started cursing like a soldier.

"I don't wanna hear their voices. I just want bodies. Give me blood, guts, shit. I'll take a man in ten pieces so long as he keeps quiet. If they can talk, they can wait. Or they can die without giving me nightmares."

Charles, the memory of the horse's terrifying moan still fresh in his mind, props his foot on the dashboard. "Would you really have shot those first three? If you'd known, I mean? Before we got them to hospital?"

The wind whips through the cab, buffering their words with its insistent whoosh. "Do we believe in the Golden Rule during war? Or is there a moratorium on all that?"

Rogerson lights another cigarette, his habit more and more urgent by the day. "All I know is I'd want you to shoot me, Reid. Put the bloody bullet through my head or my heart and let me go quickly. We heard them coughing out their own rotted lungs. We fucking listened to their throats closing. Dying from the inside out. Whatever short, joyous life they lived to that point matters none."

"Agreed." Charles nods. When he told Rogerson about the horse, his entrails hanging, slick, from his belly, Rogerson only served himself another scoop of potatoes. Rogerson had grown up on a farm, seen all kids of livestock butchered and euthanized. It didn't faze him. But Charles had been unable to sleep, remembering the weight of the horse's head once the bullet pierced it. The heat draining out and its flesh sagging almost immediately. The clap of the gun seemed to reverberate in him, making his fingers numb and useless. He'd wanted to feel his effect on the world and now he had. "But it's hard to know. I mean, what the universe might have planned. I hate to get in the way of God."

Rogerson laughs and drags deeply on his cigarette, letting the cherry crackle and burn persuasively. "God knows good and well that there is no cure for chlorine gas, Reid."

"Sure. But what about the suffering? Could it mean something? Maybe the end, painful as it was, allowed one of those boys to find a peace he hadn't had before."

Rogerson lets the ashes hang precariously over his own lap. "You're talking fairy tales now. Or a kind of devotion to God that I don't have. Nor does he, Reid. He doesn't really give a shit about us. Isn't that part abundantly clear? We are not his first priority. Who knows what is? But you took more care with that horse than God has ever taken with one of us." The ashes fall just then, singeing the seat. "God does not take care of us. We take care of each other."

Charles turns this over in his mind. He thinks of Mr. Dench and how closely his atheism resembles Rogerson's belief. "What good is it to believe in God if you don't think he can protect you?"

"Despair. I can't tolerate the meaninglessness of nothing. God exists so that I can sleep at night."

"This mess," Charles says, pointing at the relay post that has just come into view, boys spilling out its doorway, limping and bloody, "makes it all seem meaningless. Or full of meaning. I can't decide."

"Well, while you're walking the philosophical highway, I want to urge you not to be seduced by the idea of suffering. We've all got the right to happiness. Regardless of who made us or who's in control, life means nothing if it's dull and dreary. Drug addicts and boozers believe in suffering."

"What do you believe in, then?"

"Bullets, heaven, and pretty girls," Rogerson says, offering Charles the last drag of his cigarette.

Charles smiles, letting the smoke linger at the back of his throat. Exhaling finally in one long breath, he says, "Get to Rome and tell it to the pope. A finer edict has never been spoken." Laughing, they unload the first stretcher from the back of the King George.

For a reason he cannot explain, Charles once again thinks of the girl. He will not say it aloud, he can barely articulate the thought, but in this moment he has stumbled upon the idea that perhaps her few simple sentences have cracked the code. Perhaps everything he's done, everything he's doing, has all been meant only to lead him to Miss H. Dench.

Today as she looks up the hill, Hensley is still thinking about Mr. Reid's latest letter to her father. There is something different about this one. It strikes a tone of intimacy and wonder that Hennie does not recognize. It is written in fading pencil, the gray words looking more and more ephemeral as the letter progresses.

> My next move is my king's knight to KB3. I've spent parts of entire days imagining which vowels and consonants might govern the plans for the pieces with which you entice me. How strange that I can almost hear one of your gentle pawn's voice in my head, unsure of everything but its pale coloring. Your words, however, have created a self that has kept me occupied through the days and nights that masquerade here as dark, endless caves full of horrors. An English regiment took cover in the cellar of an abandoned farmhouse nearby and Rogerson and I had to meet them there to retrieve their injured, whom they'd already carried an unfathomable distance. As I stood there in the dim room, English soldiers all around me, clamoring for cigarettes and canteens, I found myself worrying about this pawn—faceless and nameless, but familiar all the same—hoping it will never recede into any

past that might be left behind. How foolish of me, you may think. Get ahold of yourself, it's just a chess game, man. But since your last letter, this gentle figure is a creature that lives in my mind, though I am sometimes sure I will die before I can see the endgame.

By the way, how is your new address? When I read that you were relocating such a great distance I was concerned. I hope everything is well with you and your family. I remember reading about the indigenous owls of New Mexico. Have you seen any? I've always admired the daring and wisdom of those birds, their round, echoing hoots making even the darkest night less lonely.

In thanks,

Charles Reid

By the end, the lead had become so dull that his signature is hardly more than a thick looping smudge. Even so, Hennie moves her index finger across the page, mimicking his script, slowing especially over his name, until she can trace his signature perfectly. Inhabiting his body, exiting her own, she crouches down under the table, imagining the cramped feel of the cellar, the roughness of chapped lips, the stale smell of urine on her clothes, the sound of artillery just outside.

She also knows exactly how she will respond, for it is clear the letter is meant for her. He has found her notes in the margin and he is intrigued. More than a chess game, he longs for her words. *My dear Mr. Reid, My father and I are political exiles here in southern New Mexico, masquerading as a mine superintendent and his adventurous daughter. I'm not sure which of us is better disguised, for he knows next to nothing about mines, and I am hardly adventurous. You see, I am a girl of just seven-*

teen, recently admitted to Wellesley College, fond of textiles, not fortresses. I'm sure your hopes will be dashed when you hear just how perfectly dull your imagination's occupant actually is, but I will make a heroic effort to give you words worth the postage. Alas, our correspondence has only begun and already I must chastise you. Please, do not invoke your death. It is not a matter to be tossed around cavalierly. Some might even say it could be used to manipulate a person's emotions. Let's agree to exist for each other forever. You are alive here on the page, here with me in our borrowed adobe house in the middle of nowhere. I will keep your pages, your words, as evidence of your vitality. Our existence can reach as far into the future as can be imagined. Look at that, we've created our own immortality. Regardless, there are lots and lots of stars out here in the desert and your safety will always be one of the things I wish for when I see one make its lucky streak across the black sky.

She is still under the table, composing her reply, when Berto comes in the front door, whistling twice, and slides a box onto the tabletop. She knows it will be filled with the items her father has chosen from the grocery: tins of smoked fish, a jug of milk, cider, fresh beans, a wedge of soft cheese, and ham bones.

She looks at Berto's boots, the black leather old and broken around the toes. To Hensley they look just like the pair she imagines on Mr. Reid. She wiggles her own toes, but they are unfettered; she is barefoot. This, even more than Berto's presence, brings Hensley back to her present.

"Boots," she says, even as she reaches her hand out and places it on one, in greeting.

It is a manly boot, but there is something overgrown about it, something clumsy. Without thinking, Hensley pushes her thumb into the toe and the leather gives way easily. There are no toes in the way; no manly foot resides in these manly boots.

Berto pulls his foot away from her reach. "I could ask what you are doing under the table, or why you are groping my boot, but I'm just going to ignore you."

Hensley crawls out from under the table. "Wait, Berto." The smell of the cheese wafts up from the box and makes her stomach lurch. She bends over, grasping the table for support. Pushing the box away from her face, Hensley stands up straight.

With her face ashen and her bare feet clutching the wood floor, she says, "Listen, Berto. I'm not like these people. I'm from New York. Manhattan. There are people of all kinds there. Just tell me. I won't be shocked. And I can keep a secret. But I can't pretend I don't know."

Berto stands there, his cap nearly hiding his eyes, and smiles. "When you feel inclined to share your own secrets, then I will take your open-mindedness more seriously." His eyes hold hers, even as she swallows hard, the nausea climbing into her throat.

Hensley runs to the open window and throws up the oatmeal she managed to eat just an hour ago. She spits the leftover sour taste out of her mouth and watches as an eager fly lands on the small puddle in the dirt. Wiping at her eyes with her sleeve, she wishes Berto would just go. She cannot bear to turn and face him.

Hensley closes the window and dries her sweaty palms on her skirt. The back of her throat is tight and she yearns for a sip of water. "Berto," she begins, but the sound of her own voice is punctuated by the bang of the screen door.

He is gone. She stands there, and her bare toes on the dusty wood seem at once bold and timid. She sighs and pours herself a cup of water.

Dear Mr. Reid,

The words form all on their own as she watches more and more flies gather and fuss over her pile of vomit.

Things you should know to better imagine me:

1. I am pregnant.

The words, imagined in black ink on her own stationery, are suddenly all she can see. As if alive, they twist and curl, stretching into every corner of the room, under the table, across the floor, around the candlesticks. Like hungry predators chasing the scent of their prey, the words surround her, threatening to obliterate her entirely.

Hensley closes her eyes.

2. Also, I am losing my mind.

Her stomach seizes again, threatening. She gathers her skirts in her hand and pulls the cloth to her mouth. Biting hard on the cotton and pushing her tongue into the bundle, she wills away the nausea. Finally, she opens her eyes and the words are gone, vanished. There is no longer any confessional wrapping the kitchen in black. She sighs again. Letting her skirt fall from her mouth, she busies herself with readying her father's lunch.

At first she blamed it on her changed diet. The small clutch of blackberries she'd picked from beside the arroyo. A bad tin of fish or an old egg. But the fear has been like a small black spot hovering in her peripheral vision all along. Now, nearly three months have passed since opening night and as noon approaches and the sun blazes, Hensley cannot deny it. Today marks the day it becomes true. The day her past transgression can no longer be ignored.

She tries to distract herself by adding to her reply to Mr. Reid's letter, but she can think of nothing more to tell him about herself that matters—everything significant is also unspeakable. It is as though her secret is burning her, charring her from the inside out, until she will soon be just ash. The black wispy remains of a fire that convey only its previous heat.

She toys with the idea of simply creating a second, better self: one who is picnicking in Central Park, taking boat rides in the reservoir, seeing theater, musical reviews, and art exhibitions; whose clothes are a reflection of the highest style, whose hair is coiffed each evening as the noise of Broadway throws its joys and sorrows up to her; who does not feel a sickness when she awakens and remembers that there is only one street in town; whose evenings are not filled with the noise of miners and misfits spilling out of the saloon onto that one dusty street, riding each other's backs like schoolboys, crooning songs that betray their own yearning for more perfect lives.

But writing false letters offers comfort to no one.

Hensley crouches, jamming the back of her heel into the space between her legs. Instead of a letter to Mr. Reid, she begins addressing the baby.

Dear Unfortunate,

You have taken up residence in the wrong place. There will be no happy announcement of your birth, no fireside toasts, no sterling spoons. Most likely, in fact, you will be taken from me at the very moment I've decided to love you most. They will hold you close, those anonymous, well-meaning arms, but then they will give you to a dreary place full of unwanted creatures who rely on strangers for food, clothing, and comfort.

She stops. Her knees throb and her head hurts. She stands up, certain of only one thing: she must tell her father. There is nobody else. There is no turning back. This is her life. It has left the realm of her own imagination and become something quite foreign and unfamiliar.

The cats surrender to the heat, jumping down from their perches into the shade of the moving crates. Isaac meows at Hensley, soliciting affection. Hensley grabs at his tail, letting it slide through her hand. She opens her palm and watches his white hairs fall to the ground in slow motion. He rubs against her in thanks, then stretches out on the bricks, happy in his solitude. Newton begins fastidiously cleaning himself, his little gray head bobbing with purpose.

Hensley imagines her father's face—its piercing blue eyes and down-turned mouth. Whether or not he can ever forgive her or look at her again without feeling ashamed, she suddenly doesn't care. She only wants company in this black hole in which she is living.

Hensley looks again to the top of the hill. The horizon is empty and there is not a soul in sight. She lets the quiet settle into her. The sky's blue seems to have been bleached by the sun into a joyless pastel, its deepest color but a memory of its own exuberant past.

Mr. Teagan is genius. That these words ever exited her mouth now seems nearly as incomprehensible as her present circumstances. That she spoke them to her brother is downright astonishing. She had simply hoped they would induce Harry to attend the show, but their effect was the opposite.

"Mr. Lowell Teagan?" Her brother put his hands to his head. "Please tell me you haven't fallen under his spell, Hen." He smiled a maddening, patronizing grin. "Of course you haven't. He is so transparent, we took to calling him Glass at Columbia." He turned his eyes to Hensley's and made his eyelids go soft, batting his eyelashes slowly. In a falsely deep voice, he mocked, " 'It is my lady, O, it is my love! / O, that she knew she were!' "

Unable to stop herself, Hensley laughed at the imitation. She threw his own handkerchief back at his pining face. "Stop it. Just because you're a brute. And a terrible actor."

Harold smiled, but then his face went dark. "Hennie. Really. He's a cad and not to be trusted. You could line the block with all the broken hearts he's collected."

She wanted to correct him then, to tell him that he'd got it wrong. That Lowell did, in fact, love her. That he'd told her he'd never, ever felt this way about anyone. But she could not speak. The doubts that she'd been swatting away like flies at a picnic were suddenly swarming her. Her stomach felt hollowed out and she forced herself to take a breath. The kitchen floor, littered with boxes of silver and plates wrapped in newspaper, seemed to dip beneath her feet. Her vision narrowed. She stared at her brother's shoes, shiny and black.

"What is it, Hen? Tell me it's not what I think." She looked up at his face. His eyes were full of judgment and disbelief. She hated him. She hated all of them. Everyone. Their greedy hands and empty words. Their votes and their guns and their stiff uniforms. Their narrow hips thrusting, thrusting, declaring absolutely nothing.

"He's shipping off in four weeks anyway. He'll probably die and then you'll be happy. I have things to do, Harold. If you're not here to help, then please let me be."

"For Christ's sake, Hen, I hope you haven't been too foolish. Don't believe a word he says."

"Just go, Harold. Go do your duty and let me do mine."

He held her elbows briefly with sweaty palms and his breath warmed her hairline. He had cried when their mother died, when her absence left their apartment a dim, quiet set of rooms. Hensley guessed it was the last time he'd shed any tears. She let him kiss her forehead in a gesture of dominion and pity and leave their apartment for the last time.

She shoved the tip of a butter knife into the palm of her hand. It was too dull to draw blood, but it left a blue dent that throbbed and ached and justified her tears.

When the telegram arrived from her brother the next day—the very same day of their departure—it said simply, *No record of enlistment by Mr. Lowell Teagan.* Hensley told her father it was simply a note of farewell.

When her father comes in for lunch, Hensley is ready. She has put shoes on, combed her hair, and powdered her nose. This is the day. The one that will change her life. Or at least the one in which she will no longer be alone with the truth of her life. Of what it's become. Of what it's going to become.

But he is distracted. There are personnel issues at the mine: unhappy men who dislike having a New York newspaperman in charge. Coincidentally—according to her father—less gold has been brought up in the past month than in any of the previous eleven months of production, which makes their animosity toward him seem justified. He does not mind being disliked for his opinions or tastes, or poor production, but this general disdain rankles him. In New York, he was the agitator, the advocate. He wrote articles about abuse, discrimination, corruption; exposed the dehumanizing conditions of sweatshops and tenements; walked with suffragists, sandhogs, and steelworkers.

Here, he is simply the boss.

Hensley watches him spread the soft cheese across a cracker. "Daddy," she says, toying with the cuff of her blouse.

"I suppose I'd feel the same way. Is that what you're going to say? Probably right, Hennie." He bites the cracker. She watches the crumbs tumble into his beard, a few scatter across his dark vest. "Did you get the post?"

"Not yet," she lies, knowing that this distraction will undermine her resolve.

"I suppose I should join them in the shaft. Take down the barrier between us. Get my hands dirty."

She tries to smile. Taking a raspberry in between her thumb and forefinger, its color deep and violent, she says, "Daddy, something happened in New York."

"Ah, news? Good. Distract me from my worries. Was there a telegram?" He looks up from his plate, his eyes meeting hers. She blinks. "Is it Harold?"

She replaces the raspberry on her plate. "No, it's not Harold. Before we left, something happened."

He blinks, waiting.

Hensley cannot hold his gaze. She looks at her cuff again, twirls the little pearl button.

"The director of the play, Mr. Lowell Teagan."

"Of course. He was to ship off not long after we left, didn't you say?"

Hensley nods but does not answer. The button is held by thin cotton thread. She put it there herself before any of this, pulling the needle through, believing that the pretty little embellishment would be admired by some charming gentleman. Believing that her own love story—like a brilliant dress pattern—was just waiting to be cut. Believing that somehow life would become simpler when she could craft her own choices.

"Has something happened? Have you got bad news, Hennie?" He has taken off his glasses, set them among the crumbs on the table.

She nods. "Yes."

One hand covers his mouth. The other reaches for her. She lets him hold her hot, damp hand, squeezing it so tight it hurts.

"What is it? Killed?"

She shakes her head. His hand relaxes slightly and she wishes it hadn't.

"Injured?"

Hensley shakes her head. But she cannot speak.

"Well, what is it, then? You are upset. Look, you haven't eaten a bite of your lunch."

Hensley closes her eyes and sees the black letters of her own handwriting spinning about her, clinging to her white skirt, the ink pooling into a stain in her lap. A sudden dark spot as though she's been shot and this is the blood seeping through. If she could be in a trench beside Mr. Reid, the plump rats so close, bullets and shells exploding overhead, she would.

"He didn't ship off. He lied about that. About signing up. About other things, too. We were close. Before we left New York. I can't explain it now. It seems so utterly foolish and I'm sorry, Daddy. I'm so sorry. But I think that he has left me . . ." She searches for a proper word. A word that will not offend him. That will save her. ". . . occupied."

He does not look away from her tears, but his forehead wrinkles in confusion and his head is cocked, as though he hasn't quite heard her.

"Inhabited, if you will," she says, wiping her cheeks with her free hand. Her other, still held by her father, is slick with perspiration. He squeezes it one last time and then withdraws. His own eyes are dry, but they appear dim, as if he were sleepwalking.

Both of his hands are spread out in front of him, pale against the dark wood tabletop. The veins bulge blue.

"Oh, Hennie." His words are quiet—barely there. But his

mouth moves with some unspoken word and a small bit of saliva escapes, clinging to his beard. This makes her cry again.

She wants to curl her body into his arms and cry with abandon. To become small again, so small that she cannot possibly be held accountable. For instance, after her mother died, the apartment was filled with bouquets from well-meaning friends and neighbors. Hennie, however, thought they were obscene—a flagrantly dark gesture. To send the flowers that her mother so loved only once she was dead. Had any of these people handed her dear mother a handful of stems when she was alive? When she was walking Hennie to school, despite the cold and her cough? Had they told her then that she was an angel? A soul that God would need too soon? A sweet woman who would be missed dearly?

When her father and brother were sorting through the large piles of condolences, Hensley gathered as many bundles of flowers as she could carry and made her way through the halls of their building, knocking on doors and handing back the white, pink, and yellow blossoms to the startled, pale-faced people who had sent them. One woman, the Irish wife of a doctor, had put her hand on Hensley's shoulder.

"My dear. Your mum would want to hold you tight right now, if she could. Won't you let me do that for her?"

Hensley nodded. She placed her head against the woman's skirts and wrapped her arms around her hips, the last bouquet still clasped in one hand. Her mother would like this—hadn't she told Hensley that she should be careful about refusing love? Hadn't she told her, even as her voice caught and her eyes closed, that Hensley would always be able to find her, that she'd always be close by?

This soft woman's embrace might, in fact, be what she'd meant. That if she closed her eyes and tried hard enough, she might find her mother here in this neighbor's arms, hiding, hoping Hensley would reach for her.

She breathed deeply, her eyes shut tight, waiting. But the woman's embrace was too gentle, ghostly, not like her mother's keen, forceful one at all. And the only thing she found there was the smell of kitchen grease and talcum powder.

The stems were damp and Hensley knew they would leave marks on the woman's skirt. Her own little hands were flecked with pricks from the flowers' thorns. She ended the embrace and peeked around at the place where her hands had been, but there was no sign of her. No water marks, no blood spots. The woman patted her head and smiled.

"What is it, love? What are you looking for?"

Hensley didn't answer. Instead, she pushed the last bouquet into this woman's arms, the petals crumpling beneath the weight of Hensley's hand. They were magenta roses and Hennie hoped some of their scarlet hue would stain the woman's blouse. She should be marked, too. Hennie's mother's death should not be just another happening; a piece of neighborhood gossip. This woman's small kindness cannot erase the tragedy. She cannot close her door and go back to her kitchen and forget. She, too, should be stained. All of them.

This was what she thought as she ran down the hallway in her black patent shoes, taking the corners quickly, daring herself to slip and fall. Wishing for her knees to be bloodied, her dress ripped. Instead, she entered the apartment with a ruckus and immediately confessed to her father that she had taken all of those pretty flowers back to the senders and even thrown the last bunch at the nice Irish lady. Not once during that afternoon did she cry. It was only when her father collected her on his lap and rocked her gently, spoke kind words into her hairline, and told her that today there would be no consequences for her misbehavior, that her tears began.

But now, sitting across from her father, in this time and place so far away from her mother's death, there is no escaping from the consequences. He will not be able to forgive her, to soothe her, to fix this.

Regardless, she continues to speak, to tell him everything. To explain how she fooled herself, gave herself, lost herself. How an act of delightful rebellion has left her stranded, irreversibly stuck in the unpleasant world of adulthood. She tells him that Lowell claimed he'd seen his own death and couldn't bear the thought of his life ending before he'd loved her completely.

Her father clears his throat, as if to speak, but says nothing. Hensley continues, relaying the conversation she had with Harold. She confesses that she is not the first girl to be fooled by Mr. Lowell Teagan, that his mastery of acting is a fierce, practiced weapon used countless times against the human heart.

He blinks slowly. When he finally speaks, his voice is firm and distant. "If I understand, you have been taken advantage of, Hennie. This Mr. Teagan abused his position and your innocence in order to obtain a selfish desire." He is silent, waiting for her to confirm his understanding. Hensley nods.

Her father continues. "Despicable. But in order to prevent this offense from creating yet another victim, perhaps we should consider that you return to New York. Surely, once he knows of your condition, this will elicit a proposal. This could be arranged quietly, easily."

Hensley shudders. She imagines her life married to a man who is ever after another woman. A man who would stand erect in front of group after group of schoolgirls or actresses or war widows, begging each of them to abandon her principles, to inhabit another role completely. A man whose hands would never be clean, whose eyes were never to be trusted. "Daddy," she begins, but she knows that all of her objections are petty compared with the injustice of depriving a child of legitimacy. "I know that you're right. But isn't there another way? Couldn't we invent another man? Give me a husband who really did sign up?"

Her father stands, knocking some milk from the pitcher. "For God's sake, Hensley! Be reasonable. This is not a game. I'm afraid life is not ours to invent. This is a very real situation, with real consequences that will not be helped by telling childish stories."

Hensley is angered by his patronizing tone.

"I know it is not a game. *You* are not the one who has been nauseous and terrified and ashamed. *I* am, Daddy. I am the one who boarded that train foolishly, silently, heartbroken, who followed you here, to this forsaken place, because I have absolutely no other place to go." Unable to speak any further, she retreats out the back door.

With shaking hands, she covers her mouth. The afternoon's heat has settled solidly against the land. Stifling a scream, she stomps her feet, sending spasms of fury up through her legs. She does not want to be here, nor anywhere. She does not want this afternoon to be what it's become. She hates her father for his calm acceptance, his staid reason, and hates herself for hating him.

Did she not entertain her father's exact suggestion on the train coming to this lonely place? Did she not sit above the ever-moving wheels and imagine what it might take to forgive Lowell? To place their beginning into a hole deep within her and never look down into it again? Has she not imagined that being his wife would immediately reform him? Turn his opportunism into a failing she would be duty bound to overlook? Hasn't she also wondered how she could possibly carry a child that was doomed to suffer an orphan's life?

But, now, coming from her father's mouth—so practical and concrete—the suggestion that she hope to become Mrs. Lowell Teagan suddenly seems contemptible.

With her brother's telegram in hand, Hensley had cajoled Marie into joining her on one last errand before she left New York; they took the train uptown to the address she'd written on a piece of paper from her father's desk.

It was a faded stone building near Columbia with an interior courtyard. The doors with brass handles were heavy but unlocked.

"I am giving him back this scarf that Sara Coe wore in Act Two. I'll just be a minute. Do you mind waiting here?" Hensley asked, motioning to the blue velvet couches facing one another in the lobby's alcove.

Marie furrowed her brow. "Which scarf? I don't remember a scarf..."

Hensley smiled. "It's in my bag. I'll be right back," she said, climbing the marble stairs.

When she reached his apartment, she pressed her ear against his door, straining to hear any private moments. She realized she knew almost nothing about his life or habits. She knocked.

Lowe stood in front of her, his hands in his pockets, and stared. She'd come with the notion that she could shame him, make him despise himself. But when he opened the door and stood before her with his black hair slicked away from his face with care and his posture ever-perfect, she knew her mission was impossible.

He leaned in close to her cheek and planted a kiss. "Hensley," he said, his voice still deeply seductive, "whatever has brought you all the way up here? Alone?"

"I thought you might like to see me," she said, stepping into the apartment. His feet were bare and the black hairs curled on the tops of his toes looked obscene. "Before you go, I mean." His apartment was spare, with just a sofa and a wooden table.

"Of course. It's just, I've been so busy. You understand. I was absolutely exhausted after the show. I think I slept an entire twenty-four hours." He shrugged his shoulders. "And now I've got to get my affairs in order. Honestly"—his eyes pulled at her with some unspoken pain—"I thought it might be easier this way..."

Hensley smiled. "But you were going to tell me a proper good-bye. I was going to get that performance, once you worked it up?"

"There is no proper good-bye for the two of us, Hensley." Here, he took her hand, gazing at her fingers as he kissed each one.

"I think there is, Mr. Teagan," she said as she pulled her hand away. "The proper good-bye begins with a confession. A sliver of honesty that may feel like a dagger for each of us. Will you do me the honor?"

"What in heaven's name are you talking about? Are you feverish?" He placed a hand on her forehead.

Hensley pulled away. "You haven't signed up at all. You will be sitting here, drinking your coffee, cultivating new fans, the whole time I'm away. The whole time the others are dying, really and truly dying, before they've had the chance to love their girl the way they long to. You never had any intention to protect or defend anyone but yourself."

Lowe closed the space between them in one large step. He was sweating across his top lip. His hands, too, were damp, as he held her face between them. Breathing heavily, he squeezed her cheeks hard. "If you're finished with the dramatics, I would remind you that lies are the currency of human society. They are written in every newspaper and spoken on every corner."

Hensley could not believe how easily and swiftly he moved

from guilt to self-righteousness. There would be no apology. Hensley shuddered with remorse and shame and a new understanding. His hands still held her cheeks firmly and just as he was about to utter some other justification, the subtle beginning of the kettle's whistle interrupted him. He let go of her face and moved across the room, his head held high.

She followed him. "You are a filthy coward," she said, surprised by her own voice. "What could be worse than lying about your service in order to seduce me? It's rotten and horrid. I hate you and your stupid rotten baby teeth."

He smiled as he unscrewed the sugar tin. This gesture was as vile as anything he'd done. "Seduction," he began, but Hensley couldn't stand it. She picked up the hot kettle, still screaming, and dumped its contents on top of his bare feet. The water steamed, nearly hissed, as it hit the tender tops of his toes. Then she threw it back on the stove and ran out, his cursing and shrieking making her at once glad and terrified.

Downstairs she grabbed Marie's hand and the two girls ran out onto the street together. Through their huffing and puffing, she told Marie that Mr. Teagan had suddenly tried to kiss her when she handed him the scarf, that he was crude and untrustworthy. Marie listened, quietly nodding. As they walked arm in arm past the huddles of pigeons, fluttering in the gutters, vying for scraps, Marie said only, "But it's over?"

Hensley had nodded, certain that it was.

Now, she stands and watches two black birds crest and dive on the blue horizon. They could be bits of trash carried by a fickle current. As they recede from view, chasing some unknown desire, Hensley imagines that she can hear their wings, flapping, moving against the thin air, pushing away all of their options but the one that says, *Fly.*

Once again, she is reminded of the letter from Mr. Reid. What scraps of her life will she send to him? What will be left of her if she returns to a life of humiliation—becoming Lowe's wife, knowing that even from the very beginning, it was all false?

Will she send that piece of herself to Mr. Reid? Tell him to hold on, to stay alive, to fight for his sanity and dignity because if he does, if he survives, he can return home for—what? Just the ashes from a different fire, the remains of another kind of warfare?

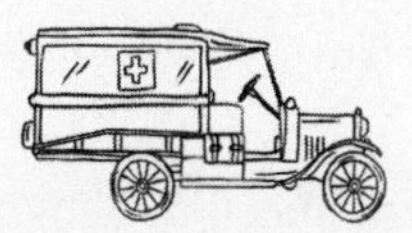

Charles drives the King George, full of casualties with injuries so serious they've not yet been fully addressed at the CCS, to the nearest train station where an ambulance train is to arrive, ready to transport the men to proper hospitals and eventually home, if they make it. Rogerson sits in the passenger seat, whistling a tune Charles doesn't know. They've been together nearly four months, but it feels like forever.

The terrain between the CCS and the train station is flat and muddy from the previous evening's rainstorm. As they drive, the mud splatters up and into the open windows, pocking their arms and cheeks.

"A year without cigarettes or booze?"

"We might be headed toward both if you don't quit smoking mine, too."

Rogerson inhales deeply and then passes the cigarette to Charles. "Sorry, Reid. I guess that's my answer, then."

Charles takes a long drag, so that only the butt is left. He tosses it out the window. "I'd give up both if we were driving along a little country road without any bloody bandages or drip bags. If we could have a decent bath and a clean set of sheets without lice mating inside the pillow. If we could walk beside her as she points out vegetation and wildlife on the way to the creek."

"We?" Rogerson says, incredulous. "Bullshit. It's you or me, Reid. Not both."

"I was being charitable, Rogerson. Obviously it's me."

"Unless you don't make it," Rogerson says, lighting another cigarette.

Charles throws a hard punch into his shoulder. "Bastard."

Rogerson laughs. "There are silver linings, eh?"

"She wouldn't have you. She's refined. Discriminating."

"But if you're gone, and I'm the closest thing to her dear Mr. Reid. You see? I'm part of your history. I've got the broad shoulders girls love to cry upon."

Charles puts his foot on the brake. He turns to face Rogerson. "That's not funny. Not at all. In fact, I think I may be sick to my stomach." He makes a production of gagging with Rogerson's lap his target. Rogerson squirms slightly, entirely unsure of the veracity of his nausea.

Finally, Charles swallows mightily and puts the King George back into gear. "I think I could defy all metaphysical limitations and haunt you so fiercely you'd beg her to leave you."

Rogerson puts his hand to his helmet and salutes. "Aye, aye, sir."

When they arrive at the train station, it is bustling with activity. In addition to the other ambulances unloading wounded from other clearing stations onto the train, there are large groups of refugees. There is an old woman with her goat tethered to her wrist, a pile of books in her arms, and a cloth bundle tied to her back. Her hair is short and thinning with barely any color, making her look like a freshly hatched fowl. She leads the crowd, mostly very young and very old, babies riding donkeys, and old men carrying chickens.

Charles and Rogerson get to work, unloading stretchers and carefully transferring the boys to the Red Cross train. Some of their bandages have soaked through with blood, but they don't risk changing them here for fear of a hemorrhage. The entire train is saturated with the salty, clotted, metallic smell of blood.

Standing back out in the sunshine, Charles takes a deep breath.

"Your face," an old man waiting with the refugees says to Charles, using an arm to gesture, "is covered in blood." His French accent is heavy and for a moment, as Charles closes up the back of the King George, he doesn't understand him.

Charles touches his cheek. "Oh, it's just mud," he says to the old man, smiling. "From the road."

The white chicken trembling under the old man's arm squawks. "Ah, mud. Looks like blood. Everything looks like blood now."

Charles nods. "Where are you headed?"

He shrugs. "Wherever the train takes us."

"Good luck to you," Charles says, offering the man a cigarette from the pack in his pocket.

The old woman just in front of this man observes his offer and she immediately leaves her place in line and stands beside Charles, her hand on his arm. She speaks no English, but her meaning is perfectly clear. Within seconds, nearly half the crowd of refugees has followed her lead, reaching for Charles, pulling at his jacket, begging for a drink, a smoke, a ride. Charles hands out the rest of his half dozen cigarettes, but that only seems to enrage them as they argue over the distribution.

One little girl no more than five has wrapped her arms around his leg, burying her face in his pants. Another old man is trying to relieve him of his helmet, buckled loosely beneath his chin. Charles holds tightly to his helmet with one hand while he works on the little girl's hands with the other, trying to pry them off.

Suddenly Rogerson lays on the horn. "Get back in line. *Retournez à votre place. Maintenant.*"

Slowly and with disgust, the old people and the babies in their charge turn away and leave Charles alone again. The little girl wipes her snot against his pants one final time and then lets go. She stands on his boot with both feet, her weight barely registering, then follows the crowd.

He walks around the King George and sits in the passenger seat without a word.

"Merci," Rogerson says to nobody as he starts the engine. The ride back is solemn. The mud splashes up and stains the opposite arm and side of each of their faces, making the dirtying complete.

"I gave away all my smokes," Charles says finally.

"Of course you did," Rogerson replies.

Rogerson is in the latrine with a stomach flu the next night when the front blows up. For weeks, there has been a pattern to the fighting, with the heaviest fire in the middle of the day, and the evenings usually spent on reconnaissance or resupply at the front and surgery and wound dressing for the CCS. But this night is different, a tremble beneath their feet after dinner, coupled with the shrill moan of far-off artillery. Charles gives up thoughts of sleep, not knowing how long it will be before things quiet enough to evacuate the wounded.

He stands outside the latrine door and calls to Rogerson, "Is it all coming out right?"

"Damn it, Reid. Shove off." Charles hears him gag and the awful sluice of vomit hitting the hole.

"At least you're escaping a night run," Charles says, leaning his back against the wall. "You'll get to sleep once your stomach settles."

"Which may be never." He hears him spit and moan slightly. "Tell me, was there a letter?"

Charles lights a cigarette and puts his hand against the envelope in his chest pocket. "Yep."

"Mrs. Immortality. Keeping us alive all the way from the Wild West of America. God, I love her."

Charles smiles. A snag of jealousy pulls at his chest when Rogerson talks like that, as though she is a girl to be shared. As though she is theirs, together, a joint adoration. But he's given up keeping Hensley to himself. He can't. He lets Rogerson read each letter, watching his eyes as they move over her words, relieved, at least, that they are real. He has confirmation of her existence, her singularity, her appeal. But he writes on his own, at dawn, usually, if they are not already in the King George. Rogerson seems to accept this. It does not diminish his participation in the fantasy. And Charles can't blame him. They both know that it matters to whom the letters are addressed. She is writing Charles's name in the salutation, addressing *his* questions and passing the sound of *his* words through her mouth as she reads.

While the soldiers at the front scream obscenities and whisper their hopeful prayers as they climb over the edge, Charles stands outside the latrine and reads Hensley's words. In between Rogerson's violent bouts of nausea and the crescendos of gunfire, Hensley consoles them both.

Dear Mr. Reid,

It's been said that we are walking on gold here. Rumor has it, and you know how rumors fly, there is so much gold that it is literally beneath our feet, just waiting to be found. I fancy this image as I walk to the small stream running not far from our house and then bravely put my bare feet into the frigid water. I tell myself, Hensley, you are standing on a ribbon of gold, worth millions of dollars. You are the world's richest girl and you can order bolts of silk and French linen, sprinkle gold flecks on your morning oatmeal, and sail a yacht to Greece. Of course, the old cottonwood trees that bend their branches graciously over the stream, giving it shadow and romance, have been twisting their roots through all that gold, pushing their way through its hard ore, for hundreds of years and they are not dressed in silk, nor have they commissioned fancy boats or golden cereal. Given their stature and the lush green leaves that joyfully host owls (!), sparrows, squirrels, and even bats, I'm told, I wonder if my aspirations are misplaced. I wonder if I would do better to emulate the cottonwood for its dreams: a strong, hidden heart that is unmoved by a dry summer or a dreary winter, but that can appreciate a powerful gust of springtime wind for the glance of past and future that it offers as it litters the sky with the tree's own tender, fuzzy seeds.

Charles pauses as Rogerson heaves again. When he's finished, he pokes his ashen face out the door and moans, "She's breaking my heart in here, chap."

"The next part is about a cabbage dish from the local Chinese place. Wanna skip it?"

Rogerson shakes his head. "Nope. I hate cabbage anyway. Lemme hear it." He closes the door again just as a particularly large shell explodes and the force knocks over a couple of empty gas cans.

"It's gonna be a rough night," Charles says, looking at the sky just over the front, bright white and pink with the excess of battle. He begins reading again.

My father and I have discovered a little place to eat here run by a Chinaman named Lin. Usually we have a quiet dinner at home. Nothing fancy, but I have been cooking since I was thirteen and I know what tastes good. In order to be a part of this place, however, my father thought it would be fun to try a night out at Lin's Chinese Cooking. It is a small wooden shack, if you can imagine...

"I can," Rogerson moans from inside, "I can." Charles continues:

... with maybe eight tables. There are no linens or silverware. Only a pair of red chopsticks marks the place in front of each chair. He makes two or three dishes nightly and we chose the one called, plainly, cabbage and eggs. I'm the richest girl in the world here, remember? Walking on gold and eating... cabbage!

But truly, it was the most delicious meal we'd ever eaten. It began with a thin, salty soup. Just broth, really, with limp, flavorful scallions and cubes of stale bread making it ever thicker as we ate. Or sipped, I should say, because there were no spoons. As we brought the red bowls to our mouths, the steam made our skin damp. Then, there were blue plates covered in hunks of sweet, tangy pork and mint leaves that he plucked straight from one of the many tin cans growing little green plants on the windowsills. The pork almost melted in our mouths and the mint made our tongues tingle with its freshness. When Mr. Lin stood by our table and asked, "You like?" my father grinned at our good fortune.

Now for the cabbage. It came, slightly browned and oily, piled over a mound of white, sticky rice. It looked like nothing. Like something you might feed to animals in a barnyard. But we were the happiest of creatures the moment we tasted it. The cabbage had taken on a kind of deep, earthy flavor, aided by garlic and onion and a spicy red paste. Nestled in among the thick cuts of cabbage were small pieces of fluffy, scrambled eggs, slightly salty and peppery and wholly wedded to the flavor of the cabbage. Does this sound crazy? I know it must. I wish I could send you a sliver of the meal to place on your tongue. In solidarity, I'm sure, you would marvel at Mr. Lin's abilities. Needless to say, my father and I have not had a happier night since we arrived.

Charles notices the quiet when he's finished reading. "You okay? I'm gonna make a run. Get some sleep if you can."

"She made me want that cabbage, Reid. Unbelievable. God, but I really want her."

Charles folds the letter. He nods but does not speak. Standing up straight, he crushes his cigarette, long spent. "I know," he says finally, fiddling with the key in his pocket. "I know."

The black kilometers that stretch between the hospital and the front are absolutely indecipherable. The sound of the engine keeps him company and he hopes the moody radiator does not quit this time. Charles drives by memory alone, hoping that there is not a new mortar hole or pile of debris since his last run. Even more than the slight curves and bumps of this road, Charles knows that Rogerson's words are his own. He wants her, too. He wants desperately for this blackened road to bend itself toward her and the obscure town in New Mexico where he might stand barefoot in a stream beneath those old trees with her and eat in a dirty wooden shack with her, letting her show him how to use chopsticks and how to be alive in the world.

Her father has returned from the mine and the two of them sit in front of the empty fireplace. He is silent except for an occasional sigh as he surveys the chessboard on the small table pulled close to his chair. He props his head between his two index fingers. It's been three weeks since her father has made a move. He is distracted, whether by the situation at the mine, or her own condition, she doesn't know. Perhaps he has been in touch with Lowell. Would he tell her?

Finally, Hensley speaks. "Isn't there a time limit on your thinking?"

He smiles, barely. "What is your allegiance to Mr. Reid, my dear?"

She shrugs, looking at her hands. Her father doesn't know she has begun her own correspondence. "There is some urgency for the poor man. He *is* near the front lines, after all."

It is now that they both furrow their brows. From beyond the front door there is a banging, as though they themselves are suddenly under attack. Soon the banging is accompanied by whistles and tambourines and joyful shrieks. They rush to their feet, knocking a pawn to the floor.

Her father opens the door, while Hensley stands behind him, her hand on his shoulder, her eyes searching the dusk.

The scene on the street in front of their house is like a dream. There are white-faced clowns juggling glass spheres lit from within by some delightful, unknown source; girls ride by on bikes wearing short bloomers and tuxedo jackets, the tails flapping behind them with alacrity; a bearded man stands atop a carriage with bars that entrap a sleeping bear curled up in the corner and three barking hound dogs; beside him sit two small monkeys shaking maracas and hooting; men in white tights stand inside black hoops that are being rolled by a woman in a bright orange evening dress; there are several small men shaking tambourines; and at the front is an adolescent boy dressed in red stripes banging a huge snare drum.

Hensley's father turns and looks at her, both of them startled by this brand-new world that's materialized as if by magic. He smiles and takes her hand from his shoulder, giving it a squeeze. "My rather astute powers of deduction tell me that the circus has come to town."

They walk arm in arm out into the street following behind two black-and-white clowns on tricycles. Other residents fall in with them, everyone smiling. The sky still holds on to the memory of the day's sun, casting a pink glow across the entire circus parade. Hensley kicks up dust as she walks, imagining that she, too, is beating the drum.

At the far edge of town, near the cutoff to the mine road, the performers begin to assemble tents. From a large sack, they produce what looks like bright orange parachute material. Soon enough, however, it is supported by long wooden posts and has become a voluminous tent, lit by lanterns and small torches. Canvas partitions are erected at the outside perimeter of the tent, allowing the performers a "backstage."

As the crowd draws around, the man atop the carriage begins hawking the amazement and surprises that await them: fire-breathers, bearded women, juggling monkeys, a strong man, acrobats, a dancing bear, mathematical dogs, music, belly laughs.

The timing is impeccable. For an entire half hour, Hensley forgets about her own life. She allows herself to delight in the wonder and amazement at the antics of these unorthodox, untethered people.

Hensley stands obediently beside her father as he greets townspeople and miners—some of whom she's met before and some she has not, a smile still spread across her face. But now she marvels at her father as he recalls each of their names. His sense of duty is never far from him. She watches his face, still burdened by what he's learned of her, and she realizes that he, too, must long for New York. This strange, dusty, lonely place cannot feel like home to him either.

She glances at the tent behind them, wishing there were a magic carpet, or some kind of secret portal straight to Broadway. She and her father could be back in Manhattan, having dinner at Polly's, and afterward Hensley might meet a school friend, one who knows all about undoing what's happening to her body. A friend who could take her to the Lower East Side, or to Brooklyn, where the gruff nurses could scold her for being careless, or corrupt, or cowardly. Their capable hands, however, would hold her tight, absorb her shrieks, wipe her tears, then send her home with warnings and pamphlets and a bloodied towel.

"Care to take a look at the strong man, Hensley?" She gasps, startled by the interruption. Berto shrugs his shoulders. "Sorry. I didn't mean to scare you."

Hensley smiles. She shakes her head. "It wasn't you. I was daydreaming. Under the influence of the circus, I guess."

He nods. "So? How about it? Do you want to see the strong man?"

"Oh, of course. Yes. Daddy?" she says, turning back to her father.

He leans his head in to hers so she can speak into his ear. "I'm going to see the strong man with Berto."

"Fine, fine," he says, all the while nodding attentively to the postman's opinion that the town should begin collecting a fund for flood emergencies.

Hensley and Berto cross to the far side of the tent where a man is just about to tear an apple in half with his bare hands. He has a delightfully long and curling mustache and he is wearing denim overalls without an undershirt. He is no taller than either of them, but his arms are thick and solid like the branches of a tree. The apple is red and shiny and Hensley wonders if it is fake. But he offers another woman in the crowd a bite to test its authenticity. She demurely takes a small taste and gives her hands a clap, vouching for its flavor.

Then the strong man puts both hands on the apple and quickly tears it into two jagged pieces, a few seeds spilling at his feet. Everyone claps. He takes a big juicy bite from one half and Hensley laughs. Berto leans closer to her, his laughter a silent, intoxicating force. Hensley laughs even harder.

Next, the strong man asks for a volunteer. Hensley is still giggling, so she is an obvious choice. He takes her hand and guides her to a stack of haphazardly stacked chairs and stools. Beside it is a little stepladder. He urges her up the steps and onto the top stool, where she sits gingerly. Berto is just smiling, watching. Hensley puts her face in her hands, embarrassed by her sudden starring role under the tent.

The strong man leans down and says, "Hold on tight, darlin'. You're going for a little ride."

Hensley grips the seat of the stool and puts her feet on a rung at the bottom, the heels of her shoes hooked around it. In a single, fluid motion, he hoists her high above the crowd. A scream of fear rises within her, but no sound escapes. Instead, the entire world goes silent. Everything slows down, even the people below, who all seem to be frozen. She cannot see the strong man, but there is a slight trembling of effort that throbs through the stack of chairs, and she can feel his presence coursing through her. For only a moment, Hensley wonders what would happen if he dropped her—if his arms buckled and the chairs careened to the ground. She imagines her head cocked at a strange angle, her legs splayed, her life, and the one growing within her, over. But this gruesome vision is soon replaced by a feeling of pure delight as she surveys the tent below her. There are bicycles—circling unmanned as though steered by a phantom, with acrobats standing on their seats; there are fat orange fruits being tossed high and then caught, without fail, in buckets and baskets strapped to the hands and feet of a white-faced clown; women in evening dresses dance with one another, dipping and twirling to the beat of the snare drum until suddenly the color and cut of their dresses changes entirely, at which point they switch partners. The entire landscape below is a beautiful, outrageous dream.

The heat that has collected in the apex of the tent wraps around Hensley and gives her the impression that her head is also being held by a pair of strong, warm hands. As though someone has placed their hands upon the back of her skull and is pushing, slightly, gently, against her. Cradling her. It is in this moment—in a small but remarkable circus tent in southern New Mexico—that Hensley remembers her mother's hands. Not just the way they looked—pale and perfect, like long, elegant gloves perched right on the ends of her slender wrists—but how they felt: the weight of them on Hensley's forehead when she was feverish; the smooth, gentle protection her mother's hand provided as they walked together on the city streets; the affection that was conveyed to Hensley each time her mother wiped a tear or stroked her back or smoothed her hair into its plaits. And even as her mother lay in her own sickbed—her eyes swollen and tired—she reached for Hensley's hand and held it, reassuring her of something bigger than the illness, something more durable than flesh. And in this moment, Hensley understands.

I come from those hands, she thinks. *That love is still in me. It is forever mine. And I can use it. I can claim it and embellish it and let it become something more. Something more than even me; an unimaginable future. Just as this man below has hoisted me with his hands to see this unimaginable circus.*

As the man lowers her down to the ground, Hensley's grip tightens and she is smiling. Berto looks surprised to see her so calm, so unfazed.

Hensley takes the strong man's hand and curtsies as he bows to her his thanks. "You're a natural, darlin'."

"Thank you so much," Hensley says into his ear. The crowd cheers as Hensley becomes one of them again.

"Maybe you should try the high wire," Berto says as she stands beside him, beaming.

But suddenly, as though doused with cold water, she is clammy and nauseous. Her mouth seems to swell and her teeth are chattering uncontrollably. She makes her way through the crowd, excusing herself as she parts couples and families. Finally, standing in the darkness outside the tent, she bends over, heaving. Her skin is damp and chilled, yet her brow and neck seem to be on fire.

Berto is soon beside her, speaking words that are drowned by the ringing in her ears. Hensley does not want him there, but she cannot speak. The rippling in her stomach is violent and unstoppable.

As she retches, she places a hand on Berto's chest to steady herself. He flinches and pulls away and only as Hensley wipes her mouth on her own handkerchief does she realize that her suspicion has been confirmed without a doubt: Berto has breasts.

The noise from inside the tent fills the quiet of the empty night. Hensley spits once more into the dirt and then moves away from the mess. Berto follows her.

They climb a small bluff that shields the circus tent from a strong easterly wind. At the top, the land in front of them recedes into blackness and the sky shimmers with an abundance of stars.

Finally, Berto places his fingertips on Hensley's shoulder. "Please don't tell your father."

"My father?"

"I need this job. Please?"

"How long have you been . . . ?"

"My brother is sick. I had no choice."

"Your brother?"

"We are twins. Luckily."

"So, *he* is Berto. And you are?"

"Teresa."

There is a moment of silence in which Hensley absorbs this revelation. The two girls then smile at their delayed introduction. Hensley gives Teresa her hand and they shake, intentionally shirking convention. "I'm sorry," Hensley says, "about that. About touching you like that."

Teresa smiles and her fierce eyes are momentarily gentle. "New York City, huh?" Their hands remain entwined.

Hensley nods and smiles. "Right. Very cosmopolitan."

A cheer rises up inside the tent behind them. Another feat of amazement on this otherwise ordinary evening. The wind pulls and twists Hensley's skirt.

"I should go," Teresa says. "Are you feeling better?"

Hensley nods. "I'm sorry that you've seen me nauseated twice now. It's so unpleasant."

The two girls let the wind's inarticulate noise fill up their minds. Finally, Teresa says, "What are you going to do?"

Hensley takes a deep breath of the dark night air.

"I've no earthly idea. I told my father. He suggested I return to New York."

"Can you make a marriage there?"

"I suppose."

"But is that what you want?"

"It's complicated."

"Then you are not in love?"

At the mention of the word, Hensley blushes. There is not a face that comes to mind, no warm memories of a kiss or passionate embrace. Instead, a phrase scrawls itself across her vision. *Your words, however, have created a self.* The man—faceless, far away—who wrote these words is the man who colors her cheeks and makes her heart race. He is the man to whom she wants to give more and more of herself, whispering secrets into his skin, giving him all kinds of words to hold on to.

But Hensley shakes her head, aware that she is prey to any fantasy of a life not her own. "Though it does not reflect well upon me, no. There is nobody. What is your brother's illness?"

Teresa's face shifts; her smile disappears. "We don't know. He cannot move his legs. He is feverish some days. He has no appetite."

"Have you sent for a doctor?"

Teresa shrugs. "We cannot afford to. But my mother has taught me a lot about medicine."

"Your mother? Oh. Is she a nurse?"

"My mother is dead, Hensley. It's just Berto and me."

"Oh." Hensley pauses. "Mine, too."

"Yes. I figured."

"Was she a nurse?"

"Of a sort. She delivered babies."

The words echo in Hensley's ears. "Oh," she says, her arms crossing in front of her chest. An image comes to her mind of a dark-haired beauty like Teresa creeping across the night, her arms laden with baskets, each of them cradling a newborn and being placed gently at the foot of its mother's bed. "And you know how to do that? She taught you?"

"I only know a few things about the body. Teas that fight infection. Treatments for fever. None of it seems to be working, though."

Hensley takes a deep breath. How in the world will a baby—no matter how small—escape from her body? The idea of it is as preposterous as some of the circus feats she's seen tonight.

Hensley makes a confession. "I had a visit from my own mother tonight. Up on the chair. It was as though I could feel her very hand on my forehead."

"Sometimes it feels like that, doesn't it? As though if we could just keep our eyes closed, they might actually be there, beside us?" Teresa reaches out her own hand. She places it on Hensley's brow. Hensley closes her eyes. Teresa's fingers are cool and slightly rough—nothing like her mother's—but Hensley likes the way they feel. The scent of the landscape's juniper bushes is carried to her on the wind. It has become a smell she now associates with this place. It's as though there is a licorice factory nearby, churning out its sweet candy all through the night. But the licorice in the local grocery is hard and stale. Not at all like the kind that her mother used to greet her with after school some days: a brown bag full of beautiful, pastel pieces of licorice. Hensley always liked the way they looked better than the way they tasted. But now, as the sourness of her own vomit coats her mouth, she thinks that she'd like to try one again. A luscious pink one or a pure black one with dainty white sugar sprinkles. Hensley remembers her mother doling them out, one at a time, as they walked the long crosstown blocks.

"Your secret is safe with me," Teresa says as she lets her hand drop from Hensley's face.

Hensley opens her eyes and the girl is gone. Berto, however, is walking away from her, down the hill to the circus tent, with a perfectly manly gait. "Likewise," Hensley shouts across the distance between them.

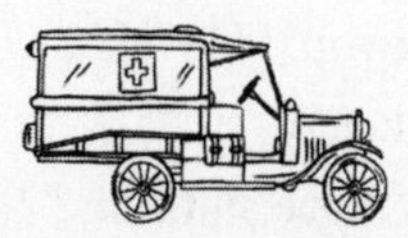

"Fuck this morning hate," Rogerson says as he pushes at a browned clump of eggs on his plate. The artillery blasts begin at dawn, marking the beginning of another day. While the shells are falling, the daisy-cutters squealing, the shrapnel bulleting no-man's-land, Charles and Rogerson spend the hours in the mess tent, waiting for the quiet that signals the end of the day's battle and the beginning of their work. With each shrill, hard rumble they imagine their effects. It's impossible to keep images of what they've seen here from intruding—a broken artery splattering its bright red blood against the sides of the King George; the disappearance of jaws, mouths, noses, ears, replaced only by a dark, haunting emptiness; a boy clutching his own innards, trying to stuff them back in; a boy's open skull, jagged and bloodied, his brain already swollen, protruding through the crack like a slick, ocher blossom.

"How long can it go on like this?" Charles says, staring at the shallow sip of coffee he has left.

"Eternity. It's hell, Reid. I think we're already dead. We carried our own still-beating hearts in our hands across some bloody battlefield and died in a hole, covered by a thousand others just like us. And now, this is our hell. Watching it happen over and over."

Charles shakes his head. "It's worse than that. It's not hell." He stands up, stomping his feet just as another daisy-cutter whistles its arrival. He jogs in place, attracting the attention of a small group of nurses playing cards at the adjoining table. He waves at them, smiling broadly. They ignore him. "We are alive. Right, ladies? I feel my heart beating. How 'bout you?" He takes a lap around the tent, then sits again, his breathing heavy.

Rogerson chuckles. "Alive and zany," he says, looking carefully at Charles's face. "What's with the calisthenics?"

Charles shrugs. He places his hand over his heart, where it pulses against his palm, a miracle. Then, he works his hand inside his jacket and, pulling out the latest letter from Hensley, as though it were an actual piece of him, an offering from deep within, he says quietly, "Have yourself a little morning love, Rogerson. Hell would be better. This bit of cruelty, this glimmer of happiness, is part of the world that our heavenly father created. Lucky us, there is not one without the other."

Rogerson gratefully takes the letter from Charles, pushing his plate away to make room for it. But before he begins to read, he says, "We're gonna be all right, Reid. It will end. It's got to."

Charles nods. As the front continues to vibrate with a showcase of man's technical ingenuity, Charles watches Rogerson absorb Hensley's words. He smiles and sighs and shakes his head. When he's finished, he turns back to the first page to start again. But before he does, he says, "If she ever saw the two of us, come on. Look at me. I'd be the one she'd love. She'd choose me."

Charles watches Rogerson place a finger against his chin, feigning thoughtfulness. His eyes are heavy lidded but a lovely shade of pine green, his jaw sloping and wide, his lips straight and chapped. Charles shakes his head. "Doubtful, Rogerson. Besides, she's not your type, remember?"

"You lucked into her because you're a rich kid with a chess habit. She wouldn't like those big ears you have. Your posture is too perfect and so are your teeth. Real men have some roughness around their edges. And what about your calisthenics routine? That surely disqualifies you." He elbows Charles and huddles once more over the letter.

Charles reciprocates, clocking him once on the back of the head before stepping outside. It is a glorious summer day, with loads of sunshine and a bank of afternoon thunderclouds just beginning to organize in the distant eastern part of the sky. He closes his eyes, gratefully letting the warmth of the sun make his skin hot and tingly. His mind wanders to a place he's never been, where people imagine gold is beneath their feet, where a circus can arrive and transform a piece of the desert into candy-colored magic, where there are rocks as smooth as a girl's cheek, where there is a girl whose cheek—soft and perfectly curved—is the most beautiful thing he can imagine.

He kicks at the dirt beneath his boots as he opens his eyes. She is not standing beside him, barefoot as she likes to be. He'd almost convinced himself that they were sharing the very same patch of earth. Instead he sees the medical tents, hovering together just across the way, and he knows that in just a few hours they will be full of boys just like him, boys who've spent the empty nights longing for the end of this war and who will die on the operating table, or come to in the evac tent missing great pieces of their former selves.

Charles kneels and unlaces his boots. Flinging his socks off his feet, he stands, barefoot, in the dirt, curling his toes. Then he gathers a fistful of the dirt in his hand. She will share his patch of earth. She will stand in the dirt where he's stood. Leaving his boots and socks, he runs to his tent and places the contents of his hand into an envelope.

Dear Hensley,

He writes quickly, hoping to make the early post.

This is the dirt from beneath my feet. Please place it beneath your own. It will be almost like we've shared this day. It will be almost like we've been together, our skin mingling in the fine remnants of yesterday's boulders.

More news later. Until then, barefoot and biddable, I remain,

Charles Reid

Unable to sleep, Hensley wraps herself in the cotton blanket from her bed and walks to the brick patio behind the superintendent's house. It is nearly dawn, but the landscape is cold, the sun's rays still just a premonition in the east. She has brought with her the second of Mr. Reid's letters to come directly to her in two days. This time her father recognized the return address in France, but as he saw Hensley's initial, he handed it to her without a word. His eyebrows, however, were precipitously raised.

> I find my mind distracted from this bloody field and I am grateful. Through the dark nights, I have figured and refigured my every move in the chess game I am playing with your father, but I cannot solve the puzzle of you.

She reads the line again and again. In her last epistle, she described the arrival of the circus, her dizzying trip on the strong man's chair, the way the air smells like licorice. She told him of her life—the dearth of dress shops, the coarse but kind miners who occasionally deliver a dozen fresh eggs or thick-cut bacon and for whom, in return, she mends their shirts and darns their socks. Her favorite, of course, is one in particular named Berto, who has escaped the savagery of the revolution in Mexico City. She also told him about the small, perfect stones that litter the yard. How they feel warm and full of some ancient place as she holds them in her palm. She'd placed a smooth gray one on top of the rock wall that runs the length of their house as she walked her letter to the post. A reminder of how unexpected and perfect his letter had been and that she sent a piece of herself across the ocean to him. And she apologized for the length of her letter, which ran two typewritten pages. *I hope you'll forgive the length of this, knowing that I am surrounded by many things, but mostly by time. Unlike you, my duties are not many and far from important.*

But she knows he wouldn't have received that letter when he wrote the one she reads now. Their lives are overlapping somewhere in the middle of the Atlantic, where a westbound cargo ship flashes its beacon at an eastbound one. Because of the time it takes for their letters to arrive, it is as though Mr. Reid has sent his past thoughts on to the future. In some ways, Hensley cannot believe he is real. She has a hard time imagining a soldier—someone so close to death—caring one way or another about the frivolous musings of a girl in the desert of New Mexico. And part of her believes that if he is real, he must be deranged. A lunacy induced by so much carnage. But his words are clear and genuine: *This is nothing but a single selfish plea: Please write again. I fear I may not have said that in my last letter. Twenty pages if you'd deign. I cannot tire of your words. What madness that across an ocean and amidst this brutality, I feel more connected to you than anything here!*

So she answers. In the barely dawn, Hensley composes the letter in her mind long before her father has gone to work when she will have her way with the typewriter.

Dear Friend,

Your last letter was an underserved windfall. I cannot speak to your madness, but, of course, I am utterly sane! Let me demonstrate. The morning has hardly begun, but I am sitting outside the house on the small patch of bricks my father insists on calling our terrace. The two house cats are nowhere to be found. Perhaps they are hunting, still. The sky in the east is the most tender shade of blue, it resembles the glow around a city streetlamp. It certainly gives no hint of the scorching fireball that will soon crest the horizon. I have a view of the back of Berto and his sister's small house on the hill above our own.

My father is following through on a threat he made weeks ago. At the end of this work day, he will accompany the night shift into the mine. It is one of his efforts to demonstrate his solidarity. I don't think he likes being the boss. His constitution is much too fueled by irreverence. However, for me, he would urge a life of obedience. A life within the bounds of social expectation. If I give up my place at Wellesley in the fall, which may be necessary, his disappointment will be palpable, but I fear it will not be his only or his greatest one.

So while he is descending a thousand feet to gain the confidence of his employees, I will be perfectly free to cause trouble here on the earth's surface. Too bad I am so assuredly sane! My chores will occupy most of the morning. There are several items to be mended and I am diligently writing to a member of the American Field Service overseas (that's you!). Since my father will not be returning for the evening meal, I will be a solitary presence in the house all day. Without anyone watching, I may eat more than my share of the pickled beets and carrots. I may also spread butter on crackers and put my bare feet on the table while I eat. Are you blushing? Surely, this will quell your desire for another letter from this heathen in the desert.

Now that I've bored you with my solitary activities, you may assess my sanity for yourself. But before you do, I must make one more confession: my attachment to your words is the sole thread that keeps my self in one piece these days. I read and reread your letters in each room of the house, before breakfast, after breakfast, to each cat, as I walk along the dry riverbank, and even in my sleep. I cannot say for sure why. Simply that I can feel your voice folding itself into every corner of my body. Though I cannot make any request of you, Mr. Reid—as you have already put your very life at stake for all of us—let me reassure you that every word you can spare, every phrase you discharge, is savored.

It is here that Hensley hears her father stirring. She returns to the house, starts his tea, and slices some bread. She fixes him a sandwich to pack in his tin for dinner. As soon as she opens the can of sardines, the cats appear. She lets them lick the oil from her fingers, smiling at the sensation of their rough little tongues.

She has not been sick for several days now. The skin beneath her apron feels tight, though, and is a nearly constant reminder of her predicament.

She and her father have spoken very little about her condition since she revealed it last week. Often, however, he is now the first to rise after their evening meal, removing her plate and telling her to sit still while he scrapes and cleans their dishes. "You need rest, Hennie. That much I know," he says, smiling kindly as he replaces the dishes in the cupboard.

Hensley suspects that he has not had the news from New York that he's hoped for. Perhaps he is beginning to understand just how poor her judgment has been. Could it be that Lowell would actually disavow his responsibility to this child?

Depending on the hour, Hensley has believed vastly different things about her future. At times, it has seemed that she could have the baby here, in this dusty place, where the fate of being an outcast would be felt less severely than in New York. Other times, she's been sure that one of the letters her father is always writing is to arrange her dispatch to El Paso or Los Angeles in order to deliver the baby anonymously and return on the train, alone, with made-up stories of parties and visits. Still other times, especially as she reads and rereads Mr. Reid's letters, she indulges a restless, reckless fantasy of escaping this fate entirely.

But there is no realistic scenario that appeases the dread in her heart. Every day brings her closer to becoming a mother, yet she knows she is mostly still the same foolish, starry-eyed girl who fell for Lowell's performance. She will soon have to become someone else's guide to life—but look at the mess she's made of her own.

She finishes packing her father's lunch supplies and butters a piece of toast for herself.

"Good morning, Hennie," he says as he reaches past her for the pitcher of milk.

"Morning, Daddy."

"I will not be home for dinner tonight."

"I remembered. I packed you a sandwich and some pickles."

He smiles, taking his time to meet her eyes. "Thank you, dear. You are very kind." He glances at Mr. Reid's latest letter, folded near her coffee cup. "I believe you are pining. Longing for an escape where there is none. Be careful, Hennie. Reality can never compare favorably to the power of our imagination."

Hensley puts her hand on top of the letter, chastising herself for leaving it out. "I couldn't sleep."

"Oh." He nods gravely. Then, placing his hand on top of hers, he says, "You should know that I wrote to your brother." He looks at his teacup. "About you."

His meaning is clear. "Daddy." Hensley turns away and pulls her hands into her lap. She glances at the plain white wall, its expanse marked by the smudges of previous summers' mosquitoes, swatted and killed without a second thought, carelessly. She wasn't ready for news of her condition to make its way back to New York. If it stays here, beneath the old cottonwoods and the endless sky, it remains small and changeable. But for Harold to know, for him to bear the weight of his disappointment as he jostles among the crowds, sits for a shoeshine, walks through the park, means it is fixed—real. "You might have asked me first. Besides, how could telling him possibly help my circumstance?" Hensley breaks the piece of toast on her plate in half.

"It is a matter of grave importance, Hensley. We are a family still."

"Really? Since when? What do we know of his life? He might have a hundred bastard children screaming all over Manhattan—how would we ever know?" She cannot explain her anger. Her words precede her thoughts.

"You cannot stay here, Hensley. It is not practical. It is hardly practical for the two of us. You must think of the child."

She puts her hands to her chest. "I think of the child every moment of every day!"

"But we have to act. Unfortunately, there is only so much time before... before he will not have you."

"Before *he* will not have me? You mean Mr. Lowell Teagan? The very man whose child I am carrying? Does he already know?

What was his response? You are so duplicitous. Have you asked Harold to sit across from him and—what? Offer him a bribe to take care of the mess he created?"

Her father takes his glasses off his face and wipes the lenses with his handkerchief. "Hensley, there is honor in facing the facts."

"Facts? Here are the facts, Daddy: *He* orchestrated this. *He* lied to me. *He* unzipped himself..."

"Enough," he shouts, louder than she's ever heard him raise his voice. Wincing, as though absorbing a blow, he puts his glasses back on and looks at her. "None of that could have happened, Hensley, had you not been alone with him. There is no way around that fact. For that, I hold some responsibility. I had no idea you were unchaperoned."

Hensley's eyes spill the tears that have been gathering, blurring her vision. He offers her the handkerchief still in his hand. Instead, she pulls her apron to her face and wipes it.

"So if he is only required to be a gentleman so long as I am a lady, and I am required to be a lady always, without fail, then I am to blame. Always. It is I who must take responsibility for his actions. For his deceit. And the baby. Is that right?"

"It is not a perfect world, Hennie. But we must live in it."

Hensley laughs at the irony of her father's statement.

"Really? You are such a hypocrite. That sounds just like something President Wilson would say about the war, Daddy. Incredible. With any luck this unfortunate child will be a boy. That way, he can rape and pillage the world with abandon. Choose just when he will stand up for what he believes in and when he will tell the girl she must shut up and take it because that's the way it is. Because for all the power he has in this world, he is too weak to own what happens when he is left alone with a lady."

Her father folds his handkerchief and replaces it in his pocket. As he stands, Hensley throws her arms around his neck. She abandons all restraint and simply sobs. His shirt smells of the juniper berries so plentiful on the bushes beneath the laundry line. Her father holds her tightly, his own chest swelling with emotion. "I thought he loved me, Daddy," Hensley says, wiping at her eyes. "I really did."

Her father places his strong hands on her shoulders. "And he still may," he says, his lips slightly unsteady. He forces a smile and drops his hands to his sides. "This conversation will have to continue later, Hennie. I must get to the mine." He moves his dish to the sink, takes his jacket from the back of his chair, and hesitates slightly in the doorway. "I wish there were another way," he says before collecting his things in the front room.

Hensley nods, busying herself with crumbing the counter. She watches him walk to the truck idling in front of the house, a well-disguised Teresa behind the wheel.

As though he could have possibly predicted the monotony of her long, solitary day, Hensley receives yet another letter from Mr. Reid when she walks to the post after lunch. It is postmarked just a day after his last letter, indicating that his new habit may be to write to her every day. Surely not, Hensley thinks, trying to keep her emotions in check. Surely this is an anomaly.

France

My dear Hensley,

Greetings from CCS #13! I'm afraid your father's sense of the war's futility may be more accurate than I'd hoped. There is so much destruction here, Hensley, and so little hope of a quick end. Yet we carry on. It seems one consequence is that I've become an amateur philosopher, brooding and questioning everything.

Today, a wise man told me that the objective of life is to be happy. Does this seem heretical? I know that duty matters, and service and charity. But is any of that useful if it is done from the depths of despair? I wish that I could observe your face as I rattle off these questions. Do you think I'm naïve, selfish, or dull? Somehow I've not given much thought to my purpose until now. How could that be? I suppose I've been busy defining myself in opposition to my parents. How trite! When I read your words, I can't help but feel that you, too, are struggling with your destiny. And, since we've already agreed that these letters will be a part of our legacy, that we will exist long after our respective deaths (I am not invoking it, I promise, only referencing our previous discussion), it would be nice if I had some clarity about life. I do not want to exist in perpetuity as some sort of foggy, ill-defined character. So, as an exercise in clarity, for you and me and the people of the future, all, I will make a list here. Things I believe:

1. Words are inherently more interesting than pictures. (Which doesn't mean I wouldn't treasure a photograph of you, if possible.)
2. It is harder to be honest than it is to be deceitful.
3. The end of the day is always the loneliest part of it.
4. A good dog can alleviate #3.
5. The strength of a person's mind has nothing to do with their gender. Women's suffrage is fair and right.
6. What's fair and right can take centuries to accomplish.
7. Cabbage should always be prepared by Mr. Lin.
8. Money matters only when it is scarce.
9. The true perfection of chocolate is clear only once

you've placed a half-melted square on a man's tongue whose fingers have been blown off.

10. God is cultural shorthand for the power of human beings to love one another when they've no reason to. God is the history of perseverance and tolerance in the face of horror. God is the celebration of the sanctity of music and art and words.
11. No matter their immortality, nor how many future readers have the pleasure of reading them, your letters could never mean more to anyone than they do to me.

Eagerly awaiting your next, I will remain,

Mr. Charles Reid

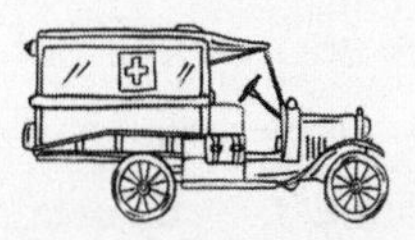

Charles and Rogerson usually only drive the wounded from a relay post near the front to the CCS, but today, because of a particularly disastrous offensive, they will trudge through the carnage of no-man's-land, following the litter bearers, trying to distinguish the living from the dead. For once, their helmets are strapped on tightly and they've both secretly made bargains with the God to whom they pray.

"This is a day for a hot bath and a thick novel, not this bullshit," Rogerson says as the King George struggles through the mud.

"Careful. *You* sound like the spoiled rich kid now."

The rain smacks the windshield in wide, heavy drops. The headlights on the ambulance look yellower than ever against the gray sky.

They pass the relay post and drive into a gulley just the other side of the support trench, where the landscape changes dramatically. The tree branches are blackened and bare; the ground is churned, like a brown and choppy ocean. It is chaos. Men are running between the trenches, their hands covering their heads, their guns swinging at their sides, their faces still tender and pink beneath all the grime.

This latest round of fighting began an entire night and day before. Nobody trusts the current peace, but there are boys who've been waiting all that time, or who've given up and are no longer waiting, but begging for another shot to finish them off, strewn across the battlefield.

A couple of the regiment's own litter bearers intercept Charles and Rogerson and lead them through the trenches to the front. They have hammock stretchers hung over their shoulders and Rogerson and Charles carry three stretchers beneath each arm. It is a dizzying walk, a macabre tour. Decaying arms and legs have been used to shore up the trench, with canteens hanging occasionally from these souring limbs. Charles knows the stench must be composed of urine and blood and rot but it is something more foul than the sum of its parts. He and Rogerson turn their noses and mouths in to their sleeves in order to quell their gag reflex. Several bodies are piled on top of the sandbags, waiting, Charles supposes, for someone to move them. All along both sides of the trenches, there are fat, white, glistening maggots undulating toward the nearest flesh.

As they approach the front trench, the litter bearers turn and motion at the ladder. They must climb over the top, which they do, despite their loads.

The mud beneath their feet smacks and sticks with each step. Suddenly the battlefield erupts with pleas and entreaties. The wounded grab at their ankles and whine profanities. Rogerson and Charles split up, each trailed by a litter bearer. Charles kneels beside the first body he sees, holding his hand beneath the boy's nose, feeling for breath. There is nothing. He closes the boy's eyes and puts a piece of black tape across his tags, securing them to his chest. He moves to the next body. This boy flinches when Charles touches his face. They load him onto a stretcher and a few privates, who've been recruited to help, carry him the mile or so back to the King George.

A low rumble begins somewhere far beyond the dark clouds and Charles follows the lead of the litter bearer, who slides himself into a wide, soggy hole nearby. There is another soldier already there, curled into a fetal position. They mimic him, with their hands held over their heads, and they wait, eyes shut tight.

As they wait for the plane they're hiding from to make its appearance, Charles realizes that the boy already crouched in the hole is not moving at all. His hands are not trembling the way his own are. Charles places his fingers on the soldier's helmet, trying to move his head slightly so that he can feel for a breath or a pulse, but the whole thing falls back against him, the front of the boy's neck all but gone. He grips the helmet, with its young face still buckled in tightly, and swears.

"Help me get him out," Charles says to the litter bearer. "Otherwise he'll be buried in here. His family won't ever know."

Charles straps a piece of the black tape to his dog tags to keep them in place, and the two of them push the boy's heavy body out of the hole onto the battlefield. The head threatens to roll back in, but Charles pushes it gently into the mud.

Turns out, the rumble they heard was a false alarm—only thunder. The rain's assault intensifies, making it difficult for them to climb out of the hole.

When they do, Charles accelerates his pace, distinguishing the living from the dead quickly. They've almost covered an eighth of the field, when Rogerson yells at him. "We're full, Reid. Help me with this one more, then we'll head back."

Charles, soaked and chilled, his hands covered in blood, nods.

As he places another piece of black tape across a soldier's tags, he calls out, "I'm really enjoying the thick novel and this bath. Outstanding."

Though he can hardly make out Rogerson's figure through the rain, he hears him chuckle. "Smart-ass," he says as another deep rumble shakes the gray sky.

They carry the final stretcher as best they can through the sloppy mud. As the rain continues, the ground is becoming less mud and more water. Charles loses his footing once or twice, but he grips the stretcher tightly so as to keep the poor boy steady. He's got a pretty good gash across his head, as well as a bullet wound in his abdomen that is clotted with thick, dark blood. Rogerson is walking backward and Charles can see the lumps of the sandbags lining the trench not too far beyond him.

Through the pelting rain, the two of them catch one another's eye. The rumble of another round of thunder begins in the dark sky and Rogerson mumbles, "Bad fucking weather for a war, Reid."

Charles nods, but he notices that a few of the other soldiers around them have begun an awkward, hunched trot toward the trench. Charles knows there are other groggy, swollen-eyed soldiers hidden in that trench, their guns ready to fire rounds into the rain.

Charles puts his hand up, the stretcher lurching. The wounded boy screams, but all Charles can hear is the rumbling that is now so close to them that he feels it through his boots in the soles of his wet feet.

"Down, Rogerson," he calls, still holding the stretcher with one hand, ignoring the boy's pleas. "Not thunder," he says, his words swallowed by the sudden rattle of bullets pelting them from the sky and the returning barrage from the trench.

Suddenly the smoke and the rain are inextricable. There is no way to tell which is emanating from the ground and which from the sky. It is as though the whole day is evaporating. He and Rogerson both hold tightly to the stretcher, running toward the trench. The ground is unforgiving, puddles and holes and mud making their progress slow and awkward. When his feet meet solid resistance, Charles looks down and notices that it is a dead body providing the traction to his boots.

He moves faster. They are almost there.

Just as Rogerson jumps into the trench, his end of the stretcher balanced on the sandbags, Charles falls. He lets go of the stretcher and scrambles to get up. Rogerson is pulling the stretcher toward him, into the trench, but Charles can't quite find his footing. He doesn't understand. He tries and falls again; the cold mud slaps his cheek like a fierce reprimand.

The buzz, the gnawing in the sky, drowns his curses. The ground seems to have vanished beneath him. Something about the physical world has changed. His balance is off; his hearing is fading inexplicably. The plane climbs higher, disappearing into the clouds. The sky goes quiet and Charles laughs, relieved that his clumsiness has not cost him his life. But once again, he tries to stand and cannot.

Rogerson grabs him beneath his arms and pulls him into the trench. It is then that Charles understands. He feels a deep burning and he is sure that his leg is on fire. The flames climb from his toes to his hip, crisp and hot. "Blanket," he cries. "Quick. Put it out." But there is no fire. There is no leg.

Or, rather, the leg has turned into a trough of blood. Nothing looks as it should. The mud-covered straw beneath him oozes through, mingling with the muck that was his leg. Charles hears Rogerson barking at the privates to find another stretcher. But what has been done will not be undone.

Rogerson heaves Charles over his own shoulder and runs through the putrid trench, Charles's own vomit falling onto the filthy, wet, exhausted soldiers whose guns are still aimed at the sky.

Rogerson props Charles in the passenger seat of the King George, the blood ruining everything. "Not protocol," Charles manages to say before he loses consciousness.

Delighted by Mr. Reid's new letter, but left completely unable to concentrate on her chores, Hensley follows the cats to their afternoon sunbath. She brings the embroidery basket with her, without any intention of working. Instead, she stares at the myriad colors of the floss, her fingers lingering on the silky, brilliant strands. With little effort, she could stitch nearly anything: cats in a garden, men in a motorcar, a baby in a cradle. But she wants none of it. She finds herself having to gasp for a breath every so often, as though even her automatic functions are in revolt. For some reason, Mr. Reid's lovely letter has only made her more despondent.

Shutting the lid of the basket, she closes her eyes and wishes for the day's end. But then, as soon as her eyes are closed, she opens them, wishing, instead, for the day to seize right here. To arrest itself and go no further. Let the sun remain just where it is, blazing hot, the other side of the earth in an eternal night. Then surely, her life, too, could be suspended, frozen without moving forward. She would not have to move forward into whatever drudgery is waiting for her. Any day now she might receive the expected proposal from Mr. Teagan (would he, really?), along with a telegram from Harold apprising her father of the particulars: the inevitable moment in which this trio of men will tell her they've arranged her future.

Just as she has decided to halt the day just where it is, she hears a loud noise from Berto and Teresa's house up the hill. Leaving the cats and her embroidery basket, Hensley steps off the brick patio. She listens intently. But it is quiet again. The only noise is a lizard or rodent rustling in the dried leaves against the wall. She ventures several steps farther. Suddenly there is a voice, hardly audible, muttering. As Hensley climbs the hill, the sound gets fainter, as though she is walking away from its source. She stops and turns, looking down at the little brick patio where the cats still sleep. A sudden breeze lifts the hair from her neck and bangs the screen door against its frame. The cats look up from their naps simultaneously, startled. Hensley's embroidery basket falls from its place on the crate, spilling the floss onto the bricks in a colorful mess. A cloud of dust circles Hennie's face and stings her eyes. She shuts them, the darkness disorienting and dizzying. Then, as suddenly as it began, it stops.

She opens her eyes and the day looks just as it did moments ago. Still, the muttering has ceased, and she feels a stinging sense of lost possibility. As though the desert has spoken to her and she has not understood its meaning. Looking for reassurance, Hensley continues on her way up to Teresa and Berto's house, hoping for a visit with Teresa.

As she approaches, she sees that the screen door is propped open with a heavy ceramic crock. There are several empty glass jars on either side of the door, like ornaments.

"Teresa," she calls, a few feet away from the door. "Are you home?"

There is no reply. Instead, Hennie hears a scraping, as though someone is pushing a broom across the floor. She peeks her head inside. Her eyes, accustomed to the bright day, are blinded for a moment and she cannot see a thing.

A man's voice comes at her from somewhere deep inside. "Who are you?"

Hennie jumps. She turns around and faces the open door, her hand on its hinges. "From down the hill. The superintendent's daughter. Hensley Dench. Please excuse me. I was looking for... someone."

"For my sister?"

"Um, I thought I heard something."

"She's not here. Probably working."

"She's my friend," Hensley says, hoping that he'll understand she is not there to snoop, that their secret is still safe. "Are you okay? I mean, is there anything you need?"

The scraping begins again. Hensley turns around, her eyes now adjusted to the dark room. There is a small cot in the far corner and a figure in it, holding on to a long wooden pole.

"Teresa doesn't have any friends," he says, with effort.

"Let me help you," Hensley says, walking across the room and bending down to retrieve the small leather-bound book that the pole is aiming for. "Here," she says, standing over the cot. "Is this what you need?"

His face is nearly identical to Teresa's, except for the dark but meager whiskers that color his cheeks. He drops the pole on the ground beside him and takes the book from her hand.

For a moment, it seems he will not acknowledge her assistance. Then he brings the book to his face, breathing in its scent.

"Thank you. I've been working on that for an hour."

"Oh, what a chore." Hensley looks around the rest of the room. In the kitchen, grease from an uneaten breakfast plate wafts across the room.

"How are you feeling?" Hensley asks, looking back at his face.

He closes his eyes. "Half-dead."

Hensley stares at his gaunt face. His hands have fallen to his chest again and his fingers are wrapped around the book with hardly any life.

"Shall I call for the doctor? I'm sure he would come if it's urgent." Hensley is confronted with the odor of urine nearby and as soon as her eyes see the metal jug beside his bed, she wishes she hadn't.

He opens his eyes. "No. This is not urgent. This is ordinary; it's how I feel every day that I can think clearly. Teresa has put the pistol far out of my reach. Even out of the pole's reach. But, really, what's the difference?"

Nobody has ever spoken to her so bluntly. Certainly not a stranger. She thinks of Mr. Reid's letters. The pistol that accompanies him everywhere. The bullets that no doubt search for him, day after day. The death that surrounds him, that he struggles mightily against.

"The difference is everything," she says, her heart racing. "It is absolutely everything."

"For you, maybe. Not for me. This cot is a coffin, only the corpse is uncooperative."

Looking at his pallor, the way his fingers hover around the book, the fatigue behind his eyes, Hensley worries he is sicker than anyone knows.

"What has happened to you? Have you become a ghost?" he suddenly asks.

Hensley furrows her brow. "Whatever are you talking about?"

"Are all my hallucinations caused by this fever? I swear I saw my mother. Right here, in this room."

Hensley shakes her head, her face blank.

"Do you know my mother?" he asks, confused.

"No, I'm sorry. I never knew her."

"Do you know how she died?"

"Your mother?" As she wonders how in the world he would expect her to know this, she is struck by an image. In a city she's never seen before, a woman runs through an outdoor market. She is being chased by something ferocious, but it is out of sight. Hensley hears the growling in her ears. Her heart races with the anxiety of the hunted. And then a blast of warmth radiates from her belly to the tips of her fingers. She folds her arms across her chest. "No. I have no idea."

Berto looks away from her, to the wall beside his cot. He begins to speak, slowly describing their history. Hensley strains to hear all of his words. He tells her that his mother, like so many, had been widowed by the revolution. They lived on a large cattle and rum plantation that covered a hundred acres outside Mexico City. His father was the foreman. It was a good job. He was tired every night. Berto and Teresa had a carefree childhood. They drank fresh milk every day, often straight from the teat, caught grasshoppers, relishing the way their legs pushed hard against their closed hands, tried to pull fish from the stream that ran behind their quarters, and never wanted for a hot meal. Their mother was a midwife and had delivered all the babies on the ranch. She knew rhymes and songs and how to treat a sour stomach or a broken bone. The parish priest taught them and the other children how to read. A nun spoke to them in English.

When Madero was shot, most of the laborers left. Things were changing. Resentment grew. Everybody was somebody's enemy.

Berto continues to stare at the wall, his voice weakening. Hensley leans over him, bound to his words.

During the upheaval, the jefe left the hacienda and went to California. Took his valet, his mistress, and a truck full of rum. His wife was left behind with the crystal and the gold chandeliers and an empty set of servants' beds. She asked Berto's father to stay. For protection. She paid him in silver goblets. One a day. Berto's mother objected. She wanted to leave.

When the mob came, there were seventeen goblets. One in every pot, two in their father's worn-out boots, three in their mother's medical bag, six pushed into the bottom of their parents' mattress, and one under each of their blankets. At night, as he and Teresa closed their eyes and listened to their mother humming the fragments of a lullaby, they each tucked a goblet under one arm like a stiff, cold doll.

Berto's face becomes still, as though perhaps he has fallen asleep. His eyes are closed. But then, he continues, his voice barely a whisper.

His father met the men—some of whom who had walked the fields at his side just months before, supplying branding irons and dirty jokes until sunset—at the door of the plantation's hacienda. His mother took him and Teresa to the barn and covered them in hay. They stayed there all night, holding their goblets tight. The donkeys were braying and stomping, the straw scratched their bare arms and legs, and the smell of animal manure was everywhere. His mother shivered between them, barely able to control her panic.

However his father tried to reason with the men, it failed. They nailed him to the door and left him there while they ran past, filling their burlap sacks with every shiny thing in the place. The doña hid in a secret passage between the pantry and the dining room. When she emerged and saw the walls stripped of their gold-framed portraits, the tables turned over, the couches' upholstery ripped and gutted, the hooks in the kitchen missing all their shiny copper pots, human feces on the marble-top dining table, and the silk rugs on fire, she ran out of the house—perhaps she never even noticed their father, sacrificed, hanging on her front door.

At this point, Hensley's knees quiver and buckle. She folds herself onto the floor beside Berto's cot. He turns to face her. "He lived three days."

Hensley puts a hand to her mouth. *Dear Lord,* she begins, but there is nothing else. Nothing. The silence gathers around them and presses hard on her head and chest. *Dear Lord,* she tries again, but fails to continue. Berto's breathing has turned rhythmic. Hensley examines his face closely. At one corner of his mouth, spittle gathers and leaks gently onto his cheek. His eyebrows are perfect black dash marks in the middle of a sentence. She does not dare wake him, but Hensley cannot help but wonder about his mother. The image of the chase has faded, but Hensley can still hear the terrified heartbeat, as if it were her own.

With great effort, she stands and moves quietly to the kitchen. As she begins to tidy up, a jar falls from the counter and shatters. "Oh, I'm so sorry," she says, turning toward Berto, but he is still, quiet.

She wraps her hand around the broom that is leaning against the wall and begins to collect the scattered pieces of glass into a pile. Mixed in with the shards of glass, there are several unmistakable flecks of gold. Picking through the pile with her fingers, she tries to segregate one from the other, but it is an impossible and bloody task. Her index finger suffers a small but painful gash. She sucks on it, drawing the blood into her mouth. Pulling a mixing bowl from the shelf, she sweeps everything into it, both glass and gold. It is a beautiful and dangerous combination of ingredients. She imagines cracking an egg and pouring some milk on top and scooping golden glass fritters onto the cast iron. It reminds her of a fairy tale—a helpless young girl concocting a deadly breakfast for a slothful and oppressive king with shrunken teeth. But killing the king will not liberate the young girl. She is doomed.

Hensley gives the bowl a shake, just to hear its noise, then sets it on the counter, embarrassed by her clumsiness.

Hensley wraps her finger in her apron. Crossing the floor again, she stands above Berto, wondering if she should do something for him. Wet a rag for his brow or brew some tea. Instead, she shoos away the flies that are gathering, landing and levitating with the alacrity of eager suitors. The book is still in his hands—or, rather, beneath his hands—since they no longer have any intention in them. Hensley tries to read the spine, but its gold letters are faded and in another language, presumably Spanish.

Letting the apron fall away, Hensley checks her finger. It has stopped bleeding.

There must be something she can do. As the sun rises higher, the air coming through the open windows is no longer cool. With the heat, the metal jug by the bed is becoming ever more pungent. The flies are drawn to it, some so spellbound that they now float, lifeless, on the surface.

Using her apron as a makeshift glove, Hensley grabs the handle and hefts it outside. Walking a few paces away from the house, she squats, turns her head into her shoulder, and holds the pail as far away from her body as she can. In a single motion, she dumps it and it pools into a momentary puddle before soaking into the ground. The slightly furry black flies are all that remain. Hensley takes a deep breath.

The cats have abandoned the sun, choosing instead a patch of shaded dirt somewhere out of sight. Her embroidery basket, weeping its colorful contents, is now the lone inhabitant of the patio. Beyond her house, she can see the post office and the bar. Farther still, the dirt road leading through the hills to the mine is visible. The rhythmic clomping of horses' hooves echoes up from Main Street.

The jug is heavy in her hand and she walks carefully, avoiding prickly pears and goatheads along the way back to the front of the house.

She pushes on the door and it opens into the room, again confronting her with its darkness. "Hello?" she says, slightly afraid that Berto may have slipped away. Instead, as her eyes adjust, the room is just as she pictured it moments ago. Berto is alone, asleep in the bed, his hands still swaddling the book, his chest visibly moving beneath it. She replaces the empty jug beside the bed.

Berto groans quietly in his sleep. Hensley wrings a damp towel out and carefully places it across his brow. Beneath its weight, he shifts slightly, falling deeper into some faraway place.

Hensley lifts a chair from the kitchen and sets it beside his bed. She closes her eyes and tries to place Mr. Reid beside her, in his own chair, in civilian clothes. Maybe even in a jacket she's tailored for him out of the beautiful gray flannel that she's coveted so often at the fabric depot on West Forty-fourth. She urges him to sit, cross his long legs, fold his hands in his lap, gaze at her in the dimness and smile. Or sigh. Or rub his eyes. Or request a story. The unfolding of a drama. Or the revelation of a secret. She realizes that despite the distance, he is her closest friend. It is he with whom she longs to be.

Reaching for the towel on Berto's forehead, she finds herself suddenly terrified. What if it were Mr. Reid instead of Berto here in the bed, with his hands splayed across the leather volume? The thought startles her out of her chair and she walks the floor, her mind racing. What if he is gravely injured overseas? With some other young woman tending to him just as she tends to Berto? Will she even know? She and her father are no relation to Mr. Reid. He might vanish and the only trace she'll ever have of him is his letters.

"You must not," she says aloud, desperate to be heard. "You must live." Returning to her place beside Berto, all of their lives conflated into one, Hensley reaches out, places her own pale hand on his arm, and leans close to his face. "Do not die," she whispers. "Please. You must survive."

Beneath her hand, his arm twitches violently and Hensley recoils.

Her tears betray some deep sorrow that feels familiar yet distant. She rewets the towel and places it with care upon his forehead. "I will stay right here," she says, collecting herself, drying her cheeks with her sleeve. Berto's book falls at her feet. Looking down, she picks it up and then returns her gaze to the bed. Berto sleeps on.

She opens the book. Its weight on her lap is reassuring. On the inside of the front cover is a list of names and dates. A family tree. Written in different hands, with different ink, this is their history, beginning in 1820. Hensley places a timid finger on the only two names she knows, Humberto and Teresa, born on the very same day, 1899. Then she places her finger on their father's name and his birth date. She closes her eyes, imagining that baby, the chubby cheeks and feathery hair. Then, at the end, his hands roughened, bloodied, torn, useless. What monsters we become, she thinks.

The book must be a hundred years old, for there are nearly a half dozen generations. Perfectly written names and dates, so carefully placed on this sacred page. How small we are, Hensley thinks, tracing the names of long-gone men and women. And then, thinking of the telegrams crossing the country, the imminent wedding gifts and baby blankets, how very large. She speaks their names as best she can, invoking history.

She turns the page. The words are in Spanish, but contrary to what she expected, it is not a Bible. It looks like a novel, with beautifully inked chapter titles. She tries to sound out some of the words, searching to hear what comforts Berto, but just then his eyes open suddenly. Frantically, he reaches out. Hensley places the book into his hands and he relaxes. Her own heart is racing, the sound of it deafening her.

"So thirsty," Berto says, his voice still thick with sleep.

"Of course." Hensley stands, walking across the floor without any feeling in her legs. She fills a jar with water and returns to the chair beside the bed. She notices that the pillow behind Berto's head is dark with sweat. "I think your fever has broken," she says.

Helping him to lean up on one elbow, Hensley guides the jar to his lips. He gulps noisily. Hensley smiles.

As he restores himself on the pillow, she says, "Better?"

He nods. "Thanks."

"You're welcome."

"You don't need to stay. Every day is like this. I am a predictable show. Nothing very interesting here."

Hensley can't help but laugh. "Utterly boring."

Berto furrows his brow. "Do I talk in my sleep?"

Hensley doesn't answer his question. Instead, hoping for distraction, gesturing to his book, she asks, "Would you like to sit up so you can read?"

His fingers tighten as he shakes his head. "No. You've done enough." His voice is not entirely kind.

Hensley is surprised but not offended.

"Of course," she says, pulling the cloth from his forehead as though it is a delicate object. Once more, she wrings it out in the sink. She refills his jar with water and places it within reach. They do not exchange any other words before she leaves.

As she walks down the hill, Hensley notices a swath of thick cumulus clouds gathering in the east. Huddled in intimate bundles of conspiracy, the sight catches her breath and gives her a focus.

My dear, dear, unexpected clouds, she begins, *how reassuring you are amid that unforgivably vast blue sky. Where have you been hiding? I've yearned for you. When Mr. Reid mentioned a pounding rain in one of his recent letters, I nearly choked on my own envy. And now, here you are. When I most need reassurance. If only you could carry messages from one part of the world to another. Glide across the sky not just into soft, moving shapes, but into gently sloping letters. I might glance up and know that he is alive and well.*

On her way inside, she kneels to replace the embroidery thread into her basket. Each bundle is hot to the touch—a limp, colorful brood. Hensley tucks them carefully away and stands up, smoothing her apron across her waist. The blood from her finger has dried in an ugly brown stain.

Just before she leaves the terrace and the burning midday sun, Hensley glances up the hill once more. The house is small and innocuous. Four walls plunked down in the middle of this desert. A flat metal roof, unafraid of storms. Windows with glass so thin that the dust seeps through, leaving small drifts in the sills and across the floor. A door with hinges that squeak, calling out their sorrows to anyone who'll listen.

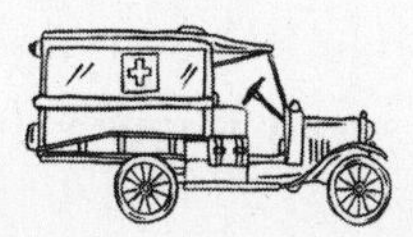

He drifts across the ocean, above the swells, but is still aware of the gorgeous spray just teasing the bottoms of his feet. The air cools all around him. *I don't matter at all,* he thinks. People die every day. Everywhere. We're all dying. The ending is always the same. You'd think life would have more variety. But it doesn't. It dies.

Then, with this understanding, Charles hears her words, as though she were beside him.

As this little stack of stones grows taller, I wonder what it will look like as our correspondence continues. Perhaps the wall will become an artifact of our friendship.

My father tells me of the miners' superstitions. Whistling in the tunnel is bad luck. Red-haired women are bad luck. Empty boots left beside the bed are bad luck. Good luck is rarely spoken of, and only in hushed voices as are used in church.

My father warns me about the dangers of fantasy. He wants me to have a cautious mind. I'm afraid, however, that my mind will not conform to any reality in regard to you. It seems that you—five thousand miles away—have become my dearest friend.

Then, finally, something he doesn't recognize.

Do not die. Please. You must survive.

Charles is terrified; she is so close but he is fading. He has no strength. If he could stay just a bit longer, he might finally see her face.

Dying is so easy. His body is ready, the fading light is seductive as it tunnels around him, blurring everything. Thinking only of her words, Charles forces his body through an ugly dark into an even uglier light.

He knows this place. He sees Dr. Foulsom's dark, tired eyes and his unshaven face and the calm, unhurried nuns with such pale hands. His leg seems to be dangling off the bed, numb. He tries to pull it back. The pain swells through him, turning everything black.

"Sorry about this," Foulsom says, his voice hollow. Charles had shared a cigarette with him before driving toward the front in the gray fog. "We've had to take the leg, Reid. Glad you're still with us, though."

A sympathetic nurse brings a canteen to his mouth. She lifts his head with a strong hand. His lips are raw and his throat tastes of blood. "Thanks," he tries to say as she sets him back down, but his tongue is thick and slow.

She wipes his forehead with a cool cloth and tells him, "*Ça va,* Monsieur Reid. You returned to us. This is all that matters." He recognizes her kindness but knows how easy it is to lie to an injured man. He feigns sleep and soon it is real.

When he wakes, Rogerson sits beside him.

"They got you on some nice morphine, Reid. Can you tell? We're all a bit envious of that."

Charles closes his eyes. His body is heavy, as though he's turned to lead. He cannot move his head or lift his arms. He smells the sourness that he knows means infection and he hardly has the energy to hope it's not from his own wound. Foulsom has pulled off the bandages and is checking the drain that he knows must be buried somewhere in what's left of his leg.

He both does and does not want to see what is left.

Foulsom lays a hand on the bedsheet covering Reid's good leg. As he walks away, he says to Rogerson, "Still dodgy."

Rogerson leans close to Charles. "He's a prick. But he saved you, so I can't hate him anymore."

Charles tries to smile. If only to assuage Rogerson's worry, which is palpable.

Sacha knows the mine has given up fifteen million since 1915. His wife's cousin, Thomas Wright, rode into this valley as an act of youthful rebellion almost ten years ago. He'd left his family's home in California, intent on proving that his mother was wrong about his poor manners and sullen expression. His father had deserted them five years earlier, and though he swore he'd never forgive him, Thomas thought he understood. Rumor has it, Thomas visited the red-light district in Kingston, spent three nights and all his money on a girl with a glass eye. He thought she might have loved him, but when his money was gone, she danced with one fellow and let another follow her up the stairs with his hands on her waist.

Thomas stole a bottle of gin from the bar and rode his horse into the star-studded desert, intent on dying, his gun pressed against his hip like an eager lover. He drank until morning, reviewing and extending the list of grievances he'd endured in his twenty-two years. Then, as the sun came up, he discovered that he'd fallen asleep with his face in the dirt and his horse unhitched. He stood, kicked the empty bottle, and reached for his pistol. Instead of shooting himself, now he was intent on killing the ungrateful horse. With his head pounding, Thomas began tracking the beast. It was a miserable morning, with slow-moving flies lingering on his face, the sky nearly white with the summer heat, and no breeze at all. He threw rocks at birds and ached for any small spot of shade. There was no sign of the horse.

Finally, weeping for his own stupidity, yearning for the comforts of home, wondering how he ever thought life could get better, he shot his gun at the side of a rocky cliff. The noise cracked the day open, filling the quiet just after it with fear. Even Thomas was afraid of what might happen next.

But here's what did: his horse whinnied and ran right out of a deep gash in the cliff, and a heavy piece of rock fell away, throwing a dust cloud into the heat. Where the bullet hit the rock, it revealed a milky white quartz bleeding all through the side of it. Having grown up in California, with rumors of gold fortunes swirling around his cradle, Thomas's fingers and toes vibrated with the possibility of that ore. He walked slowly toward the horse, lifted its reins from the dirt, and leaned against it, basking in the reassurance of the animal's deep, steady breath.

Believing the quartz must have been a hallucination, Thomas stood there for a long time, pleading with each and every force he could imagine. The tears he'd already cried stung his cheeks and reminded him of his cowardice. Eventually, though, he gathered his courage and faced the rock again. To his surprise, the quartz was, in fact, there. Startlingly pale against the expanse of brown. Like a shock of lightning trapped in a dark sky. With the horse's breath still hot and reassuring on his neck, Thomas approached the rock. He laid his hands on the cool face of the ore. From this moment forward, he would be a very rich man and his tears, when they were cried, would never sting his cheeks again but would be caught by a fine linen kerchief, monogrammed with silk thread.

Thomas Wright married Ramona, the girl with the glass eye, and built a large house in Kingston, hoping to fill it with their offspring. When this didn't happen, he took her to doctors all over the world to find out why. It was during one of these trips that she disappeared—crawled out a bathroom window in Baltimore and hasn't been seen since.

Thomas swore he would not return to Kingston without her, so he spent his money following the trail of his fugitive wife, the same pistol that he'd shot that desperate morning ten years ago strapped to his hip. The mine in southern New Mexico that continued to fund his quest required a new superintendent at the very same moment Sacha Dench resigned his position at the *Times*. Through family connections, each man learned of the other's needs.

The miners know of this family connection and have distrusted the newspaperman from New York from the moment he arrived. The first thing they did was begin cuffing their pants again, a practice that every previous superintendent had outlawed. But Sacha didn't suspect that small nuggets of gold could be smuggled out of the mine, hidden in these cuffs, when the men ascended the shaft, their faces blank and tired.

Despite this new perk, the other consequence of Sacha's inexperience was a swift decline in morale. Working in the mine, spending twelve hours thousands of feet below ground, requires that each man trust his coworkers. With a naïve superintendent, the men suspect that not only are the others all cuffing a few nuggets for themselves, but that there are other weak spots. Is the hoist man sleeping on the job? Can they be assured that their shift will be returned to the surface on time? Will there be food in the cook tent when they return? Are the tram lines being maintained? Is the spark man stingy with his fuses?

Though Sacha Dench is not a miner, he does know something about human nature. The suspicion and mistrust at the mine are palpable. It reminds him of recent months in the newsroom at the *Times.*

When he arrives just before dusk in dungarees, tall boots, and his own carbide strapped to his head, the miners snicker and tease. This does not bother him. The foreman, Henry, greets him with a handshake and directs him to the crew cart they will ride into the mine. Sacha folds his legs into one of the carts and sits beside Henry. The night shift piles in behind them, and he can smell that few of them have bothered to bathe. Their picks and hammers rattle against the side of the cart as they begin their journey into the tiny black tunnel, carved into the side of the mountain. The air is cool and thin in the tunnel and as they descend an invisible track the miners whistle high-pitched good-byes to the daylight. Sacha closes his eyes, thinking he will adjust to the darkness, but there remains no difference in what he can see whether they are open or shut. The darkness is so complete it's as though he himself has disappeared. Momentarily, he feels weightless and empty. He clasps his hands in his lap to reassure himself of his own existence.

Hensley's words still nag at the edges of his thoughts. Has he become a hypocrite? The truth is, he doesn't want to urge her into a marriage of necessity. Whatever rare happiness she might claim on her own terms might be better than marrying the very louse who assaulted her. But, fearing his own sentimentality, he wrote to Harold so that someone else—someone more practical than he—could help shoulder the burden of persuading her to make a wise decision. Her situation reflects, to some degree, his own failings as a father, his own inability to recognize the perils of ordinary life. For a young girl to grow up without a motherly influence is unfortunate, but surely he could have done more to protect her. Perhaps his own preoccupation with his work has had more dire consequences than ending up here, in this desolate place.

Regardless of the cause, he now doubts his own objectivity. He fears his own cowardice. Despite the shame of Hensley's situation, he loves her more each day. She is a lively, fearless girl. Her spirit is so much like her mother's it both soothes and pains him. Olivia's death often seems so long ago, the phenomenon of being loved receded so quickly, overpowered by the terrible loneliness left in its wake. He often coaxes himself to remember her ways, her mischievous sense of humor, her easy affection, her contagious smile. Though painful, he knows that there are lessons she can still teach him. How to be attentive to the children, how to laugh more easily and often, how to forgive himself when he does not. Somehow, Hensley has emerged every bit as sweet and smart and loving as Olivia. If she were to go now, if he were to watch her train pull out of the station in El Paso on her way to marry the man who defiled her, the drive back to this arid place would be an extraordinary hardship. And every day thereafter.

But this is nonsense. It is utterly irresponsible. He is her father. However he has failed, he knows his duty now must be to see her begin a life of her own. To become settled in a marriage. And how much easier that would be if her mother were alive. She could tell Hensley, with some authority, that real love is not the stuff of cheap novels but, rather, a force to be cultivated and cajoled, separate and apart from desire. Is this what Olivia would say? In the darkness of the tunnel, he wipes at his eyes. A new grief swells as he must acknowledge that he would like to share this burden. Regardless of the pain it might cause her, he wants Olivia to be here now more than ever. To look into his eyes and love him again. Together, they could long to undo what cannot be undone. Together. What a lovely word, he thinks.

Their own courtship had been chaste. He hadn't even touched her lips with his own until the night of their marriage. But he'd memorized the curve of her lashes, the length of each finger, every freckle on her face, the scent of her breath after tea, the way her nostrils flared when she stifled a giggle, the beads of perspiration that flanked her temples when the sun was hot, the fierce look in her eyes when she disagreed with him. These details accompanied him through the long months of their betrothal.

It's true that he often infuriated his wife. She always wished he were more diplomatic, less ideological, lighter-hearted. But there was never any doubt of his love for her. He cherished her. He cannot endure the thought that his daughter would be any less treasured by her husband. But he also cannot conjure an honest man who would treasure the mother of a bastard child. The world is not a very imaginative place.

Henry leans close to Sacha and says, only, "Sunrise." Their cart mates turn on their headlamps and he follows their lead. Now he can see that the walls of the shaft are supported by thick wooden beams overhead. Soon the passage widens and they enter a huge cavern. A half dozen men disembark from the cart and Henry directs them to take their places with their hammers and picks to chip away at the quartz. Henry is a tall man with a thick black beard that covers most of his face. Only his eyes, a startling green, prevent him from being a creature drawn completely from black and white. He watches the miners studiously, directing their steel chisels in his soft voice, then returns to his place beside Sacha.

On the wall hangs a wooden block with a series of black bells that are connected to the hoist man who sits in the small office adjacent to the mine's entrance. This is the way all messages are delivered between this blackened universe and the lighted world.

The cart keeps moving and the black ahead of them gives way to their headlamps. Sacha's ears plug with the change in altitude. Their beams throw shadows against the rock. That this whole world exists below the ground they walk on seems as improbable to him as the circus that drove into town.

In the next shaft, the muckers jump out and move toward the shovels that line the wall like single girls at a dance. They confront the piles of loose rock that are waiting to be loaded into the ore carts parked on the adjoining track. In places, the ceiling is so low they have to shovel while nearly doubled over. The noise of the metal shovels scraping against rock echoes into the dark tunnel ahead of and behind them. And as the rock tumbles into the ore cart, there is no room for thought. Sacha wonders that they are not all deaf from the noise. But Henry seems to be speaking to some of the men, gesturing to the carts and then to his watch.

The cart descends farther now, the din swallowed by the steep shaft behind them. Sacha pictures the map of this underground world that hangs on the wall of his office. It is a series of lines, both vertical and horizontal, with shaded sections of ore overlaying the shafts. It could very easily be a map of the subway tunnels in New York. But this is not New York and there is no stop at Times Square.

Finally, the cart yields in an opening no bigger than a child's fort. This is where the most recent ore has been found. There are only three of them left in the crew cart. Henry turns to face Sacha.

"Mr. Dench, you know our powder man, Amador."

Amador reaches his hand out to Sacha's. "Sir. Not many superintendents wanna be around for the blast."

Sacha nods, his throat dry.

Amador steps out of the crew cart but cannot stand up straight. His work focuses on a new vein of white quartz that's been located. There has already been deep holes drilled around the ore and now Amador will set a fuse in each of the holes to blast away the surrounding rock. There is a wooden ladder on the opposite wall that descends down a small hole.

Pointing, he says, "That's the escape hatch. I will meet you there after I've lit the fuses."

Henry leads the way. Sacha follows him. The wooden ladder sheds a splinter into his forefinger and he winces. Henry crouches and Sacha does so, too, his hands spread over his ears. They wait.

Eventually, Sacha's legs tremble with the effort of kneeling. He is not accustomed to such physical feats. It reminds him of his age. He begins to question the sagacity of this endeavor. He is the superintendent—not a young man seeking their approval. Yet he cannot deny his esteem for the men who make this their living. This daily descent into a labyrinth of dark chambers, where a breath of fresh air becomes a luxury of which one could spend the entire day dreaming, requires a strong will. To Sacha, the sensation of fresh air entering his lungs is starting to seem as unlikely as one more kiss from his long-dead wife.

"How's it coming, Amador?" Sacha says loudly, removing his hands from his ears, his voice echoing through the closed chamber.

"Yep," Amador says, giving no other hint to his status.

Henry crouches beside Sacha, their shoulders and elbows touching. He shakes his head, admonishing Sacha for the interruption. Whispering, he says only, "Live explosives." Sacha is confronted by the smell of Henry's last cigarette, now stale on his breath.

Sacha nods, willing the bones in his legs to cease their aching and the muscles to release their cramping. He imagines climbing up the ladder, just to stretch his legs, have a peek at what that damn powder man is doing. How long might he be expected to wait like this? He realizes how little he knows about the workings of this underground world. Like a rodent in a crowded nest, he starts dreaming of escape. His fingers scrape mechanically at the hardened dirt in front of him.

It is at this moment that the call comes from Amador, "Fire in the hole!"

There is a silence broken only by Amador's feet, scuffling across the dirt above them. His satchel sails in first, like some frantic, disoriented bird. Then, forsaking the ladder, Amador jumps in as well, his legs pulled in to his chest as though the cavern where Sacha and Henry are huddled is a swimming hole on a hot summer day. Amador's hand grazes Sacha's neck when he's airborne as he tries to avoid landing right on top of him. There is something in his hand—something cold then hot, hard then soft, that easily sinks into him.

"No!" Amador says as he falls beside Sacha.

Just as his tumbling subsides there is an explosion of magnificent proportion. Sacha's hands reach for his ears and his eyes shut tightly. There is a pain in his chest that seems to come directly from the noise of the blast. He curls his body tight around the pain, expecting it to subside in the quiet.

But the quiet comes and the pain remains. His hands are still tucked tightly around his ears and he can hear the ocean's strong tide drifting in.

"Shit," Amador says. "My steel."

"What?" Henry says. "Where?"

Sacha understands that Amador has lost something. The two men are quietly panicking, but he is not yet sure why the location of Amador's chisel is so important. The ocean's soft, rhythmic noise dulls his reasoning. He opens his eyes. It is smoky, which has made their cavern even darker. A warm, wet stream trickles down his neck and he wonders if they are sweating as much as he is. The pain has subsided, but there is an ache that remains. He shifts his eyes and sees Henry's face, black with dirt.

"Should we take it out, boss?" Henry asks, and then Sacha realizes just where the chisel is. He moves one hand to the dull ache in his chest, but there is nothing there, only the subtle beat of his heart. Henry shakes his head. He puts his hand to his own throat.

Sacha follows his lead, surprised when his fingers graze against the cool metal of Amador's steel chisel. It moves slightly underneath his touch and the pain accelerates, driving hard into his chest and all the way through his legs.

"Oh, hell," he says, realizing that the constant warm oozing is blood, not sweat. When he tries to turn his head, the pain squeezes tighter, as though it is a rope twisting around and around his neck.

Amador's face is at Sacha's periphery—his eyes red, his face blackened, his lips trembling. Sacha pities the poor man.

"I don't think we should take it out," Sacha says. "But I would like a bit of fresh air." His own voice sounds very loud in his head, but he can tell that Henry is struggling to hear him.

Sacha decides to let Henry wrestle with the problem of their exit. He fixes his eyes on the dirt just above him, in a position that corrals the pain into that dull ache in the center of his chest.

It seems nearly unbelievable that the entire world exists a few thousand feet above his head, that everything is continuing out of his sight. Hensley preparing her own dinner, the dry goods store busy with inventory, the mournful cooing of retiring doves. All of it goes on without him. The miners hammering out nuggets of gold,

Mr. Lin preparing the day's specials, the fight for suffrage and workers' rights on the streets of New York and Boston, the brutality of war, and, finally, the baby, his own grandchild, becoming eyelids and ankles and fingertips.

Sacha closes his eyes. He travels through the layers of dirt, reversing the recent journey down. And then, with great and sudden clarity, there is the burst of dusk, so bright compared to this hole. The thin, clean air stings his lungs and he breathes even deeper for the thrill of it. Far away, a bell is ringing, summoning children to school or men to work.

The sound of the bell conjures the only memory he has of the crossing from Germany to America. His mother and older brother were standing on the deck, awaiting the view of New York's harbor. Behind them, he was bouncing a small red ball, trying to catch it on its first, then second, then third bounce. A strong hand grabbed his shoulder and Sacha immediately clasped the ball and shoved it in his pocket, afraid it would be confiscated. Instead, a large man in a smart blue uniform asked if he would like to ring the arrival bell from the bridge. Sacha nodded and followed the man up three flights of narrow stairs to a large metal bell that hung above even the officer's head. He lifted Sacha into his arms and held him up so that Sacha could reach for the fraying brown rope that hung from the bell. Pulling hard on that rough rope, Sacha smiled so much he felt his chapped lips split and bleed, even as the loud metal clang rattled his teeth and made his fingers numb with its reverberation.

Even now, Sacha can taste the blood on his lips. He smiles at Henry—who is suddenly beside him, his face clean, his shirt white—wishing he had the energy to tell him about his first glimpse of America, that bell buzzing through the small length of his body.

Instead, Henry is telling him to breathe slowly in through his nose and out through his mouth. The blossoms of the fruit trees—pale pink, lavender, even yellow—have such a sweet fragrance that Central Park has become young love's delight. Everything so full of raw possibility and hope—from the nectar collected in small dusty clumps by the honeybees to the electric, tender skin of his young wife's fingertips when she wraps them around his arm. The future is unknown and thrilling. Their good fortune swelling between them on a Sunday afternoon—everything yet to come.

Straining to move, Sacha urges a shoulder forward. There is a whistle coming from his own body. A teakettle screaming that it's ready. He wants to hold her there in the park. Olivia Wright. He wants to study the complex coloring of her golden emerald eyes one more time. Feel the heat of his own breath moisten her skin. Watch her lips move ever so slightly as she reads over his work. Give her more reasons to smile, more babies to swaddle, more trips to the seashore.

Tell her not to take the hot loaf of bread to her aunt's apartment uptown. Forget the tea towel and the twine and silk shawl from Shanghai that she'd never wear again. Not after she shed it upon her return later that afternoon, a headache just setting in as dusk did. Taking a cup of tea beside him in the living room, her coloring fading, even as Hensley skipped through, the ribbons in her hair flapping like crimson warnings, and Harold recited his verses, stumbling with shame around the forgotten ending. She descended into a fever that night as she slept beside him—the first grip of the influenza her aunt would recover from just days later, but that she never would.

Just as Sacha had put his own linen to her face, hoping with each touch that she might soon recover, Amador wipes Sacha's face with his dusty handkerchief. But Sacha does not want to be bothered with the poor man's grief and regret. He only wants to see each of his children, now so grown and fierce that their previous chubby cheeks and short fingers reside only in his memory. Their contagious giggles and stormy tantrums. Pink rosebud lips and shell-shaped ears. Gone, soon. Recalled by no living soul. A worse death than his own.

That their sweet little legs pushing against his chest as he held them high will not be remembered after this. That the memory of their sleeping faces cradled by their mother's arms, so dear to him, will be lost. That the countless details of their treasured beginnings will be buried here, too. Beside him, beneath him, within him. This is the sadness that presses against him, beginning with the steel embedded in his neck and filling him with its black, leaden weight. He cannot move his arms, nor his legs. It is as though there is a gigantic magnet just below him, pulling at all this metallic sorrow flooding his veins.

With great effort, Sacha rubs the fingers of his right hand in the dirt. If he can just keep moving, there may be a chance to resist the infiltration of the steel's blackness. You cannot die if you are moving, he thinks to himself, wondering if this realization is as significant as it seems. Just stretch your fingers out, let their vague movement save you. Slowly, the dirt gives away beneath his efforts, creating five small divots of defiance.

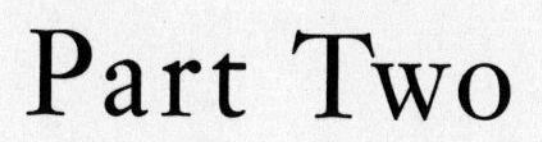

Part Two

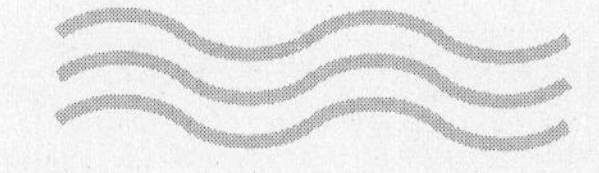

When Hensley opens her eyes, there is a woman beside the bed. Her posture erect, her arms folded patiently in her lap. The room is dim—she has no idea the time of day, or even what day it is—but Hensley feels sure it is her mother. The woman doesn't touch her. She doesn't speak. Her face is composed, unmoved. But she worries over Hensley. Hensley knows, could sense, even before she was fully conscious, that this woman has been sitting here for hours, watching her sleep. In fact, could it be that at one point her mother's hands were actually on her, smoothing her hair, easing her shoulders onto the pillow, stroking her temple?

This memory wakes her, tears seeping from behind her eyes into her throat. It was this presence, though, this reassurance, that allowed her to sink so far into the blackness that gathered around her, pulling at the edges of her mind, pushing its weight onto her chest. She simply gave in to it. She left all resistance to her mother, knowing that she would pull her back when it was time. It was as though she'd been loaded into a small rowboat, sack upon sack tossed on top of her slight body, until she could no longer move. The undecipherable rhythm of the water as it sloshed against the hull filled her ears with its urgency. She floated in those dark waters, bearing the weight, grateful for the grief that did not need words. That it was not hers alone.

But it was not her mother who pulled her back. It was Teresa who sat beside the bed, waiting for her. And Hensley hates her for it. Hates her for being here. For being real at all.

Her hair is not folded beneath Berto's hat, nor are his boots on her feet, nor his high-collared shirt buttoned tightly around her neck, but, rather, her long hair is parted gently, falling across her shoulders, a full skirt wrapping her slender hips, a sheer cotton blouse buttoned nowhere near her neck. To Hensley, her beauty seems more of a disguise than Berto's clothes.

When Teresa sees Hensley's eyes upon her, she smiles tenderly but says nothing. Hensley turns her own head toward the window, its curtains pulled tight. This single fact tells her that it is true. All the details of her loss rush at her. The boat that carried her through an ocean of murky sadness is suddenly gone and she is on the shore, alone, unprotected, searching the horizon for the people she loves. The words and images that suddenly overwhelm her mind are what she feared most. The truth of the accident.

The bells that started ringing just before dawn, the horses' hooves that seemed to never stop, the chaos in town as she walked Mr. Reid's letter to the post, the miners solemnity along the side of the road, their heads bowed, nobody's eyes meeting hers. The whole thing had seemed like a stage play; an elaborate show designed to test her. So she did what she thought she should. She busied herself composing a telegram to Harold, writing a letter to Mr. Reid, and brewing the morning coffee. She'd thought that once she completed all the tasks required of a grieving daughter he might reappear. She would pass the test and be rewarded with his approving nod, his gentle smile.

But instead, even after the simple burial at the top of the hill, the house remained hers alone. The days were empty and without rhythm. She washed his clothes and hung them out to dry, taking special care with the shirt collars. When she couldn't sleep, she read and reread the letters from Mr. Reid. She stared at the chessboard, wondering if she should dare to make the next move; if this act might finally complete this excruciating charade. She held a pawn, then a bishop in her hand, straining for some insight, but soon replaced it. She pulled the curtains and took to her bed, where she's been now for a week.

Both cats are stretched out long on the bed beside her. "What time is it?" she asks.

Teresa tells her just after dinner. "There is soup. Just broth. Shall we give it a try?"

Hensley nods. She'd agree to nearly anything just to have the room to herself, to be rid of Teresa's sympathetic gaze. It only confirms her worst fear—there is no one else.

Alone, she shoves the cats onto the floor.

Her grief is like an impossibly heavy blanket, smothering every inch of her. She wants to destroy it—to push against this weight, set fire to it, escape its iron hold. The only way this seems possible is if she wreaks some damage of her own, takes a piece of this blanket and throws it over someone else. Watches it suffocate them, stifling their movement, choke their breath.

The cats land on their feet, as cats do, undamaged and unfazed. They saunter away from her slowly.

Hensley stands on her bed and places her hands against the ceiling. Pushing as hard as she can, Hensley hopes to break through. Climb up and out, stand on the roof, survey the new, ravaged world. But the mattress beneath her bare feet sags, preventing her from achieving her desired effect—destruction. She turns her hands to fists and bangs until a piece of the plaster buckles, disintigrates, and falls into her eyes.

She crouches on the bed, her eyes blinded, momentarily, by the debris. Behind her closed eyes she once again sees the horse-drawn coach that brought her father's body back to the house. She gasps. She'd almost forgotten. Those dreadful, innocent horses, so useful and large. In vain, she tries to push the image away, tries not to see its arrival in front of this house. Though he must have died hours earlier, it is this bleak, irrefutable evidence that haunts her and that she wishes to undo.

If only he'd gone on a train to Chicago or Los Angeles or anywhere instead of into that mine shaft. She could accept the abandonment, the truth of his absence, if only she didn't have this image in her mind. The stubborn, vile memory of him with his bloodied shirt still tucked into his dungarees; the wide metal wedge awkwardly cradled in his neck, like a child's prank, a circus stunt; his mouth agape, utterly abandoned by the vibrancy of a working jaw; his fingers on both hands stretched long, as though with a yearning, a profoundly hidden desire. She wants to eradicate the piece of her brain that has stored this, that will undoubtedly torture her by replaying it every time she isn't entirely fortified. But the plaster in her eyes has only shut her in with this memory and she is unable to escape it, trapped in the darkness.

From the doorway, Teresa's voice intrudes and rescues her. "Have you plans to destroy the whole house or just the ceiling?"

Hensley tries to open her eyes. She blinks away the lingering dust. The first thing she sees is Teresa's bare feet, so brown and alive on the wooden floorboards.

"Either," she says, noticing the tray in Teresa's hands. "Any scrap of this horrid place."

There is a long silence between them. Hensley looks at the welt on her knuckle that is beginning to show itself. This pain snaps her to life. She scrambles from the bed in a shock of movement and drags all the bedclothes off. Throwing them to the floor, she howls at the insult of this comfort. This suggestion that life could go on. As though the bed and its covers are mocking her. She rages at them, beating at the mattress that remains, at the dreaded pillows. Her face reddened and wet, she finally throws herself back on the bed, defeated.

Teresa is not moved. "I once saw someone go up in flames fueled by grief. As if her very soul was a box of dry timber. There were ashes dancing in the breeze even as her flesh charred and melted."

"God." Hensley's heart races with the possibilities. Destruction frolicking around her like a harlot with lifeless eyes.

Teresa nods.

"God," Hensley says again. Might that happen to her? Might she simply ignite?

Teresa places the tray on the cane chair beside the bed. Without invitation or hesitation, she climbs onto the bare bed beside Hensley. The two girls hold each other, trying desperately to affirm some community, some solidarity that neither feels in her heart. But each girl's tears dry on the other's skin in thin, salty tracks of protest.

Immediately after hearing her father was dead, Hensley sat in front of the typewriter, still in her nightclothes, her hands streaked black with ink. She imagined Mr. Reid, living in that time warp of their letters, innocent of the events in the mine. He would exist there, with her father still alive, still a solid opponent, for a few more weeks.

I've woken early, the room still dark. I wonder, in fact, if I actually slept at all. Only the occasional birdcall breaks the silence—an eager finch or mourning dove. And I must confess that even now I am contemplating an act of forgery. Mostly to spare you, but also, perhaps, to spare myself. I think I could surely mimic his terse, rational prose—his voice will always be in my head—but I would be a hopeless failure when it came time to determining the next move in your chess game. You would wonder and worry what fate had befallen your partner and I would eventually have to confess to my crime. So, as the sunlight shed its rays onto my pillow, I knew the terrible truth of the day. I would have to form these detestable words and send them across an ocean to you: My father, Mr. Sacha Dench, has died.

Next, she went into town to send the telegram to Harold.

Dear Brother. With immense regret I must inform you of our father's death. I am heartbroken.

She maintained her composure while she threw a handful of New Mexico dirt onto the coffin that held her father's body, walked down the dusty road back toward town, toward the trunk of her father's clothes and the untouched chessboard in the living room. But when nothing changed, when the awfulness of his death only seem to amplify instead of recede, she took to bed.

It was Teresa who told her they would eat lunch because it was time. It was Teresa who tied on an apron and cleaned the stack of plates and bowls that littered the sink, bought a slab of bacon from the butcher, and knew that the house needed the smell of garlic and onions browning in oil.

Now, Teresa has left her alone to check on Berto. She glances at the damaged ceiling above her bed and hates it. Pulling Isaac onto her lap, she wonders what animals know about death. She scratches the stiff fur between his eyes and marvels at the strength of his purring. There is a knock at the front door and Isaac leaps from her lap and beneath the chair.

Henry, the foreman, stands outside the screen door, his hat in his hand.

"Ma'am," he begins, his eyes dodging around Hensley's. "I've got a couple telegrams for you here. They came to the mine."

Hensley takes the yellow envelopes from his hand. "Thank you," she says.

"I sure hope that you know how sorry we all are. Especially Amador and me. Really sorry for what happened. Your father was decent to all of us."

Hensley can only nod.

"What happened—it will be with us the rest of our days. It will haunt us," he says with conviction.

Hensley bows her head. "Me, too," she says quietly. With this agreement between them, she watches him walk away from the house, returning the hat to his head.

She goes to the kitchen, places the envelopes on the table, and stands in front of the stove. She holds the wooden spoon in her hand, poking at the beans as they simmer. She watches the golden oil gather on the surface.

Finally, she sits at the table, the telegrams beckoning her. The first is from Harold.

Dear Hennie. Heartbroken here too. Together we
will remember him. I am prevented from travel due

to the necessity of my presence here. I have spoken to Lowe. Your return to New York will be a great relief to both of us. Your loving brother

His words seem to exist somewhere far away from her. She can hardly absorb them. She moves quickly on to the next.

Dear Hensley. I am sorry for your recent loss. It is my understanding that you will be returning to New York. I would be remiss if I did not extend the offer of a marriage when you do. Whatever our disagreements have been we can surely agree to leave them in the past. Awaiting your reply. Lowell Teagan

Hensley closes her eyes. She is short of breath. Her heart bangs recklessly in her chest. Finally, she stands and walks to the stove. She lifts the pot of beans from the flame momentarily and replaces it with Lowe's telegram. She watches it ignite. Then she replaces the beans and lets his words wilt in her hand as the flame turns them into graceful black ashes. Finally, just as the heat singes her knuckle, she lets it go—watching it cascade to the floor, weakened without its fuel. Hensley steps on the small remaining flame, buoyed by the sound of its sigh as it is extinguished.

"You are intent on destruction, aren't you?"

Hensley shrugs her shoulders with disbelief. "I've just burned up my one and only proposal, Teresa. My one and only chance to salvage a life of respectability."

"Pity," Teresa says, with absolutely none.

Hensley smiles for the first time in days.

"Well, you *do* wear boots and suspenders most days. What would you know about a woman's respectability?"

"Precisely. The moment you wear a skirt and blouse is the moment you've given the world license to decide for you about things like respectability. In dungarees and a hat, I have it so long as I am standing up straight."

Here she pulls her skirt tight between her legs, throws her shoulders back, and puffs out her chest.

Hensley mimics her and the two of them walk the floor of the small kitchen, imagining what it might be like to have their own place in the world. They bite through apples like abandoned love affairs, stir the beans with the carelessness of a vote cast for war, swing their arms about with the ease of dismissing unwanted children.

But they soon tire of the charade and Teresa spoons them each a bowl of beans, while Hensley pulls off two chunks of bread, and they walk through the ashes left by Lowell's telegram, smudging the soot across the floorboards that will have to be cleaned later.

Later that night, unable to sleep, Hensley walks through the house, looking at all the things that are so familiar to her. All the things that used to comfort her. The things that she's lived among for as long as she can remember. Her father's desk set: the sterling inkwell shaped like an acorn, his fountain pen and luscious paper, waiting, expectantly; the chunky brass candlesticks that stand guard in the front window, their white candles awaiting a match; the gray linen pillows that adorn the sofa, perfectly finished by her mother with lavender silk stitching; the three porcelain angels that once belonged to her grandmother Wright, each with a slight golden halo hovering above its head.

The night brings with it all the fear that it did when she was a child. Afraid of some unknown danger lurking, waiting for her around nearly every corner, she finds herself imagining that even

Lowell's presence might be better than none. These beautiful things, these pieces of her previous life, cannot console her the way a familiar voice might. They have no warm arms, no temperament, no capacity for tenderness, or even brutality.

Timidly returning to her room, she goes straight to the small wooden box on her vanity that holds Mr. Reid's letters. They are the closest thing to solace she can find. But in their solace is also the enormous chasm between here and there.

In the deep middle of the night, Hensley yearns for something more. Some way to bring him closer. From her father's desk she takes the ink and pen. Cradling the inkwell in one palm, she fixes her eyes on the wall. In its blankness is the abyss that breaks her solace. Its expanse mirrors the distance between their two selves. She stretches out on the bed, feeling the rhythm of her heart's singular beat—at once miraculous and disappointing. The weight of the inkwell could be his hand in hers.

She imagines lying beside him on some battlefield, the ground beneath them trembling with the impact of nearby shells. It wouldn't matter—the proximity of death. All that would matter is that they could each finally see and touch the body from which their words emanated. His eyes, lips, hands, neck, elbows, fingers, hair. There would be no end to her desire to hear him speak—the voice in her head becoming his, his words unfurling themselves directly into her ear, the heat of his breath all the warmth she'd ever need. And as the violence nears, as the sky fills with smoke and they have to close their eyes, as he wraps his arms more tightly around her, she would place her hand across her own belly, hoping that however little the child can sense, it senses this. Curled into his side like this, she would let the bullets drag through her flesh, opening up her skin, revealing her insides to the dirt and the sky of a foreign land. Shredding her to minuscule bits that will sink into the mud, fortify the countryside, feed the rats, haunt the future. But each bit will have in it the whisper of his voice, the feel of his hand in hers.

Her skin raw, as though already ripped open to the evening's breeze, she gazes at the spot on the wall just below the window. The inkwell cajoles her with its fullness. Hensley stands, her bare feet sure beneath her. With his very first letter between her lips, the paper damp and woody in her mouth, she transposes it, nearly entirely from memory, onto the wall. The first black mark sends a thrill from her fingers up her arm and into her throat. Her skin is consumed with goose bumps. With a deep breath, she continues, vandalizing the plaster with alacrity.

I've spent parts of entire days imagining which vowels and consonants might govern the plans for the pieces with which you entice me. How strange that I can almost hear one of your gentle pawn's voice in my head, unsure of everything but its pale coloring. Your words, however, have created a self that has kept me occupied through the days and nights that masquerade here as dark, endless caves full of horrors.

By the time she places her head back on the pillow, her fingers smeared with black, his words are permanently stretched out before her. She stares at them until exhaustion prevails.

When she awakes the next morning, his words prod her into consciousness. She wants only to begin another letter to him. She wants to exist only within their correspondence.

Teresa, dressed in her brother's clothes, watches from the doorway as the typewriter keys fly up and strike the ribbon with incredible force.

Hensley looks up at Teresa. Her hair in her brother's hat, his boots on her feet, she is dressed for work.

True to form, Harold has sent his third morning telegram in as many days, and Teresa hands it over without ceremony:

> I must speak to you. This loss is ours to share.
> Grief spans the distance but my voice cannot.
> Please travel to El Paso this afternoon to receive
> my call at 3pm.

In her other hand, Teresa holds a black metal dish and a small trowel. She sets them down on the coffee table.

"These are for you. Berto says there is a place just west of town. Past the dry creek bed. There are three cottonwoods whose branches nearly overlap. Just beneath their canopy, where the dirt feels cool. You might get lucky."

"I know that place," Hensley says, then scoffs. "So—what? I'm going to pan for enough gold to buy a ham? Or a bolt of linen?"

"How else? If your inheritance is like mine, you will starve waiting for it."

"Harold will settle things. I will have something to live on." As she says it, Hensley realizes the totality of her dependence upon him.

"Until he does you that favor," she says, pointing at the tools. "Or if you'd rather, I have an extra pair of boots at the house."

Hensley drops her hands to her sides. "Why did he go down there, Teresa? He should be *here*." She stomps her foot for emphasis and looks at the chessboard, still fielding its current game. "Right here. Playing this stupid game." Through her tears, she mocks him: "Protect the king. Respect the queen. Use the bishop. Know the next three moves. See the future. Understand the end." Hensley picks up the board and hurls it, with all the pieces, onto the floor. She is pale, stunned by her own anger.

Teresa bends down and picks up a black bishop that has landed near her feet. "My father liked the game, too. Some nights, he played with his boss." She sets the pawn on the table beside the pan and the shovel. "I bet they would've liked each other—our fathers. Played chess all night long. Lamented the destructive capabilities of their own species."

Hensley wipes her eyes, the scent of ink lingering on her fingers. She nods, smiling. "Perhaps. Wax poetic about the dangers of power and its misuses."

"Exactly. Are you going to town like that?"

Hensley looks down at her nightclothes. "I suppose not. I better change. I wouldn't know the first thing about how to use those," she says, motioning to the tools.

Teresa nods. "Suit yourself," she says and heads for the back door. Isaac scoots between her feet, eager to follow her out. With her hand on the screen, Teresa—the spitting image of her brother—turns to face Hensley again. She looks handsome and strong. "Nothing ever ends, Hensley. Games were made up so that people could impose a beginning and an end. Feel powerful, in control of time. Life is not a game. Even when it's over, it is not the end. He will always be with you."

Hensley crosses the floor, her sheer nightgown clinging to her changing body. She wraps her arms around Teresa's neck but doesn't say a word.

How she'd like to believe her! What she'd trade to possess this certainty!

Teresa holds her as tightly as she can manage, stroking her uncombed hair.

"I wish..." Her chest heaves with regret. She buries herself further into Teresa.

Their embrace—if seen from the street—resembles the desperation of the final good-bye in an illicit love affair. But it is not. Nobody passes by, nobody misunderstands their love for something sordid.

Soon Hensley is dressed and ready for the Ready Pay truck that picks her up just outside the house.

Harold has arranged for the El Paso Mutual Telephone Company to host his call to Hensley this afternoon. The office is cooled by a large fan in the corner that pushes Hensley's hair up and away from her face with its power. She holds the line while the call is originated in New York.

"Hensley? Can you hear me?" Her brother's voice is suddenly in her ear, sounding just as it always has.

"Yes, I'm here." Hensley pictures her brother, his nearly always chapped lips speaking to her from the Naval Yard office in Brooklyn, his pants perfectly creased, his shoes polished, his brown hair clipped close to his scalp.

"Oh, Hen," he says, sighing heavily, his voice momentarily thin. "How are you managing?"

Hensley looks at the dirt underneath her fingernails, a geographic hazard. She wills herself to speak without crying. "I am just in a daze, really. Trying to understand…" This is as much as she can say before her voice withers beneath the weight of her thoughts.

"You are very brave. And I will be always grateful to you for handling all the arrangements. I'm sure it was just what he would've wanted."

Hensley pictures the brown hillside where her father is buried. "He would've wanted you here, Harold." The line crackles with static as though she has spoken too loudly.

"This is not an ordinary time, Hennie. I would have been there if it had been at all possible. Can you forgive me?"

Hensley nods. "Of course I will. This is just the worst thing, Harry. The worst..."

"I know. He was just so stubborn. If only he'd stayed here. If only..."

"For God's sake, it's not his fault, Harold. He's the one who's died. Don't blame him for that, too." Hensley wipes at her eyes with a handkerchief.

"But now what, Hensley? Have you answered Lowell's telegram?"

"What did that cost you?"

"Not as much as this telephone call."

Hensley glances out the window at the traffic in front of the train station. A man in dungarees and a big straw hat lugs two suitcases behind him. Three women share a parasol as they stand in the sun, waiting. Two horse-drawn carriages are loaded with crates that have bright red stripes across their middles and the word *dynamite* written in block letters inside the stripe.

"Well, then, get to the point. Let's be efficient and not waste time on the trivialities of our emotions."

"Don't overreact, Hensley. I only wanted to hear your voice. To make sure you are safe."

"I am, yes. Safely devastated."

"And we do need to determine how and when you will return. Have you a schedule in mind?"

The authority in his voice irks her. "Who says I am? I have no plans to do so."

"Don't be unreasonable. If you're angry at me, or Lowell, don't let it foul up your life."

"I didn't think we had time to discuss our emotions."

"I know you're susceptible to all those romantic notions, Hensley. But regardless of what I've said about Lowell in the past, he is willing to be honorable now. Let go of your girlish ideas. Every life is full of mistakes. There is nothing unusual about that. Forgive him for the past. Begin again." His voice is earnest and pleading.

"I appreciate your advice, Harry. But I have no immediate plans to return to New York." She closes her eyes and pictures the wall in her bedroom back in Hillsboro, the words being the very closest thing she can imagine to a home right now. "Girlish ideas are more tenacious than you'd imagine."

"So I've heard. But, Hennie, I know that's not you. We were both raised to think. That's his legacy. Use your mind to solve this problem. I know you'll come to the same conclusion as I have."

"But it's not *your* problem to solve, so your thinking is different from mine."

There is a silence in which Hensley thinks he may have been disconnected.

But then his voice returns. "How is your health, Hen? Are you eating?"

"Yes, I'm fine. I've a dear friend. She's taken care of me through it all."

"What a relief. I hadn't thought there'd be anybody there but miners and Mexicans."

Hensley smiles slightly as she fingers the telephone cord. *"El burro sabe más que tú,"* she says, using the only saying Teresa has taught her.

"What's that?" he says. "I think our connection is going bad."

"I'm here, Harry. I appreciate the phone call. And the telegrams. I know that you want what's best."

"Okay. Good. So you'll think about it? You will let me know?"

Hensley nods, but then realizes he cannot see her. "Yes, I will," she says, wondering if Mr. Reid has yet received the letter about her father.

"Good. We've only each other now, Hen."

Hensley feels her throat tighten with emotion. "Yes," she manages to say. "I know."

"Much love to you," he says before the line goes quiet and then turns to a flat buzzing signal.

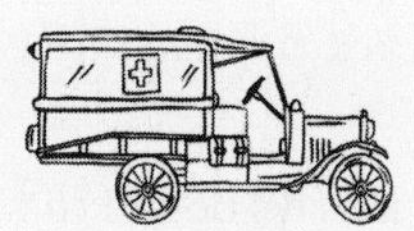

Nearly a week after his injury, Foulsom thought Charles had a decent chance of surviving the train ride, so they loaded him with some other gravely injured soldiers onto a Red Cross train to Rouen, where an ambulance from Base Hospital #12 met them.

Gradually Charles has become able to spend more than an hour sitting up and he's glad to hear lots of American voices, men from St. Louis who took over this abandoned racetrack from the British a couple of months ago. Charles's bed is with several others in the small room adjacent to the administration building. The nights are getting cold and he often reads Hensley's letters just to try to remember what sunlight feels like.

This evening, Rogerson appears in the doorway, his eyes glancing across the room, searching for Charles.

"Looking for me?" Charles says, running a hand through his unwashed hair.

"Reid. I never figured you for a gambling man. But here you are hiding out at the racetrack while I drive those muddy roads by myself."

They shake hands, Rogerson careful not to look at the place where Charles's leg should be. He's had four nights in a row full of evacuations, so they let him take a day of personal leave.

He stands in the corner watching as two nurses transfer Charles into a wheelchair. Rogerson sits beside him in the dining hall. The dinner includes chicken thighs stewed in a makeshift tomato sauce that is thick and syrupy. Both Charles and Rogerson have rings of the red sauce clinging to their lips.

"Is it really tasty or just not white mash?" Rogerson asks as he licks the back of his fork. "I can't tell."

"Not sure it matters, really, does it?"

"Right. Not really. Just curious."

"It's all relative. Isn't that what we've learned? Otherwise, I wouldn't find myself suddenly envying that fella who blew off his own toes, oozing blood through the leather of his boot—remember him?"

Just as he says it, a nurse calls out his name, a letter in his hand. Rogerson bounds off the bench and collects the latest dispatch from Hensley. As he returns to his place beside Charles, he smiles and says, "See? Good day."

But when Charles reads the letter, his mood darkens. He wipes hard with his napkin at the sweet sauce stuck to his lips.

"What is it?" Rogerson asks, gnawing a bit more on one of the bones on his tray.

"Hell," Charles says, "he's dead. Mr. Dench." He hands the letter to Rogerson and brings his head down on the table, banging it twice so that the rattle of cutlery and dishes echoes in his ears.

He is gone. Charles goes over her words again and again. Just ink on paper. What does it really mean? It is not the same death that resides here. It is not visceral and indisputable. It is simply a scattering of letters, an assortment of words that litter the paper. Could she be mistaken? Is it really true that the man is gone? Will he never receive another letter from him?

Though they are just words to him, he understands that somewhere in New Mexico, their meaning is real. She is now an orphan, bereaved and alone. The sweet dinner has turned sour in his stomach. He longs to see her now more than he ever has. He wants to comfort her in some way, to alleviate her suffering. But he is stuck here, useless to himself and to the heartbroken.

Rogerson grimaces and hands the letter back to Charles. "Sorry, Reid."

Charles nods. He glances again at Hensley's writing. He pictures her sitting in the dawn in an empty house, choosing words just for him. His eyes burn and he quickly folds the letter and replaces it in his pocket.

He wipes at his face again with his mucked-up napkin, then watches Rogerson take the remnants of their meal to the trash bin, where he scrapes the bones from the trays.

"Shall we get some air?" Rogerson asks as he takes the handles of the chair and begins pushing him toward the doors.

"Not sure I'm allowed."

"Since when has that mattered?"

Outside, dusk is just descending, turning the figures outside into black silhouettes. The compound looks quaint, almost like cardboard cutouts from an amateur stage production. There is the wide center of the racetrack, filled with tents and makeshift buildings. Several ambulance trucks wait near the operating tent.

Rogerson offers him a cigarette.

"Paint them black and it looks like evening," Charles says to nobody, taking the cigarette between his lips.

Rogerson offers him a light and Charles accepts. "It is evening, Reid."

"Right. The bad evening of a good day."

"Exactly."

"But he didn't die today. There was an evening all those days ago when he died and we didn't know. Just like this. She's no idea."

"You should tell her."

"He died and we were unaware. We went right on. We went right on and got my leg blown off."

"Yep. We went right on."

"She should go right on. She needn't know about this. What grief she's already got."

Rogerson nods. They sit together as the night darkens and their cigarettes burn brighter.

"But if you want another letter. If you want it to reach you sooner rather than later, she'll need the address of this first-rate racetrack."

Charles pulls hard against the burn of the cigarette. His chest tightens. He wonders if it was always this hard to breathe.

Each night, Hensley has transposed another letter so that now the entire eastern wall of her bedroom is covered in his words. From the living room, through the half-open door, it looks like an act of vandalism or deterioration, as though the bedroom is sure to be condemned. But as she lies in bed, Hensley is transported, conversing with the sentences he has written to her. Existing in the curves of the black letters, she can easily imagine that he is there with her. His unknown face is irrelevant. She knows his syntax, his fear, his logic.

She cannot help wondering, however, if she's jinxed everything with this vandalism. She has not had a letter since. Each day when the post arrives without an airmail envelope, she aches with unfulfilled desire. Like a hunger that cannot be satiated, this need cuts a hole right through her, rendering her weak and listless. The cats mirror her despondency, lying with her on the bed, their eyes lazy, their tails languid.

Finally, she holds another letter.

As you know, death walks with us here, always bringing up the rear, or shoving its black hood through our ranks so forcefully that we can never escape its threat. Alas, I've not escaped unharmed. I am recovering at an American hospital in Rouen. Please note my temporary address. Your letters and those of your father have been my reprieve. A generous shelter into which I've retreated over and over again. I now understand that my desperation created a fantasy—believing that the carnage here—the very worst the world has to offer—might be enough. That the rest of the world, the people for whom all of this blood is let, would be safe. I scoff now at my ignorance. But your words, Hensley, shattered me. Eager to be transported by you—to you—the ink was blurred before I even fully understood your meaning. I am not ashamed of my tears but of their uselessness. I can do nothing for you, offer no comfort or consolation, no nourishment or companionship. Even my words can offer no relief, I know. But let the arrival of my letter at least provide you with the knowledge that you may add my name to the long list of others who will forever count themselves lucky to have known your father.

I will treasure the remains of our correspondence and confide to you a truth that my pride prevented me from telling him: he was bound to win.

Another confession, Hensley: Your words have become as necessary to me as my own heartbeat. It is terribly selfish, I know, to request that in your time of grief you would remember me, but I live in fear that I will not receive another of your letters.

This ocean and this war prevent me from taking your hand in mine, placing a warm stone from the earth into your palm and closing our fingers around it. Hold on, I whisper. And I know it is meaningless, these words spoken so confidently into the din of this forsaken place, as if this stone made by or from the earth so many years ago could sustain us. But

I know much more than I ever wanted to about the ability to live through the worst circumstances. This, if I could, is how I'd love you. I would see us through to a happier day.

Hensley finds herself smiling, trickles of perspiration rolling from her armpits down her rib cage. Before she's finished reading the whole letter, she is dipping the pen into the inkwell, eager to write his sentences, to inhabit his pattern of speech, to see the words he's chosen for her written large across the room. Making it real, inking it onto the wall has become more pressing, even, than reading. But she stops on that sentence and gasps. *This is how I'd love you.*

The ink dries quickly on the smooth plaster. As soon as the fresh sheen has faded, she breathes a sigh of relief. Every word he's ever written to her is here on this wall. She sits on the bed and reads a sentence from up high, and then another from below the window. The afternoon passes easily this way, with short, dream-filled naps punctuating the hours.

Hensley hears the screen door open and shut. Teresa, just back from the mine, stands in the doorway, her boots caked with dirt and her face stern. Even though she knows it well, Hensley startles at the perfection of her disguise.

Teresa's face absorbs what Hensley has done to the wall.

"He is the chess partner? Your father's?"

Hensley nods. A faint, but insistent, tickling begins in her abdomen, as though there is a small stringed instrument, rather than a baby, growing inside of her and it is being plucked—without any rhythm or tune.

"But he is in the war?"

She nods again, touching the place on her stomach where it

seems she should be able to detect some movement from the outside. But there is nothing. It's all inside. Unreachable.

Teresa crosses her arms across her chest.

"Are you angry?" Hensley asks. The thought reminds her how quickly she has adjusted to being beholden to no one.

"Thomas Wright has given up on his wife. He's returning to look after the mine himself for a while."

The bed seems to recede beneath her. She pushes her hands against the mattress. "What do you mean?"

"I'm driving to El Paso on Saturday. His train arrives at noon."

"Well, our mothers were cousins. Surely this is good news. He will let me stay and perhaps..." Hensley locks her eyes on the wall, on Mr. Reid's words.

Teresa furrows her brow. "Hensley. This is *not* good news. *He* will be living here, but you will not. His mood will be blacker than ever now. Cousin or not, he is not a kind man."

There is a long silence. Teresa does not remove her eyes from Hensley. Hensley wishes she would look away; cast her eyes down to her brother's boots on her feet, her own cuticles, the pale floorboards. But she watches as Hensley clutches her jaw tight, bracing against the ache that has begun in her throat and travels a direct path down the center of her body.

The words on the wall—the very same ones that have reassured her for weeks—are suddenly useless. She cannot bring a single one into focus. The black just hangs like a curtain, blurry and far away.

Teresa stands there, waiting for an answer. Finally, fiddling with a suspender, she says, "You have no place to live. That's what I'm telling you."

Hensley stands and walks to the desk, fingering the stack of envelopes. "I understand, Teresa. You have been very clear." Hensley thinks of the pile of mending she's just finished for Amador. The fresh buttons and perfectly tied threads that her own fingers placed will remain here. She will not.

"The eastbound to New York leaves at two o'clock on Saturday. I can drive you in when I go."

Hensley cannot move her jaw. Even if she could, though, there would be nothing to say. Her gums ache beneath the pressure of her clenched teeth. She blinks her eyes slowly.

Dear Nobody, I have nothing left. Not even words. There is just a deep, hollow hum, like the reverberation of an oversized metal bell that has long since tolled.

When Teresa leaves her alone, Hensley sits at the desk and scribbles some lines on a scrap of paper from her father's desk. Just to see how they look. It is not something she's accepted yet. It is a terrible answer to a worse question.

> Dear Mr. Teagan. I received your proposal. A friend here has offered to teach me to pan for gold. It involves staring at a filthy pool of mud until a single fleck glints in the bottom of the pan. Perhaps that will serve us well. I will arrive at Grand Central Station on Wednesday the 21st.

It is only as she stands in the post office, the flies buzzing against the front window, and dictates the telegram just as she's written it, that it becomes clear to Hensley that she will, in fact, be returning to New York and marrying Mr. Lowell Teagan. Her hands seem disconnected from her body as she counts out the correct change. She forces a smile across her lips as she hands the clerk her payment.

Walking slowly back to the house, her shoes knock against the wooden sidewalk and she counts off her steps. She passes the grocery and the saloon. She passes Mr. Lin's restaurant and the hotel, the foundry and the bank. Within a hundred steps exist all the businesses of Hillsboro except the mine. Hensley wonders how it can be that this small town is the place that killed her father. He'd covered strikes, fires, and murders in New York City. He'd interviewed gangsters, exposed crooked politicians, and opposed the war. He'd made a difference—his one slight body had meant something in that big city. But here, he'd done nothing, meant nothing. He'd become a gruesome tale set in a gruesome landscape. Returning to New York will mean reclaiming the place where both of her parents lived the best of their lives. It will mean remembering each of them in the places they loved: Central Park, the coffee shop on Varick, the theater, dinner at Polly's. She walks with surer steps.

It will also mean becoming a proper mother to this child. Walking without shame, loving the baby without reservation. For the slight swelling above her groin will soon be an actual baby. Then a child. And they will be a family. Maybe she will find solace there. In the chubby fingers and sticky mouth of her own little one.

She is buoyed by this logic—Mr. Teagan's presence in the equation receding—until she reaches the gate and sees the stack of stones. One for each of her letters. Then, in her bedroom the black words still adorn the wall, words that have become like an entire gospel, committed to memory. Rife with meaning, sentiment, and history. Read and reread when she has been most desolate; consoling her through doubt-filled days and nights. Though she doesn't need to see them to know them, the appearance of their sloping lines and circles strike a fear in her. She realizes that although she can take the letters with her, they will have to be hidden. They will become her past, her history. Nothing more. Any comfort she takes in them will amount to a betrayal. This word—*betrayal*—nestles itself beneath her breast.

When that train departs for New York, what will become of Mr. Reid? What will she tell him about her sudden silence? Because she mustn't write to him anymore if she's to be a married woman, a mother. And more painful, even, is the question of what she will do without him. Without his letters.

She knows then, in the very same moment that she knows she must live without him, that she loves him.

She is not sleeping when the light shines into her window. A handful of pebbles are thrown across the glass with the elegance of a percussionist. Her heart races beneath her nightclothes as she pushes open the back door.

The night is so dark here it sometimes feels as though her eyes are not open at all. She blinks twice, looking at the glow of the lantern. It is Teresa, dressed in her own skirts and a loose T-shirt of Berto's. Her dark skin appears deep and sturdy beneath the yellow light. In contrast, Hensley feels barely there—a pale wisp in the dark.

"Sorry. I need some help."

"What is it? Is it Berto?"

She nods.

Hensley returns inside, grabs one of her father's cardigan sweaters, and slides into her flat shoes. She closes the door behind her and pulls the sweater tight.

"Let's go," Hensley says as they begin to ascend the hill.

"It's not what you think," Teresa says.

"What do you mean?"

"He's not dying. I mean, not tonight."

Hensley slows her pace, but they are both breathing hard.

"Is he in distress?"

Teresa nods. "It's you. He says that he wants to see you. You have the key."

Hensley stops walking. The absurdity of this statement hangs between them. She giggles. Placing her hand on top of the one Teresa has gripped around the lantern, she says, "He has a fever, Teresa. I have no key. Literal or otherwise. He is hallucinating."

"I do not disagree. But I can no longer argue with him. He's convinced that you're our mother."

"Are we in a dream? Are you in my dream? I know it's the middle of the night."

With her other hand, Teresa pinches Hensley's wrist and leaves her hand there, threatening another.

"Ouch." The pain pricks through her skin. Hensley is surprised how clearly she can see Teresa's eyes.

Both girls have their hands on the lantern, as though it is the cause of their disagreement. A toy they cannot share.

"Don't waste time pretending that you are so refined that you cannot understand what is happening."

Hensley pulls her arms away from Teresa, relinquishing the lantern. "But I have no idea what *is* happening."

Silently, Teresa continues to walk up the steep grade, the lantern swinging by her side. Hensley follows, afraid of the darkness that she's left behind.

The small, slanting house is dark, but delicately shifting shadows across the windows convey some activity within.

Teresa throws open the screen, letting its shriek pierce the night. Hensley follows her in.

Berto is propped up in the small bed against the wall. He has a white rag thrown over the top of his head so that it appears as though he is wearing a small child's ghost costume.

Hensley has not been in the house since the day of her father's death. She has not thought much about that morning, but now she has the feeling that time has not passed here. That Berto's fever has not changed, that his legs are still immovable, that the book he would not release is still held close, his hand gripping it, even in sleep.

She cannot help but think that if she had stayed here, in this room filled with illness and this half-dead body, she would not know of her father's death. She could have nursed Berto, wringing out the wet rags, spooning broth into his inquiet mouth, massaging his limp legs, and never heard of the accident at the mine. Never seen her father's poor, slack jaw, his fingers spread, as though in midgesture and midthought—his death both an uninvited and unwanted guest—the blood pooled beneath his chest in jagged, blue puddles.

She might still be ignorant. Returning to their own house only after dark, believing in her father's untroubled sleep just behind his closed door. Believing the chessboard had been studied, the dishes in the kitchen dirtied, the cats stroked by his very alive hands.

But she had left. Though not before she'd imagined her dear Mr. Reid—not her father—wounded and helpless.

"He won't give up this idea," Teresa says, as she moves a jar of pickled vegetables from the edge of the counter to the back of the counter. "I'm sorry. But I've asked you for nothing. I don't know what else to do."

Hensley hesitates. Everything inside these four walls is disorienting. The sound of agitated insects hovering around the windows seems to be magnified and ominous. There is a strange damp cool-

ness that moves through the room, like an ocean breeze. She shivers and pulls her father's sweater even tighter across her body. "What do you mean?"

Hensley loses her balance and catches herself against Teresa's arm. It is as though the house has become a boat and a sudden swell of water pushed the whole starboard side up, off balance. But there is dirt all around the outside of these walls. The house has not moved. There seems to be absolutely no cause to the effect.

"I am desperate," Teresa says without meeting Hensley's eyes. She throws a rag onto the counter. "I don't know what else to do."

Berto says something from his place in the corner.

"Is that you? Mama?"

Hensley looks at Teresa, but she will not meet her eyes. Her face is exhausted, dark shadows hanging below her eyes.

Hensley imagines the short distance back to her house. She could easily turn around and go. Teresa might even be grateful, saved from her own shame. She remembers how she wished Teresa would leave her alone with her grief. But she didn't. She stayed and spooned broth into her mouth. This knowledge allows Hensley to be braver than she'd imagined herself to be. She walks toward Berto and sits close to him on the bed.

A thin white line of dried saliva runs around his mouth. His lips are cracked and pale.

He speaks again, quietly, his eyes closed. "Mama? I knew you'd be here."

Hensley lifts her hand from her lap and places it gently upon his forehead. It is damp and hot. "Of course I'm here," she says. "Right here."

"I'm scared. Nothing makes sense. I can't move."

"Everything is going to be fine. You'll see," Hensley says as she

remembers her own mother saying these words to her, both when Hensley was small and feverish and later, when she herself was lying in the big bed, dying.

"It's all over. I don't remember how it starts. Just this. Just this terrible ending." His fingers wrap more tightly around the book that is still resting upon his chest. The scent on his breath is putrid.

Hensley turns her face away for a moment. She tries to picture Berto as a small child, smelling sweetly of warm sugar. She knows that his mother loved him, so she says this. "I love you, darling boy. There is much more than the ending. I know you remember. Remember when I held you in my lap and we sang? Remember all the wonderful stories? Some mornings you couldn't wait any longer for a new one. You'd climb into bed with us. You'd push your small knees into my back and ask for another."

For a moment, Berto is calm. His eyes are turned toward Hensley, but they are looking far beyond her. He releases his grip slightly on the book. Hensley says quietly to Teresa, "Should you read?"

From across the room, Teresa bristles. "It's a stupid novel. About a guy and his parrot. My father read it to us as kids." She wipes her hands on her skirt. "Berto always loved it, but he doesn't want me to read it. I've tried."

"But your family—its genealogy is written in there. Not in a Bible."

Teresa smiles. "I suppose my ancestors were rebels."

Hensley sighs. "I have no idea what's going on here. I could try to get a doctor for Berto. I probably have enough for that."

Berto moans. Hensley looks at his face. His cheeks are the inverse of Teresa's, not full but sunken. He grips the book and thrashes his torso. Then he's still again. He reaches out for Hensley. As she places her hand in his, he whispers.

"Don't leave me. Please, Mama. Don't leave."

Hensley sighs. Once again she strokes his temple. "I'm right here."

Teresa stands beside the bed with her hands on her hips. "Maybe it's your condition."

"Maybe. It's okay. I don't mind," she lies. She can only close her eyes and try to imagine how her own mother loved her. Regardless of her tantrums or sickly breath or stupid ideas, she knows she was loved. So she holds Berto's hand as she knows her own mother held hers, and she tells him that things will work out. She tells him that there will be another day when everything will look a little brighter. As she does this, she hopes it is true.

Yet again, she wishes this crazy world would hurl her up and out of this house, fling her across the black, salty ocean, and throw her into the tawny French dirt upon which Base Hospital #12 is planted.

Suddenly Berto opens his eyes. He looks at her without recognition. "What are you doing?" he says, pulling his hand away from hers and pushing her slightly with his elbow so that she is forced to stand.

Hensley is stunned, terrified by the look of disgust and fear on his face, as though it was she who was responsible for conjuring an intimacy that did not exist. Teresa takes Hensley by the arm, squeezing it with surprising force. "Come on," Teresa says, her long black hair framing her wild, sad face.

Outside beneath a sky lit up with stars, Teresa puts her head close to Hensley's. "I'm sorry. But thank you. You gave him some comfort. And me."

"I'm not so sure. But you're welcome."

She takes Hensley's cheeks into her hands. "The balance of

things we do not know far outweighs what we do." Hensley looks into Teresa's dark brown eyes, which seem as black as the night, but far more mysterious.

"Why do you seem so unflappable? This"—she gestures to their small house—"this is a nightmare."

Teresa does not smile. "The world likes us to be delicate." Teresa drops her hands to Hensley's abdomen. "How, exactly, is your body forming another? Doesn't that seem impossible? An act of incredible strength? Just as unfathomable as any of this?" Hensley feels the warmth of Teresa's hands through her nightdress. "A little heart, beating its own rhythm. Fingers and toes and a tongue with all its own taste buds. Think of that."

Hensley's cheeks are damp with tears, but she makes no move to wipe them. "Yet the simplest of things—boarding that train on Saturday—seems impossible."

Teresa closes her eyes for a moment, leaving Hensley to her own thoughts. She remembers the morning she spent with Berto. "Why are you here?" she finally asks Teresa. "What is this place to you?"

Teresa opens her eyes. "The last place my mother was alive."

"So it was here..."

"She left something behind. Our inheritance."

Hensley thinks for a moment. She remembers Berto's story.

"The goblets?"

Teresa drops her hands from Hensley's body. Her eyes narrow. "How do you know?"

"Berto told me. That day that I was here. Is that it? You're looking for the goblets?"

Teresa blinks her eyes in affirmation. "She ran. For days, dragging the two of us and those goblets through the desert at night. She thought we were being chased. She imagined horrible fates would fall upon us. We heard the hooves of Obregón's army and watched from the far side of a canyon as they raced south, past us. She didn't care. She was sure they would take us from her. That she couldn't protect us. It was more than she could bear. One day, she left us by the creek. She was distraught, worrying that the goblets were too loud, too shiny. When she left she carried them with her, wrapped in a bedsheet. While she was away, Berto caught a fish. He was so proud. We waited and waited. When we couldn't anymore, we walked upstream. Berto and I stood up there, just beyond the ridge, and watched as a strange, misplaced fire burned just in front of the bank."

Hensley has seen the view from the top of the hill many times. She imagines seeing her own mother burning in the middle of the street, an irrecoverable, impossible pile of debris left to clean up. She reaches her hand out to Teresa's. "They could be anywhere. Will you dig up the entire desert?"

The darkness seems to deepen around them as a wisp of a cloud covers the moon's glow.

"Once Berto is well. Stranger things have happened," Teresa says without any humor in her voice. She leaves Hensley's side and goes inside to be with her brother, whose noisy, raspy sleep is audible through the screen.

Hensley walks quickly back down the hill without Teresa's lantern, her feet slipping often over the uneven ground. She holds her hands out in front of her like the newly blind. When she finally reaches the brick patio, she is desperate to lay her hands on the bundle.

Her fingers frantically untie the ribbon and she unfolds the paper to see his carefully slanted words filling the entire page, his commas and periods and exclamation marks like the stars that anchor the myriad constellations in the night sky.

Dear Life, she thinks as she sinks to the floor, her feet and hands bleeding from their brief encounters with the junipers and hackberry bushes on the hill. *Thank you for letting this part be true.*

As the dawn arrives, casting its restrained light upon the wall beside her bed, Hensley's eyes rest on the black ink listing that in which Mr. Reid believes.

With a terrible weariness, she pulls herself from the floor and writes one last letter.

Dear Mr. Reid,

What a strange night I've just had. I hope to tell all about it someday. For now, though, I must address your recent letter about what you believe. It is a lovely letter and it's made me want more of myself. For you, too.

Things I know:

1. It is easier to lie than tell the truth.
2. Your words are the ones I would hold to my chest if I were dying. True or false, they are everything.
3. You will make it home and I will live out my days consoled by the fact that you are in the world.
4. I am pregnant.

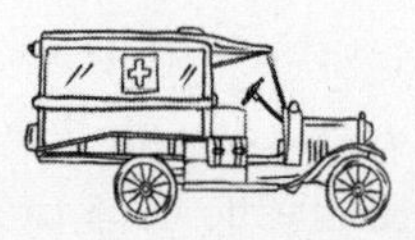

Charles's convalescence has been delayed by a fierce bout of pneumonia. By now, he might've been home, on his way to find Hensley. Instead, he has endured long days of feverish sleep, prickly skin, and impossible lethargy followed by nights in which he sat up, unable to breathe, straining to force some scrap of air into his lungs. He'd bang against the metal bed frame with the bedpan, panicked. Inevitably, his noise would wake the other fellows and he'd be shushed by a nurse, who would hold his hands above his head until the fit had passed.

He has no idea how many days have passed when he awakens to see Rogerson sitting beside him, his shirtsleeves covered in mud. For a moment, he believes he has overslept, that it's all been a terribly vivid dream and that he's about to catch hell. He wonders if there is time for coffee.

But as he looks around the room and feels the ache in his chest, the dull throbbing in his head, he knows.

"Still raining?" Charles asks, closing his eyes again.

"I'm waiting for my hot bath."

"A good novel."

"I've got something for you," Rogerson says. "A letter."

Charles opens his eyes slightly, just to see the familiar slant of her handwriting. Everything is blurry, but the shape of the envelope is clear.

"Apparently you've been so sick that you couldn't even be roused for this. Shall I?" Charles cannot speak. "Of course I shall," Rogerson says, clearing his throat. The sound of the envelope torn between Rogerson's fingers sends a chill across Charles's body.

His voice begins, articulating her words carefully.

"Dear Mr. Reid, What a strange night I've just had. I hope to tell all about it someday. For now, though, I must address your recent letter about what you believe. It is a lovely letter and it's made me want more of myself. For you, too." Here Rogerson stops, then adds in his own voice, "More, yes. We love more, Hensley. Right?" When Charles says nothing, he continues, "*Things I know.* It's a list, Reid. Ready?"

Charles tries to nod his head. Rogerson continues. "*One. It is easier to lie than tell the truth.* Don't we know it? *Two. Your words are the ones I would hold to my chest if I were dying. True or false, they are everything.* Sweet. God, she's good. *Three. You will make it home and I will live out my days consoled by the fact that you are in the world.* She loves you, Reid. I mean, really. This is getting serious. *Four. I am . . ."* But Rogerson's voice halts here.

Charles opens his eyes. "What?" he manages to say. "She is what?"

Rogerson folds the letter and replaces it in the envelope. Charles reaches his hand out, but it falls onto the bed, impotent.

"She is waiting for you, Reid. That's all." Rogerson's hand is heavy and warm against Charles's shoulder. "You've got to get the hell out of here, okay? Get out of here and go get her."

Charles nods, weeping. The tears are warm, then cold, and he cannot hide them.

Hensley changes trains once again in Chicago, painfully aware of her solitude this time around. For several hours she settles herself onto a wooden bench near the ticket booth. As trains arrive and prepare to depart there is a great surge in the size of the crowd, but then it diminishes. It is as though the terminal is a beach and the passengers are its rhythmic, if irregular, waves.

Luckily, Thomas Wright's arrival was delayed by more than a week and Hensley was able to pack her things properly and conjure a traveling skirt that allows the slight swell in her waist to be accommodated by a soft, pleated waistband. She knows it is ridiculous, but she wants to step off the train and shame Lowell by her beauty. She'd like to arrive more desirable than when she left.

On the morning of her departure, Hensley stood in the kitchen where she last saw her father alive. She cooked herself an egg in the cast-iron pan that was there when they arrived and would stay on, serving the house's next resident. It was a good pan, well seasoned, with a shape somewhere between a circle and an oval. Just the sight of it made her hungry. So many slices of ham and bacon had been fried in it that everything came out slightly smoky. She ate the egg right out of the pan, imagining the face her father would have made to express his disdain for her slovenly manners.

Her father's desk, her own sewing machine, the silver tea service, and several boxes of personal items including her father's chess set were bundled in the corner of the living room, to be sent to New York separately. Hensley just had a trunk and one valise to take on the train. Mr. Reid's letters were tucked into her own satchel, which would not leave her side.

The truck sat in front of the house, idling. Teresa came in, her boots striking hard against the wood floor.

"Ready?" she called, her voice pitched low like her brother's.

They had spoken little since their middle-of-the-night encounter a week before.

"Almost," Hensley called from the kitchen.

Teresa poked her head in the doorway.

Hensley had her fork in the pan, scooping the eggs onto it. "You caught me. Want a fork?"

Teresa's boots clomped across the floor. She took a clean fork from the dish rack. "I'm starving."

They ate the buttery eggs in silence, like an old married couple. The truck idled outside, filling their thoughts with the imminent journey.

Finally, Teresa pulled the brim of her hat down hard and said, "We should probably go."

"Okay. I'll just clean this pan."

Teresa turned away from her. "Good eggs. Thank you," she said. Soon, Hensley saw her carry the impossibly heavy trunk and suitcase out and heave them into their place in the truck bed.

Hensley wiped the pan dry and then scooped up Isaac, who had been slinking between her legs all morning. Rubbing his little white face with her knuckles, she told him to be good. Newton was nowhere to be found, but she placed the last of the milk into a dish and left it by the back door.

Hensley stood once more in front of her bedroom wall, wishing she could take the whole thing with her, wondering how she would bear to awaken each morning without his words being the first thing she saw. Despite the trouble it might cause, Teresa had acquiesced to Hensley's pleas to leave it until she'd gone. Hensley leaned her cheek against the wall, the morning sun already making it warm.

You are going to become another man's bride, she told herself. *This has to be the end.*

Hensley tried to conjure the way Lowell's face looked to her when they first met. When it had appeared innocent, handsome, even. But instead she could only picture the words of his telegram. *I would be remiss if I did not extend the offer of a marriage.* She understood how loath he was to see her again. Could this be, in fact, their only commonality?

Hensley opened her eyes and her fingers traced the words just beside her. But she finally pushed herself away from the wall and closed the door behind her.

The two girls drove away from Hillsboro. Hensley kept her eyes on the dirt road that brought her here.

Dear Mr. Reid, she began, *I wonder how it is that this desolate dirt road is somehow connected to the chaos of Times Square.* But then she stopped. She gripped the handkerchief in her hand, willing her mind to be quiet.

She had not written to him again since she'd confessed the truth. And there had been no reply. So, just as she'd suspected, it must be finished. Their short love story had ended with a blank page. Their effort at immortality, in the end, sabotaged not by death, but by life.

What would he do with her letters now that he knew the truth? Perhaps they would be thrown into a rubbish bin in the mess hall, piled on by clumps of that uneaten white mush. Or maybe he and

Rogerson would take a match to them, throw them on top of a fire, eliciting some final heat from her words.

Still, she longed to know that he was safe. She'd left her forwarding address only with Teresa, not the postmaster. If a letter from him did arrive, Teresa would send it along, bundled in her own correspondence. Hensley knew she must not imagine that possibility, just as a hungry man must not imagine a roast.

As they drove, flies buzzed against the inside of the windshield. "I'm sorry you'll have to explain about the wall."

Teresa shrugged. "I don't expect he'll care. I'll just have to fix it."

Hensley reached out her hand and laid it on Teresa's. "You're a good man."

They giggled as the heat of the day assaulted the truck.

"Yes. I am Berto Romero with hair on my chest and a cock between my legs and you're a nice, refined, virginal girl sitting here beside me."

"Two peas in a pod."

Their smiles faded gradually. Hensley stuck her hand out into the hot air. Teresa wiped the sweat from her brow with her shirtsleeve.

"Will it be terrible? Marrying this man?" she asked.

Hensley let the question settle into her. She pictured the way he looked when she went to his apartment, his bare feet flimsy and awkward and slightly grotesque. When he acknowledged his deception without flinching, she'd known it was not the first or the last time he would lie to satisfy a desire.

"Perhaps people change."

Teresa nodded. The journey was long and hot and hostile to cheerful thoughts. By the time they reached El Paso, Hensley didn't care if she never saw another long-eared jackrabbit or the shadow of a red-tail hawk as it hovered, darkening the desert.

Teresa parked the truck beside the curb while Hensley flagged down a porter. Suddenly their good-bye was imminent and they were in public. There could not be an embrace between a lady and her driver.

Instead, Hensley handed Teresa an envelope. "I saved myself the cost of postage and already wrote you a letter."

Teresa smiled. She glanced at it and read the sentence written in small script on the outside. *Parting advice: If you have hair on your chest and a cock between your legs, you should not use the women's restroom.* She smiled and folded it into her back pocket. She touched the brim of her hat. "Many thanks."

Hensley watched her move into the crowd, a young hired man entering the station in search of Mr. Thomas Wright.

Soon enough, another train disembarks and the station is full again with finely dressed men and women walking hurriedly across the marble floor. Into this chaos, a man enters from the street, rolling two large, upright cases. His face is familiar, but Hensley doesn't know how that could be possible.

At the very moment that she is studying him for clues to his identity, he sees her and approaches.

"Well, hello," he says in a surprisingly deep voice. "You don't recognize me in my street clothes. But I never forget a face. Especially not one I might've killed."

"Oh," Hensley says, excitedly. "From the circus. Of course. Your mustache is not... curled."

"Right you are. Remind me where I had the pleasure of holding you? Was it California?"

Hensley shakes her head. "No. New Mexico. A little mining town in the south."

His eyebrows vault high up on his forehead. "A long way from home."

"I was, yes. I'm going home now. Back to New York."

He nods approvingly. "The whole troupe will be there next month. Will you come and see us again? Articus McDonald. Everyone calls me Arty." He takes Hensley's gloved hand and brings it to his lips.

"Oh, I'd love to. It was a wonderful show."

"I will curl my mustache for you."

Hensley smiles. "Then I will recognize you."

"You don't seem as happy as most people who are on their way home."

"Don't I?" Hensley puts a hand to her throat, trying to ease the lump of emotion that is lodged there.

Arty shrugs his wide shoulders. "The road is my home, so forgive me. I wouldn't know anything about going home."

The noise of travelers is receding all around them.

Quietly, Hensley says, "I'm to be married. In New York."

He nods. "Well, that is a terrifying idea."

Hensley smiles. "Like being lifted in a chair way up high by somebody you've never met before."

Arty laughs. "Precisely. What did I tell you that night?"

"Um, you told me to hold on tight. That's all I remember."

"Well, it's good advice for marriage, too, I guess."

Hensley nods. "I suppose it is."

"I was married once. The holding on is everything. When you get lazy, let go a little bit, that's when she will find another strong man. Even if he's a short lion tamer who needs red whips and sedatives to control his creatures. He will know something about captivating a creature who is feeling neglected."

"That's a sad story."

Arty winks. "But it's mine. And I use it all the time to my advantage."

Hensley blushes. "Lemonade from lemons, as they say. Right?"

"Load on the sugar," he says, pushing his carts slowly away from Hensley. "My last bit of advice. Lots and lots of sugar."

Hensley watches him cross the empty station and wishes she could follow him. If she'd any courage at all, she might just join the circus and swing from the trapeze. Her baby would learn how to juggle and eat fire. They would live in train stations and on wagons, amid midgets and giants. She could write letters to Mr. Reid from every single town and city, hoping in each one that he might make himself known to her. That he would step into the spotlight, surrender his arm to her sweaty, chalky hand. Then they'd reinvent themselves and a whole new act could be developed: the three of them holding tightly to one another while they sailed through the heat of the tent, untethered from any earthly concern.

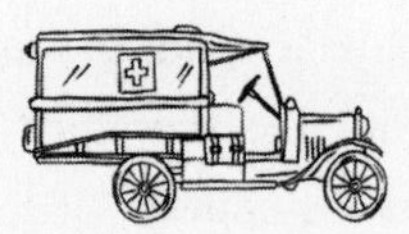

Six weeks after the crude amputation, Charles sits on the deck of a transport ship with a pair of crutches beside his chair and a stiff blanket covering his lap. His eyes are closed to the sun. The ocean spray makes the blanket damp and heavy across him and he doesn't move for hours at a time, convinced that if he can just be still long enough his leg might reappear. At times, the sensation is so visceral, so urgent, he is sure that it has. He wiggles his toes on the gone foot and the coarse wool scrapes against his overgrown toenails. The abrasion is as welcome a feeling as he's ever had.

Slowly, so as not to disturb this miracle, he opens his eyes and lifts the blanket. But beneath it, there is only one leg; where the other should be, the hem of his pants is folded up and pinned nearly to the pocket, redundant. This sight is still an affront to him. A raw feeling that he's becoming accustomed to rises up from the wound, through his thigh and groin, and lodges in his chest. Each breath scrapes against this rawness and makes him cringe.

From the hospital bed in Rouen, he dictated letters to his parents, his uncle, and a few friends from college. It became easier after the letter to his parents.

> I am safe, but I am not whole. I am sorry for the pain you will feel when you read this, but the tragedies of this war are innumerable. There is no accounting for why I am alive and able to write these words and many thousands of others (boys I picked up myself) have perished. But the truth of the matter is that I will be coming home forever changed. I have lost most of my left leg. The Red Cross has given me a crutch, but they tell me that there are many options for prosthetics.

Even before his father told him he'd arranged for him to see a specialist in Chicago, Charles knew that he would wind up on a train headed west.

He has not revealed to Hensley, however, the totality of his injury because he could not bear to deliver more sad news so soon after her father's death. Her last letter, the one he vaguely remembers Rogerson reading to him while the pneumonia still gripped him, is strangely missing from his bundle. He's read each of the others daily during these long weeks of recovery. All he can imagine is that Rogerson kept one for himself. Pocketed it as he drove the King George away from Rouen.

He doesn't blame him, really. Or, he wouldn't if it were not so important to him that he have every word she meant for him to have. He cannot remember many things from the last month. Nearly everything has faded to just a few dark memories, the most vivid of which is Foulsom pulling away the bandage, the cotton sticking slightly to the pus, and exposing his stump. The lucidity of the pain as his wound met the stiff, cool air of that morning is still enough to provoke tears.

Also, he remembers the hymns that the nuns would sing just before dark. Standing in a small circle, the gathering of black robes just beyond the last bed like a holy shadow, their voices called upon

God and the Holy Spirit with modest charm. He remembers believing that he would soon be dead and that this was why he could hear their songs, which he'd never heard before on his way to or from the mess hall.

And he remembers Rogerson sitting awkwardly beside his bed on a stool too short for his long legs. He held a letter in his hands, a forced grin glued upon his face. *Dear Mr. Reid,* he can hear him say in his perfect Midwestern cadence. But nothing more. An aching blankness surrounds that moment. Then again, he thinks, perhaps he has imagined it all. Perhaps there was never another letter from her. But why not?

Either way, as he occupies a small part of a large ship in the middle of the great Atlantic Ocean, Charles feels as insignificant as he ever has. His leg has been blown off, but it will not change the course of the war. For the rest of his life, he will be reminded of his sacrifice and its irrelevance. Even if a million boys each left a limb in the mud, learned to survive with only three-quarters of themselves, it would not matter. The war would go on until there was nobody left to fight.

But he also acutely believes that, despite his insignificance in the world, there is still a girl to whom he matters. Unable to picture her face, he only imagines a figure seen from behind, her shape unremarkable, her bare legs standing in the middle of a slow-moving stream, the sound of her words coaxing him into believing that though the water is cold, it is worth the plunge.

As soon as the train pulls into the station, Hensley scans the platform for Lowell. Her feet feel heavy in her shoes and her fingers tingle. She says the word *fiancé* in her mind, thinking this is the first step toward acceptance.

When she descends from the car, however, she still has not spotted him. She looks at the large clock over the station door. The train is on time. Many other couples are reuniting on the platform and for a fleeting moment she hopes to see him, standing beside a porter, smoking a cigarette, looking at his pocket watch.

When she has looked all around and lingered for a moment beneath the track sign, she begins to walk on her own. Entering the station, she finds a bench and sets down her valise and her satchel. Just as she did in Chicago, she watches the crowds swell and ebb. Finally, she lugs her valise and her satchel to a phone box and calls Harold.

"He's not here," she says when Harold answers.

"Hen? Where are you?"

"At Grand Central. Under the big clock."

"And Lowell?"

"Not here, as I said."

"Well, perhaps he's been delayed. Stay there. I will come directly."

"Thank you, Harry," she says, wondering how in the world Lowell will explain himself.

It is past dinnertime when Harold arrives, his own face flushed with worry. They embrace and then Harold's eyes glance at her figure, so perfectly hidden by her handmade clothes.

"I can't believe he's not here. We spoke last night. He assured me this would be his first priority now. You would be, I mean."

Hensley sighs. "Well, his assurances are often hollow, aren't they?"

Harold picks up her valise. "This will not do. Follow me. We'll find a taxi."

As they drive through the darkened streets of New York, Hensley looks carefully at the people walking on the sidewalk. Suddenly there is more than her eyes can absorb. She marvels at the hats and heels and bags decorated with sequins and beads and feathers. Though the colors are demure beneath the streetlamps, it is dazzling.

Hensley remembers Berto's shirt that she'd finally altered for Teresa, its thick collar and manly cuffs. She looks down at her own traveling skirt and fingers a snag Newton made in its loose weave by his insistent claws. She misses the mischievous little cat.

Harold's profile is worried. Hensley reaches for his hand. "I'm sure it's just a misunderstanding," she says. "I do have his reply, though. He certainly knew of my arrival."

"Oh, it's more complicated than that, Hen."

"What do you mean?"

He shakes his head. "People have complicated needs. It's exhausting."

"For example?"

"You need a husband. He doesn't need a wife."

Hensley furrows her brow. "Why? Why doesn't he need a wife? What *does* he need? I don't understand."

Harold nods. "That's why this is my concern. Don't worry. We will sort it out." He looks at her and smiles. "Thankfully, the lady who cleans my place left some potato soup for me. We'll split it and you can get some rest."

Hensley smiles. Harold squeezes her hand and she turns her eyes back to the streets of her home that are newly strange and beautiful.

Hensley spends the next afternoon preparing a dinner for Harold and washing dishes. As she folds and refolds petticoats that still have Hillsboro dust coating their hems, she allows herself to remove the bundle of Mr. Reid's letters. The heft of them in her hand is familiar and reassuring. Now she curses her decision to leave her forwarding address only with Teresa. How could she be so reckless? What if Teresa, too, leaves Hillsboro? If there was the hope of another letter, she would at least have that to project into the future.

As the afternoon light fills the room, she imagines no greater pleasure than anticipating and reading a new dispatch from Mr. Reid. Even if he chastised her, or despised her for her weak character. From him, she would welcome it. She would at least have one or two fresh letters to add to her bundle. Its increasing weight a buoy to which she could cling throughout any storm.

For now, she unties the ribbon holding them together and the sight of the first envelope—her own name written in his familiar script—sends a thrill through her spine. She sits up straighter, as though he might be able to see her.

> Your very name, which now pulses through my head with nearly every footstep, is like a magic wand that can conjure idyllic days in which I stand by your side as you tend to a pot of beans or stroke Newton's fickle head or kick off your shoes and dance with me.

She shoves it back in its envelope and stands up, feeling the urge to see the street below. Looking out the bedroom window, she can see the bustle of the Manhattan afternoon. It is so strange, so different from Main Street in Hillsboro. There are dozens of men walking quickly, hats on their heads and briefcases hanging from their arms, and several women, one pushing a baby carriage, another holding a young girl's hand.

Hensley realizes with a new sense of urgency that she hasn't seen a newspaper in weeks. She ties on her hat and ventures down to the street to buy one.

Returning home, the newsprint already blackening her gloves, she settles in with a cup of tea and the news of the day.

She reads carefully about the latest tactical maneuvers overseas, trying to place Mr. Reid among them. The Red Cross has announced it will administer aid even to German soldiers. There are plans for Ford to build tractors in Ireland, a teacher has been fired for refusing to register with Selective Service, the Yankees played fourteen innings and finally defeated the Red Sox, and stocks are surging for no apparent reason. Two workers were killed when the tree they were trying to take down crushed them against a stone wall, Lord Wellesley quietly married his brother's widow, and a Mr. Moller of Tenafly left thirty-five thousand dollars to his housekeeper and nothing to his wife.

These accounts of events in the world leave her feeling both comforted and vulnerable. We are all stumbling, she thinks. The grass is just as weedy on both sides of the fence.

Then, as she reads the editorials, she finds herself crying. On the very page where her father's words once appeared so regularly, he is absent. His voice is no longer a part of the world. And the opinions of these other men interest her very little. In fact, it angers her that they exist at all.

On the back page, there is a list of names. They are the men most recently killed in the war. Terrified, Hensley scans the list quickly, her eyes blurred by tears as she looks for any Reids. When she finds none, she wipes her tears and sighs.

Her eyes go back, reading each and every name, knowing that there is no good reason to be relieved. Each of these lost lives will be grieved; somewhere this page will be torn out and added to a maudlin scrapbook of the great war that took everything.

Her tea has gone cold and she winces as she sips it. The baby stretches, reminding her that she is not alone. Hensley pulls the gloves off her hands and extends her fingers across her belly. Closing her eyes, she hums a lullaby she doesn't remember learning.

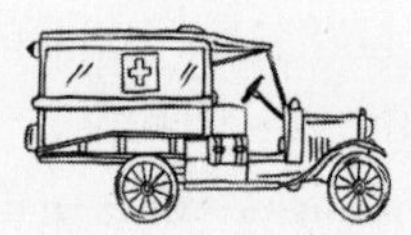

The first thing Charles notices as the truck hesitates at the eastern edge of Hillsboro is the dry goods store. In the very last letter that he has, Hensley told him about a mummified child who had been placed in the window. It was found—the way nearly everything was—while a prospector was hacking away at the earth. The child, crouched as though searching for her own pot of gold, sat in the window, a petite, forgotten piece of humanity. As alarming as it is, it thrills him. He knows that he is looking at something that she has looked at, too. Their lives are finally intersecting. Her description of it runs through his mind. *It is eerie, maybe even gruesome, but I cannot take my eyes from the shriveled brown bundle. Life's mystery looks stubborn and cruel when you see the little fingers curled in perfectly silent requests.*

The hired driver is going on to Kingston and Charles tells him to leave him off right there.

"You sure, sir?" the driver asks, glancing at Charles's leg and his black cane.

"Go on, please. I'm fine," he says, slamming the door. He stands outside the window studying those little fingers, relieved that this is the right place. Within moments he might be gazing at the face that for so long has eluded him. It is lunchtime and there are not many people out, but he still feels the terrifying thrill that he may glance her actual face at any moment. The street is not long, hardly the length of a crosstown block in New York, but he takes his time.

Across the street, he notices a small wooden sign in the window, lettered in red, that reads **Lin's Chinese Cooking**. His mouth waters at this sight and a smile forms on his lips, but he keeps walking. Could she, in fact, be sitting inside right now, eating a plate of cabbage and eggs? Will he know her when he sees her?

Charles would like to remove his jacket, for the heat is dry and unmoving, but his appearance matters more than his comfort. He lingers in front of the post office where she mails her letters. He walks in, smiling at the clerk and laying his hands on the counter. There is a brass slot for outgoing mail that he fingers carefully.

"Help you, sir?" the clerk says, without looking up from his sorting.

"No, thank you. Just getting acquainted," Charles says and he is nearly floating.

The prosthetic that he acquired in Chicago fits tightly around his thigh with a leather strap. As he leaves the post office, it seems as though it alone is keeping his entire body from levitating.

The sound of his own gait on the wooden sidewalk announces his wound, his deficiency. The shoe carved into the end of the wooden stump is stiff and heavy. Will his loss forfeit her affection? He won't blame her. Or will he? Surely she will have some physical flaw. Can any flaw ever match his own?

As he makes his way closer to her house, the sweat trickles from his hair across his temples. Removing his handkerchief to wipe his brow, he wonders if her affection is even real. Has he inflated something trivial into something grand? Has he given her words more meaning than she intended? He wants to pull the letters out right then from his case and reassure himself.

But then he sees the rock wall that she's told him she is in the habit of adding to. Three stacks of smooth little stones, just there by the black iron gate. One for each letter. Meaningless to anyone else on earth but him.

The sight of this might as well have cut a hole in his chest. He nearly stops breathing. The heat of the afternoon whooshes through him as though he has a great big wound that has turned his body into a cavern of hot air. It seems impossible that those are the very stones she picked and placed while he trudged through mud, loading the lucky ones onto stretchers—unaware that his own leg would soon be obliterated into scraps. Which rocks did she choose while he was still whole?

Afraid to touch them, to disturb their careful placement, he walks past. He opens the gate and stands before the door. Leaning hard on his cane for support, he raps three times on the screen.

A Mexican opens the door. Beneath his hat, his eyes are friendly; white paint is splattered across his work shirt and one cheek.

"I'm sorry," Charles says, "I was looking for a Miss Hensley Dench."

The man stares at him, then nods. "She's gone. We got a new superintendent. He's moving in here this weekend, after I get the place cleaned. You can find him at the hotel."

"I'm not looking for the superintendent. I'm looking for Miss Dench. Where has she gone?"

"Back to New York."

"When?"

"Weeks ago. I drove her to the train. She was ... torn about it."

The man stares at Charles, his cane, and his black case. Then, without any inflection, he says, "Are you the soldier?"

"Why didn't she tell me?" Charles says, banging his cane once against the concrete porch.

The Mexican stands there, looking at him. The questions are not meant for him. They both know that. Nevertheless, he shrugs. "Women," he says under his breath with a slight smile and walks into the house, leaving the door wide open.

Charles inhales. She is not here, but this is where she lived. Where she stirred those pots of beans and let Isaac tickle her legs. Where she mourned for her father and filled entire afternoons composing letters to him.

Carefully, he maneuvers the threshold.

He stands in the nearly empty living room. Long white curtains hang from the windows, taming the zealous sunlight. There is a single walnut desk, a chintz-covered armchair, and a trunk meant to serve as a coffee table. Through the back screen door, he observes the patch of bricks Mr. Dench called their terrace. A black-and-white cat lolls in a bright spot.

In the kitchen, there are several pans hanging above the stove. He wraps his hand around the handle of each. The cast iron is cool and rough to the touch. He holds it tightly, letting the coolness transfer to his hand. Then he presses his hand to his cheek.

He stands at the sink, staring out past the yard to the street. Is this really what she saw? Is this view really the one for which he spent all those months yearning? It is utterly ordinary. Sighing, he turns back to the table and sits in a chair, letting his eyes close against the smudged walls and the uneven counter. The magic of her words has faded. His body is tired and he dreads the trip back to El Paso.

Following the clamor coming from another part of the house, he walks back through the living room and peers into a bedroom, where the Mexican is pulling a canvas cloth across the floor, setting up a ladder. A paintbrush and a little can of whitewash sit in the corner. "Mr. Wright didn't want me to touch it at first," he says, adjusting the ladder. "He seemed nearly fixated on it. But then, after a few days, he decided to go again. And when he left, he told me to cover it up. Get rid of it."

The wall looks a mess, as though it has been tattooed, or burned in a fire. Only as he stands there with his vanished leg aching and his temples throbbing does Charles realize what it is.

With no idea how much time has passed, he finally speaks. Though he knows he has absolutely no authority to do so, he instructs the Mexican to leave the room. "Get me a drink," he says, his voice a quivering whisper. "Something strong."

The young man kneels down, wiping the brush off carefully. Then, with a sudden movement, he is gone.

Alone, Charles reads the entire wall. All the words that he'd carefully chosen and written himself, suddenly new and different written in her hand. These words from before, from far away, from when he was whole. He pushes his forehead into the plaster, letting the black ink blur in his periphery, nearly surrounding him. Dropping his cane, he stretches his arms out wide, pressing all of himself against the cool plaster.

Finally, he retrieves his cane and inches back toward the bed. He sits on the bed—her bed—then lays his head on the pillow, letting the sweet pain of desire encompass him. He can almost hear the whistle, the whine, of a faraway train screaming the impossibility of the distance between them. It feels as though he's been hollowed out, all of his blood and organs drained through that same mysterious opening that emerged when he saw the stones piled on the wall. With each breath, he seems to lose more vitality. He will wander through life like this until he can hold her head to his chest, look into her eyes, and hear her voice. Only then will this aching vacuum be filled. Only then might his breaths fill him, instead of empty him.

Charles's wooden leg hangs off the bed, its weight pulling against his groin. Suddenly, in the doorway, the Mexican appears again. His face has transformed—there is a wild look in his eye and a smile, wide and white, brightening his face. For a moment, Charles fears he's gone mad. But, still, he is unable to move.

There is a cup in his hand. Silver. A tall cup with a stem, like a goblet. Charles is grateful, hoping it is filled with some blindingly strong liquor. But the man does not hand the goblet to Charles. Instead, with that mad look on his face, he places the goblet on the writing desk just inside the door and takes off his hat. A mane of thick, shiny black hair falls across his shoulders. Then, without changing expressions, he unbuttons his shirt, revealing an ample, womanly bosom. He unbuckles his belt and lets his trousers fall to the wood floor. Stepping out of them, it is quite apparent that he is not a man.

Charles does not move. He assumes he is hallucinating.

But finally, she does pick up the goblet, the work boots still on her feet but the rest of her completely bare, and brings it to Charles.

"This is for Hensley," she says. "I have her address in New York. I know you will take it to her."

Charles reaches out for the silver stem. "I will," he says to her. "I will." Her brown skin is sturdy in the most beautiful way. It seems an affirmation of life, of resilience, of metamorphosis.

She turns away from him. Then, in the doorway, she pauses. "I had no idea there was a cellar in this house. Until you came. Until you asked me for a drink. All that time. Right here in front of me. Or, rather, below me. Filled with glass canning jars. And these."

Her face is beaming. Charles cannot find a single word to say to her. He clasps the goblet tightly in his fingers.

"I suppose I'll never know why. Or how. But they are actually here. What madness. I'll always be grateful for your visit. Always," she says.

Charles watches her walk away, listens to her footsteps descend stairs.

A dry breeze blows through the open window, bringing invisible flecks of dust into the room, some of which collide with his wooden leg, giving noise to the maraca that is his heart.

He stands on the brick patio and imagines himself back in France, her bare feet where his are now. The sky is that tender blue that made her crazy with its enormity. He closes his eyes and pretends his skin is hers. He feels the warmth and it is almost like they are there together. Right there, inhabiting his own body. The thin desert air makes him breathe deeply. A sweet scent lingers on the edge of each nostril. That desert, vast and desolate, reassures him. Charles climbs up the hill just as the sun is setting.

Inside the shack on top of the hill, there she is. The Mexican. But now she is dressed in a skirt and a blouse, her hair braided down her back, her face clearly feminine. In the corner, her brother appears to be asleep on a cot. They are the inverse of one another.

"What's the trouble?" Charles asks her, gesturing to the invalid.

"He's sick."

He nods. "Still? With what?"

"We don't know. But we will soon, hopefully. I will take him to El Paso and pay for a doctor to examine him. We can afford to now. We can afford to lose this job."

"May I feel his pulse?" From this distance, his condition appears similar to the typhoid Charles saw in France. The way his face twitches and his legs are stiff beneath the sheet. "How long has he been like this?"

"Are you a doctor?"

Charles shakes his head. "No. But I was an ambulance driver in the war. I learned a few things."

"It's been months. Since May."

"Oh. That's too long to be typhoid. High fevers?"

He places his fingers on the man's neck. His pulse thrums, with barely any space between its beats.

"His heart. It's flying. Get me a cold cloth."

For the next several hours, Charles dresses him with cold compresses, just the way they did it at the CCS, trying to bring his body to a normal temperature. Occasionally the man opens his eyes and asks for Teresa. This is how Charles learns her name.

She speaks to him in Spanish and tries to take the book that he has clenched in his hands away from him, but he won't let her. She tells Charles it was once their father's book. And his father's before that for five generations. It is the place they've written all the births and deaths and marriages since the time of Hidalgo.

"This is part of the fever. Hallucinations. He's afraid I'm going to write his name in there. His date of death."

"A doctor needs to see him now," Charles says, alarmed by the constant whir of the man's heartbeat. He does not say it, but he suspects polio.

Her eyes make it clear that she understands him. Without warning, she begins to remove her clothes again. Charles turns and faces the window.

Through the fly-ridden windowsill, he looks down at the house where Hensley and Mr. Dench lived. He sees the brick patio, the windows of her bedroom, the chimney they never used. For months he's thought of the place where she existed as some completely other world. A place so far away from his own that it might as well be in another universe. He'd been sure it would only ever exist in his mind. But now, as he stands in the small house on top of the hill, he feels remarkably buoyed. As though he is visiting another person's dream—her dream. If he has found this place and confirmed its existence, perhaps he really will find her. Perhaps they might still have a chance.

Teresa has transformed herself again. Her hair hidden under her cap and her dungarees tucked into formidable boots, she's become a man.

"I will park the truck just outside the super's house. Do you think you can get him down the hill?"

Charles glances down at his own boots, one wooden. What would have been a simple task so recently was now impossible. He says only, "I will wait with him. Perhaps together..."

In the end, she does it all. Charles only cradles her brother's feet in the crook of his elbow as Teresa handles his torso with surprising strength. Covered in blankets, he rides in the bed of the truck all the way to El Paso, the box of sterling goblets rattling beside him.

"Do you think he'll survive?" Teresa asks, midway through their journey.

Charles nods. "Yes," he says, the ease of so many lies returning to him quickly. He really has no idea. There is an insidious danger in the unseen injuries. But had they come across him on the battlefield, they would have given him a chance. They would have loaded him in.

She seems reassured. They speak very little. Charles keeps his eye on the horizon, the way the vast blue sky seems to fade slightly at its edges. The world wearing out.

The outskirts of El Paso appear with their fences and long, low buildings of ranches and dairies. Teresa suddenly places her hand on his arm. It is a strange gesture, neither affectionate nor necessary.

Without reason, she removes it just as suddenly.

"Whatever you find there, in New York, she wished it had been you. All along. From the moment I met her."

"I don't understand," Charles says. "Tell me what you mean."

But she will say nothing else. They are soon in front of the doctor's office and Charles stays with them only long enough to determine that her brother's treatment is assured. Then he crosses the street and waits for the next eastbound train.

It is not until ten days later that Hensley finally sees Lowell. Instead, she's seen her dear friend Marie almost every day and the two girls have spent afternoons walking arm in arm, looking in windows and sharing lemon bars from the corner bakery. Marie is being courted by the owner of a shoe store whom she met when he fitted her mother for new boots.

"He has all the prettiest shoes in his shop, Hen. I can't help but think about that. Is it terrible?"

Hensley laughs. "Of course not. Practicality is highly valued in these matters, I'm told. Beautiful shoes are a real, tangible benefit."

The girls giggle, wiping powdered sugar from one another's cheeks. "Have you seen anyone since you've been home that you fancy?"

Hensley blushes. "Oh, Marie. You know me. I'm too aloof to attract anyone's attention."

"You certainly got Mr. Teagan's."

Hensley is quiet.

"I'm sorry, Hen. I didn't mean to..."

"Don't be silly, Marie. You're right. I got his attention and my brother seems convinced that we are right for each other."

"No. Harold? What use would he have for Mr. Teagan?"

Hensley shrugs. "I don't know. Did I tell you about the time I was riding that enormous horse, Thunder, and two hawks dived right in front of me and each grabbed a lizard?"

Marie's eyes widen. "Oh, Hen. You were like an actual cowgirl or something. I know some people might not, but I love how brown your skin is now."

"I wore a hat every day, I promise. But it's impossible to avoid the sun. Oh, Marie, you'd love it. Wading in the creek and eating a picnic beneath an enormous cottonwood tree. I could walk out the back door in my bare feet and see lizards and rabbits and even snakes."

"I'm just so glad you're home," Marie says, squeezing Hensley's arm. "Really, I am."

Hensley leans her head against Marie's. "Me, too," she says, wishing she could tell her the truth.

When her brother left early that morning, he was agitated by yet another unanswered telegram. He'd been mysterious about Lowell's whereabouts, his intentions, the misunderstanding of her arrival. Finally, that evening when he returned from work, something in his demeanor seemed shifted.

"You are to meet Lowell tonight for dinner. It's all set. It may still be redeemable."

"Your arrangement or my life?" Hensley asked wearily. She had spent the last three nights at her sewing machine, trying to accommodate the changes in her figure. Using a bolt of awful taupe silk, which must have been her mother's, that she'd found in Harold's closet, she'd made a draping of cascading pleats to attach to a tunic. She would have preferred feathers worn long like a necklace, or roses made from some ethereal chiffon, but when she held up the pleats against herself and looked in the mirror, she was pleased.

"Let's try to leave the drama to the playhouse," Harold said, pouring each of them a cup of tea. "Or to Mr. Teagan." Harold smiled at her as he stirred a lump of sugar into his tea.

Hensley let the steam collect on her palm, condensing into small, cool drops. "He doesn't love me, does he?"

Harold sipped his tea carefully. "Again, Hensley, it's time to be practical. Words like that can only confuse things. They are fraught, and their meaning changes with the decade."

Hensley wiped her damp palm across her cheek. "I really thought he did. I thought I could tell. It seemed perfectly simple."

Harold loosened his tie and said nothing more.

She meets him at an Italian restaurant on the east side. They do not touch. Lowell seems not to know what to do with his hands and so he places them firmly on the table.

"Hensley," he says, quickly, as she sits down at the table across from him. "Would you like a drink?"

"Maybe something cold would be nice. Thank you." Hensley looks at the charcoal gray wool of his suit coat. With a deep breath, she surveys the landscape of the table. He's already ordered a Scotch and water for himself, which is sweating. There are red flowers on the table, and for a moment she thinks he's brought them for her. But as she looks around, she sees that there is a bunch on each table. Glancing at his face, Hensley tries to find something new or changed in him. Instead, all she can see is that his hair is darker than she remembered it.

"You look well, Hen," he says finally. "How are you feeling these days?"

Hensley blushes. The question seems too personal. Then she reminds herself that he is her fiancé. It is his baby twirling inside of her right now.

"I'm fine, Lowell. I feel good. Just a little tired. It's a long journey. I thought you were to be at the station…"

"I can't really tell. I mean, you're hiding it well. It's not noticeable at all."

Hensley smooths the front of her dress and shrugs. Is this a compliment?

Then, after another sip of his drink, he adds, "Are you sure?"

"You mean, might you be off the hook?" Hensley says, her heart racing.

He shakes his head, his brow furrowed. "Don't start. I'm just curious. I'd like to see, that's all." He winks. His small teeth make an appearance as he smiles. "Husbands are allowed."

Hensley shudders. "You are crass. Would you like me to lift my skirts right here and let you inspect me?"

"Settle down, Hen." Lowe reaches for a cigarette. "I only meant that you aren't fat yet. That's a good thing."

"Yet?"

He ignores her. "I've had a lot of time to sort this out. We are embarking upon a sort of living play. We've been cast in our roles and we must do our best to render them with passion. I hope you can remember how this started."

She takes a deep breath. "Passion?"

"Love, then. Is that better? Charles has things arranged with a judge next week."

"Next week?" Hensley is suddenly short of breath. She imagines what her poor brother has had to endure, fixing this mess. Fraternizing with a man like Lowell Teagan is not his idea of fun.

"Not soon enough for you?" Lowe finishes his drink and signals the waitress for another.

"I just didn't know it had all been worked out. I mean, I wasn't even sure... when you didn't meet my train I thought..."

"The sooner the better. While you can still pass for respectable, right?"

Hensley pushes back her chair. She wants to hurl her glass of water at him. Dirty him, shame him, hurt him. Why did she ever think this would work? Does he care at all for her? Will he ever learn to be thoughtful, to be kind? Will she?

"It's a joke, Hen. Look, we're in a predicament. Or, rather, you are. But I helped you get there, I know. So I'm trying to do the right thing. But don't make me feel as though by marrying you I am shackling my entire spirit. Can't we be light? Be frivolous?"

Hensley is still. His words do absolutely nothing to quell her anger. In fact, she cannot remember ever feeling so offended. She is certain she has never hated anyone until this moment.

Though she wishes she could stop them, the tears begin as soon as she speaks. "Nothing about this is frivolous, Lowell. This is forever, what we are about to do. You are to be my husband, not my jester. I do not feel like laughing about such a horrid mistake."

The consonants in the word seem to spark in the air. The din of the restaurant continues all around them, but between them there is nothing but the echo of her word. *Mistake.* This word is somehow worse than his. How did that happen? In defeat, Hensley pulls in her chair. She brings her hand to her face to wipe away the tears.

"Please forgive me," she says quietly.

Lowe's face is expressionless. He smiles a quick, bitter smile and says, "Well, at least we agree on something."

They sit across from one another without speaking until they've finished dinner. A heavy sadness presses against Hensley's chest, but her eyes are dry.

As the sidewalk outside bustles, a million lives in transit, Hensley can think of only one. She reminds herself not to address him, that it is a useless endeavor, but she cannot help it. It is a cliff that she throws herself right over.

Even as Lowe sits across from her, Hensley drafts a new letter in her mind. *Dear Mr. Reid, Have you ever felt betrayed by your very own self? As though you've locked yourself in a burning room and swallowed the key? This is how I feel as I sit across from my fiancé, the father of my unborn child, the man beside whom I will lay my head. I fear that I've grown up just a little too late. If I were the girl I was when I met Lowell, I would run away. Pretend that my own happiness matters more than any other's. But just as I realize that I am part of a much bigger story, that someone else's history has already begun inside of me, I know I must stay. What a foolish owl I am.*

Finally, Lowe stands and offers Hensley his arm. She forces a smile and takes it.

They walk out into the evening, their betrothal like a wedge between them.

When she arrives back at Harold's apartment, he is already asleep. Hensley paces across the living room. *Next week.* Her thoughts are incoherent. She doesn't know what to think. The abstract notion of becoming Mrs. Lowell Teagan has become an actuality. They dined together. She took his arm as they left the restaurant. He walked her past his new apartment building on Seventy-second, where she, too, will soon live. He kissed her cheek when he left her at Harold's door.

None of it seems right. But she knows that when she put herself on that train, this was precisely the destination she'd chosen.

Unable to sleep, she sits up late at her sewing machine with his words a refrain blurring her thoughts. *Next week.* She works on a veil. There is a scrap of lace in her sewing basket that she thinks she can fashion into something sweet. A Juliet cap or perhaps a headband. But after hours of standing before the glass, folding and piecing, ripping out stitches and rethreading her needle, she falls asleep, with only discarded bits and pieces strewn around her.

Hensley spends the week before her wedding on entirely domestic pursuits. She prepares a cut of meat for dinner, irons laundry, tidies the living room, washes the windows, and sweeps the floors. She does not mind having the apartment to herself. But she knows it cannot go on like this. In the glass above her dresser, she marvels at her changing figure, letting herself smile at the baby's clandestine movements. Beneath her full skirts and long tunics, her belly is becoming round and tight. She likes its weight, the fullness of her body. This baby has become her only ally.

In the afternoons, she walks rather aimlessly, trying to ignore the hourglass that seems to be falling ever faster as her wedding day approaches.

She sees the flyer pasted up against the wall by the Seventy-second Street entrance to the park. The circus will be in town all week. She remembers holding her father's arm, walking with him behind the clowns and the tricycles and the spinning hoops. How desperate she felt then, and now, looking back, how she longs for such a simple time.

It is not in good taste to leave the apartment after dark alone.

Harold would have no use for a circus. She can just imagine what he'd say.

A circus? With clowns and fire-breathers? There's enough of that in this city without paying for it.

She thinks of sending Arty a note, just to wish him good luck, but decides she'd better not. She walks on home, lingering on the memory of how he snapped that apple right in half.

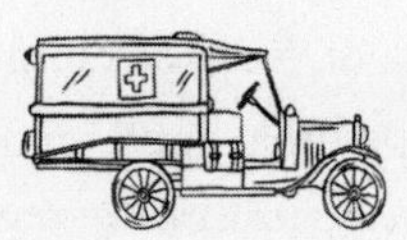

When Charles returns to New York, his father brings the car to the station. Neither of them acknowledges the cane in Charles's grip, nor the slow pace used to navigate their way out of the station. They drive directly to his father's club, where they dine in a corner booth. The steak arrives so thick and rare, Charles has a hard time eating even half of it.

"You must get your appetite back," his father says, passing him the front page of the evening newspaper. "I'm sure the food was awful over there."

Charles takes the paper from his father, nodding. He doesn't really care about anything he reads. He is thinking only of finding Hensley. The strange silver goblet is wrapped in newspaper in his luggage along with an address on West Seventy-second.

He has written to Rogerson about his encounter in Hillsboro. *You can imagine my surprise when the man transformed before my eyes into a woman, a beauty. The Wild West is as wild as anything, my friend. I know this one anecdote will keep your dirty mind occupied for many days.*

Several times on the train he began a letter to Hensley, but he cannot bring himself to tell her of the severity of his injury. Of course, he must. It is all that matters now. Will she care to be courted by a crippled, handicapped man? A veteran who has not come back stronger but who has, in fact, come back a shell of his former self. Of course, if one can survive with a quarter less of himself, perhaps that does make him stronger than those who remain whole. But as long as the question remains unanswered, everything remains possible. And so he's thrown every attempt into the trash.

At home, he stands in front of the large mirror centered over the dark mahogany bureau. In the falsely lit night, he unbuckles his belt and lets his pants fall to the floor. Then, loosening his prosthetic, he leans it up against the chest of drawers. There in the glass, he can see the butchery of his stump. He has felt its wide, uneven scar with his fingers and imagined how it must look, but he has never had this view.

Its bluntness is animal and indelicate, like the sole of an elephant's foot. He can lift the stump with his thigh muscles, but the absence of a knee joint or the slender slope into ankle and foot makes the job seem ridiculous. He is acutely aware that he will never appear whole again. This is the way his body will remain. There is no recovery, no therapy.

He sits on the bed to remove his tie and shirt, so that he is completely naked. With the support of his cane, he then stands and lets the full image of this new identity sink in.

His own unforgiving eyes avoid looking at the left side of his body. He turns slightly, hiding his lack. His body is still young, the skin full and buoyant across his torso and biceps. From this side, he is a whole man, virile and healthy, his buttocks the strong beginning of a long, solid leg. But he turns back, letting his full figure show in the mirror. He looks unfinished, deformed, and, worse, he cannot cross the room without strapping on the wooden leg that waits against the bureau. He hangs his head and throws his cane at the lamp to extinguish it.

The next morning, he travels uptown in a taxi and stands in front of the building that matches the address Teresa wrote down for him. Will he know her if she's on the street? Will she be anything like what he imagines? He looks carefully at the women who pass him, their languorous strides and wide-brimmed hats revealing nothing.

The apartment is just a block from Central Park. He stands beneath the awning and peers into the lobby with its small, upholstered settee cradled between the two curving staircases. The doorman greets him with a sorry look on his face. "Can I help you, sir?" Charles detests this look of sympathy. He shakes his head and walks on past.

Later, as he sits in the parlor having a drink with his parents, he loosens the strap from around his stump so that the prosthetic falls away, leaving his pant leg flat against the chair. His mother's face fills with horror. He'd only wanted to massage his aching stump, but instead he folds his hands in his lap, allowing his mother some peace in her own house. "Excuse me, Mother," he says finally, reaching for the wooden leg. "I didn't realize…"

"Good God, Charles," she says, pulling a handkerchief from between the cushions of the sofa. "Have you lost your mind, as well?"

She stands and leaves the room, her eyes clouded by tears, leaving Charles to reassemble himself.

When his father enters moments later, the newspaper tucked under his arm and an umbrella in his hand, he says merely, "Good evening, son."

Charles nods a greeting and swallows the last of his drink.

"Are we smoking?" his father says, offering him a cigarette from his case.

"Love to," Charles says.

His father fixes himself a straight glass of whiskey and refills Charles's glass. He sits across from Charles with the newspaper on his lap, reading the headlines. Without looking up, he says, "Don't let your mother trouble you. She is sentimental. Still thinks of you as her own flesh."

Charles nods.

"When you're up to it, I'd like for you to come into the office with me. Nobody there will give a damn about your leg. You're a Reid—that's all that matters."

Instead of telling his father that he still wants nothing to do with the business and that he will continue to pursue medicine, he says, "There's a girl. She wrote me letters. First her father did. We played chess. And then she chimed in. She's remarkable."

His father looks up from the paper, smiling briefly. "A pen pal, you mean?" He takes a sip of his drink.

Charles nods and reaches for the ashtray beside him. Holding it under his cigarette, he says, "Yes. You might say that."

"Well, where is she, this girl?"

Charles swallows. "Here."

"Manhattan, you mean?"

"Indeed," Charles says, letting the burn of the nicotine swell against the back of his throat.

His father grunts. "Let's meet her. Bring her for dinner one night. Just give your mother some notice so that they can prepare an extra plate in the kitchen."

Charles puts out his cigarette. "Yeah, it's a bit complicated."

His father wrinkles his brow. "How so?"

"She doesn't know about this," he says, motioning to his leg. "She doesn't know."

His father looks back at the newspaper. "Says here they are putting a woman in jail who was speeding and refused to pay the fine."

Charles sighs.

"And it looks like that little Pitcairn Island received their first mail from America."

The room goes quiet except for the occasional rustle as his father turns the pages. Charles uses his cane to stand and cross the room, removing another cigarette from the silver box. He opens the window slightly, letting the warm, noisy air of the street enter the parlor. As he lights his cigarette, his father says, "What I mean is, you cannot let this defeat you. If this girl doesn't want you, another will. But get on with it, Charles. You lost the leg honorably. Shame is ugly."

Charles watches the leaves of the oak tree turn ever so slightly in a breeze he cannot feel. "You've not seen it," he says quietly.

His father shrugs. He refills his whiskey and joins Charles by the window.

"I will always be this way. Always," Charles says.

They stand side by side, watching the world go by.

"Bravo," his father finally says, clinking his glass against the windowpane.

In the hours before she dresses for her wedding, Hensley walks alone through the already busy streets of New York. Her shadow stretches in front of her, darkening her own path. She is walking west, toward the river, away from the noise of Broadway. The sun swathes her back, heating her freshly washed hair and neck, while the bare skin on her face stings with the lingering coolness of dawn.

She is following no route, simply walking. Looking for a reason to believe that something about today might surprise her. When vows concerning the length of love and honor in the face of sickness or death are spoken, surely the chemistry between two people changes. Surely they will no longer be the disappointments to one another that they've been. Surely, if anything, the air between them will be suffused with solemnity. They will transform, like the work of the very best illusionist, into kinder, more beautiful partners.

She watches a young boy hurl trash onto a growing pile in the gutter, his pants too short and his hair too long. He nods his head at her. "Mornin', ma'am."

She smiles and continues toward the water. The baby turns and stretches somewhere deep inside.

Hensley would like to know how this life will unfold; how the unimaginable future will actually turn out. The fact that a child can be made without love or intention still startles her. She wonders about the destiny of such a world. She wonders if her own parents ever imagined that she would face a morning like this. What choice will her own child face, twenty years from now, that she cannot imagine?

As she comes upon the next block, the shimmer of sunlight on the black Hudson blazes white. Hensley thinks of the heavy pan Teresa had offered her in Hillsboro. It was a gamble, a chance that had seemed foolish. But what is it that she's doing now? Will it feel as though she's found a small speck of gold in the bottom of a black pan later today when she promises her life to Lowell Teagan?

She imagines Mr. Reid walking beside her, this same sun warming his own neck and shoulders. They could stand here, gazing at the barge moving coal up the Hudson and into the unimaginable future, and it would be thrilling. It would be theirs. As far as she can tell, solidarity is life's one comfort.

The barge blows its loud, flat horn. *Even now,* Hensley says to herself as she turns her head uptown, *you are a simplistic fool. Have you learned nothing of the mirage of romance?* A horse pulling a cart up Riverside Drive whinnies gruffly, as if in answer. Hensley nods as she watches the creature bow its head, straining slightly as the incline gradually rises. *Forget your hypothetical life. This is your wedding day.*

She puts her back to the water and begins the return to Broadway. Now the sun is on her face and she looks down at her own feet to avoid squinting. She hears the young voice call to her again. "You lost, ma'am?"

Hensley holds her hand up against the sun, looking the boy in the eye. He is now stocking a cart in front of the store with buckets of carnations and roses. She stops, admiring the blossoms. They are white and pink and yellow and red, with fat drops of water clinging to their petals.

"Wanna buy a flower? Three stems for a half-dollar," he says, wiping his hands on his pants.

Hensley smiles. "I like the small roses. What do you call those?" She bends over to smell the pink buds.

"The spray roses. Ain't no cheaper, though. Still three stems for a half-dollar."

Hensley smiles. His voice is unexpectedly firm.

"Okay," she says. "I'll take three of the pink spray, please."

As he wraps her flowers in a sheet of newspaper, Hensley wonders about the circumstances of this boy's conception. It might have been utterly romantic or ruthless, ordinary or remarkable. Just around the corner, up against a brick wall in the darkness of a summer night, or halfway around the world in a refugee camp amid gunfire and bitter cold. Does it matter? Did his mother ever imagine that the slight stirring deep inside her body would one day be selling flowers on a bright fall morning, counting out change carefully, in need of a haircut and a new pair of trousers, sparking this moment of imagination in another soon-to-be mother?

He places the small bundle in Hensley's arms and smiles at her. "Have a nice day, ma'am," he says and returns to his chores.

Hensley holds the roses to her nose. They smell of warm days and tall grass, burned sugar and small hands. "Thank you."

The boy nods, calling out to another woman passing, hoping she, too, might want a stem or two.

Harold stands in the small, wood-paneled room looking more like her father than she's ever realized. His hands are buried in his pockets, a look of serious contemplation on his face.

Hensley is wearing her mother's wedding dress—a bone white silk empire gown with a lace collar and long, sheer sleeves. It is exquisitely made and lovely in its simplicity. There is no veil, but she has pinned three small pink rosebuds into her hair.

"Harold," Hensley says, pulling him out of his reverie. The two siblings embrace.

When Harold pulls away to look at her, he smiles. "You are quite a picture, Hen. A real beauty."

"Thank you, Harold. But I don't know what I'm doing. I just wish things were... different."

"That's a bland wish. If you are going to spend time making wishes, at least make them colorful. Exotic. Worthwhile." His voice is full of effort, trying to be cheerful. Hensley doesn't mind, but it is not contagious.

Hensley nods. "You're right. Certainly you're right, Harold. We should not waste our wishes on imprecision." Immediately, though her toes are cramped in her satin wedding shoes, her hair demurely pinned up, her eyes lined carefully with kohl, just moments away from promising herself forever to Lowe, Hensley begins. "Dear brother, here is what I wish: I wish I'd never met Lowell Teagan, never been seduced by his practiced moves and his foolish self-importance. I wish I'd had sense enough to avoid his earnest eyes and cloying hands. I wish this morning when I put on this beautiful dress, I didn't worry about how it would be taken off. About how my new husband would certainly feel entitled to that. I wish I hadn't cried for an hour, cursing my own stupidity and Daddy's. He should never have gone in that shaft, Harold. Never. And more than all of those wishes, I wish I could marry a different man. A man I've never met but who lives in my heart and in my mind. I wish that he would walk through that door—short, fat, pimpled, sloppy, toothless, I don't care—and take my hand, lead me away from you and Lowell and this whole charade. That is my wish. Better?"

Harold shoves his hands back in his pockets. "Bravo. Toothless, huh? Much better. But you know I'm not a genie and I cannot make your wishes come true." He smiles at her, but his face is still sad.

She nods. "I know."

"Things will work out. You'll see. We are a stubborn lot, us Denches. We don't like having decisions made for us. But life made this one for you, Hennie. There is no disputing that. This is the right thing—the only thing, really—to do."

She hates him in that moment. She wants to tell him so, too. To tell him just how foolish his optimism is. But the sound of footsteps striding down the hallway ends their exchange. Harold cocks his head and then extends his hand and Hensley knows, without turning around, who it is.

"Lowell, good man," Harold says, continuing his act. "You look utterly groomish. I think you know my sister..."

Hensley faces him. She and Lowe manage a smile and briefly allow their cheeks to touch. It is they who seem to be the amateur players in this drama.

There is a dull silence in the room punctuated only by a fan that whirs and clicks in the corner.

"You look really nice," Lowe finally says, acknowledging Hensley's dress, shoes, and makeup. "Really nice."

"You do, too, Lowe."

"So, we all agree that you two make a handsome couple. Now, let's get this show on the road," Harold says, checking his wristwatch. "I've got a million deadlines today."

Just then, the judge enters and smiles at the three of them. "Good morning, folks. Happy wedding day. It looks like we need another witness. Give me a moment and I will employ my secretary."

He returns with a middle-aged woman wearing glasses and a gray cotton dress. "Good morning, lovebirds," she says, smiling easily.

Hensley tries to mimic her smile.

The judge stands before the four of them and reads from a book. Halfway through, Lowe takes Hensley's hand in his. Both of their palms are cold and clammy. Hensley hears the judge's voice, but his words are muffled as though she is behind several closed doors.

She notices Harold pull a box from his pocket and hand it to Lowe. Lowell removes a ring that Hensley has seen before and fingers it, waiting for the instructions.

Tears blur her eyes as she stares at the gold band with its single embedded diamond. It is her mother's. This is the ring her father gave to her mother so many years ago. This is the ring her mother wore until she died. Somehow, before his own death, her father must have sent it to Harold, anticipating this very moment. His last gift to her. It should reassure her—his blessing right here. But it doesn't.

The judge asks Lowe first if he promises to love and honor her, cherish and care for her according to the laws of man and ordinance of God in the Holy Bond of Matrimony. Without hesitation, Lowe says, "Yes, I do."

Now the judge looks at Hensley, his voice repeating the same question. Her ears are ringing. She shakes her head.

"Miss Dench?" the judge asks.

"I do not," Hensley says, finally. "I cannot."

Somehow the city has changed. Everything all around her appears different, amplified. Even her body is different, her heart beating so quickly and insistently it is as though she'd never before realized its power. Her skin is hot, then cold. Her legs move effortlessly beneath her, but she has no idea how. There is not a single coherent thought in her mind, only disbelief. Only a buzzing, rumbling noise that will not stop.

She returns to Harold's apartment and removes her mother's wedding dress. Carefully she folds it and replaces it in the box where it is stored. She disposes of the roses in her hair. Sitting in her knickers, the pale sunlight falling into a rectangle on the floor beside her, she begins to realize what she has done. Instead of the dread of spending her life with Lowell, there is now a disquieting blankness stretching out for as far as she can imagine.

Dear Teresa,

What have I done? I've come all this way to make a fool of myself and everyone else. I cannot stay with my brother much longer—I've brought enough trouble to him. I'm not sure where I'll go, but I do hope Berto has recovered and that you are free. I miss you terribly.

When Harold returns, he throws his key onto the front table and walks past her into the kitchen. She has made dinner, but he reaches over the pot on the stove and fixes himself a drink.

"You are angry?" she says, following him.

Harold raises his eyebrows. "Anger is way too simple an emotion for what I am. To begin with, I was humiliated. That judge does not need to have his time wasted, a melodrama played out in his chambers. It was a favor. Now I'm indebted and embarrassed. But that's just the beginning, isn't it?" He takes a long drink and then sits in a dining chair, untying his shoes. "I cannot keep you here forever. We are not gypsies, Hen. You will soon be unable to hide that," he says, gesturing at her waist.

Hensley nods. "I'm sorry," she says, trying to control her voice. Trying to conjure a certainty, a bravery that she imagines another girl having. "It was just wrong. You were asking me to tie my life to a man who betrayed me. A man for whom lying is a habit, a tool. I saw Mother's wedding band and I knew she would never approve."

"She'd also never approve of what you've done. Let's not forget your part in this."

Hensley bows her head. "I know that." She pulls a plate from the shelf above the sink. Putting a piece of braised meat and a pile of rice onto it, she places it on the table in front of Harold. "There are beets as well."

Harold turns his body toward the food. "Oh, Hen," he says, rubbing his eyes. "You'll be ruined. Just give him a chance. He might make you happy."

She nods, placing the bowl of syrupy beets on the table. "You've done all you can. My life is no longer a problem for you to solve. It's mine."

He shakes his head, utterly disappointed. "You've no idea, Hen. The world will not be kind to you. To your child."

Hensley does not protest. She lets his words hang between them, punctuated only by the scraping of his knife against the plate.

After dinner he goes out without explanation. Hensley is left in the apartment by herself.

Before dinner, Charles reads through her letters once more. He doesn't want to have survived only to give up. As he is dressing, he takes a fountain pen from its place on the desk and tries it out on his wooden leg. Imagining Hensley's impulse to apply his words to her bedroom wall, he inscribes the prosthetic with the words of her first letter. The ink smears slightly on the finish, but the entire letter fits lengthwise from knee to ankle, around half the circumference. This makes the appendage less of a burden. In fact, it will be his secret strength.

He dresses in his best suit and goes out after dinner, the silver goblet in his briefcase.

This time, he tips his hat to the doorman and waits patiently for the elevator to the third floor.

When a tall, disheveled man answers the door, his surprise renders Charles mute. He assumes he must be in the wrong place. Checking the apartment number Teresa has given him against that on the open door, he confirms he is in the right place.

"Can I help you, mister?" the gentleman asks, his voice full of misery and phlegm, the stench of an abundance of drink on his breath. Perhaps this is her brother, he reasons.

"I apologize for the intrusion. I am looking for a Miss Hensley Dench. Are you Harold?"

"Lowell Teagan," he says, shifting his stance and glancing at Charles's cane. "How do you do?"

Charles holds tightly to his case. "Is she here? I was told I could find her here," he says finally. "I've something for her."

The man smirks, amused by something unsaid. "No, she's not here, actually. Though she should be. First yes, then no, then me, then her . . . it's never-ending. Tell me," he says and pulls out a cigarette. "You courted her once?"

"No," Charles says, a low buzz flooding his ears, making it difficult to think. Had he? "Nothing like that. I've been overseas. In the war."

The man's face loses its color. "Oh. Excuse me, then. Would you like a drink?"

Charles barely hears him. He sees his mouth moving, his body language full of apology. What has happened? Who is this man? This dreadful noise like a swarm of bees encircles his head. He grips his cane tighter and sets his case down. "I have something for her," he says again, unable to hear his own voice. He leans over carefully and his fingers search out the bundle. "From a friend in New Mexico," he manages to say, despite his diminishing strength.

"We're engaged to be married, but there's been a bit of drama. Courthouse drama. I could've staged it much better, though, really. Those flowers in her hair were simply too innocent. Or perhaps too cloying."

"Drama?" Charles says, clinging to that word, certain that surely it is over. Whatever this was, it could not be what Hensley wants.

"Don't tell anyone, but she's with child. Mine. Progeny already.

Cart before the horse, but... You can leave that with me," he says, gesturing to the goblet in Charles's hand. "I will make sure she gets it."

"How kind," Charles says, handing it over, his fingers trembling. "May I ask... I don't mean to be rude, but is it recent? The engagement?"

The other man drags a hand across his forehead in a gesture of weariness and nods. "Quite."

Charles retrieves his bag from the floor, wishing for the first time that instead of just his leg, his entire body might have been obliterated in the French mud.

He halfheartedly tips his hat and leaves her fiancé there, blowing his nose into a handkerchief as he closes the door.

He waits in the corridor for the elevator, all thought obliterated by the horrible sawing noise that has moved into his body, dismantling each piece of the scaffolding their correspondence has built around his heart. His mouth hangs open and his chest heaves.

The endless days of carnage, moist insides falling out of ragged openings, pungent in the hot French air, are not nearly as vile as that man. Her fiancé! With child!

The horrors of the war are quite apparent. Violence is not hidden or disguised. Hatred—whether real or imagined—is expressed in loud, riotous shots and explosions. How, how is he to release this ugly rage? What can he possibly do with it all?

Charles wanders the streets well past midnight, cursing everything in sight. Ugly, dirty pigeons roost in awnings. Newspapers riddled with lies and propaganda, their obsolescence at the end of every day marked by the overflowing trash bins. Insipid horses sleep on their feet, shitting in the gutter. Impatient, anxious drivers blare the irritating horns of their trucks. Buoyant clouds hang low, reflecting the city's light back on itself. The smiling faces of couples, their arms linked in solidarity, oblivious to the foul stench emanating from the corners and alleys of the city. Loathsome. All of it. Yesterday. Today. Tomorrow. He cannot imagine his despair ever ceasing.

When he returns to his parents' house, he pours two strong drinks in a row. The effect is just what he'd hoped. Everything becomes slightly blurred and unreal.

As he undresses, he is newly devastated when he unbuckles his appendage. There are her words, in his own hand. There she is. Mocking him. Revealing his tender, foolish heart. He lets it fall hard against the floor.

The knock on the door wakes her. She presumes Harold has forgotten his key. But instead, it is Lowell. He stands there with a lovely bunch of white daisies—perhaps purchased from the same boy who'd earlier in the day sold her the roses for her hair—and a single silver goblet.

"Hensley," he says, pushing the flowers toward her. She blushes, terrified of explaining herself.

"That's sweet," she says, taking the flowers from him. "I'm sorry about today. I hope you don't hate me."

"Well, I'm confused," he says, stepping into the apartment. "This was to be our wedding day. There is no denying that I'm hurt."

She sighs. "Lowell, you don't want to marry me. You are just . . ."

"Trying to be honorable, Hennie. Trying to save you from a life of misery."

His tone is strange. She recognizes it as the way he spoke to her so many months ago, in the theater. It is as though he's speaking from a script.

"Since when do you care about saving me? I don't believe you've ever cared about me."

His face drops. He holds out his hand to hers. "Hennie. Don't say that. Our road has not been easy, but I've always cared."

His voice is deep and convincing. He takes a step toward her, his dark hair falling slightly to one side. The day has worn her out. He smiles, casting a gentleness over his face that she'd forgotten he had. She lets her head fall onto his shoulder and struggles with a bittersweet feeling. Would this do, she wonders, as the sun descends over the Hudson and the air cools with the expectation of fall?

But the moment he places his mouth on hers, the world contracts. She feels short of breath and restrained. And there he is, that open mouth that has brought her here, humiliated and desperate.

Is this affection, she wonders, as he forces her mouth open with his? Is this what husbands and wives allow each other to do? Push their needs into the space between them, demanding that they be met no matter the coarseness or cost?

But they are not married. And despite his best efforts, she is only more certain that she does not want to be married to him. This morning cannot be taken away from her. She turns her face away from his and holds her arms across her chest.

"What is this?" he says, his face flushed with desire. He holds up the goblet. "I understand cold feet. But I don't understand another suitor."

"What do you mean? I have no other suitor." Hensley takes a deep breath.

He turns around and takes two steps toward the door. Then, as though just realizing something, he faces her again. "The baby is mine. You have no wherewithal. For God's sake, you're not even of age. Don't think you can just run off with some new fellow."

"What are you talking about?"

"He came to see me tonight, Hensley. He was looking for you. Lovesickness all over his face. And he had this. Not a mere friendly trinket, is it?"

Hensley reaches for the goblet. Was it Teresa? Had she come for her? "Who was it?"

"Don't be stupid. You've nowhere to go. We both have an interest in making this work. And he's a cripple. Damaged."

Hensley takes a deep breath. "Please explain. I don't understand."

But he doesn't. He sets the goblet down on the dining table and takes her hands in his. "Hennie, today was just the dress rehearsal. We can still make it right."

"And what is your interest in that, Lowell? What have you been promised to make it right?"

"I'm actually quite good with figures. I've a head for both poetry and balance sheets."

"You think I have money?" Hensley is incredulous. "If I had money, I would already be gone. I certainly would not have put on that dress today."

Lowell squeezes his hands into fists at his sides. He shakes his head. "You are a tease. I have the scar to prove it."

He bends over, unties his shoe, and pulls it off. With his sock in one hand and his shoe in the other, he holds his pale foot up for her to inspect. Across the arch there is an amorphous pink scar.

Hensley trembles at the sight of it. "I am sorry about that. But you deceived me. Do you remember that part?"

"You did that to yourself."

Hensley places her hand on the back of the sofa. "How is that possible? Do you remember what you said?"

Lowe throws his shoe across the room and it hits the wall, leaving a small, angry divot. Hensley shrieks, hoping desperately that Harold is coming home.

"Do you remember what *you* said? You recited Tennyson. *If I were loved, as I desire to be?* For God's sake, you were to become my wife today. I won't play these games with you."

He tries to grab her arm and Hensley pulls away. She shrinks behind the couch, afraid. She listens as he unties the other shoe and, with less force, throws it near the other. In his bare feet, he stands above her.

"Please don't, Lowell," she says, watching his nostrils flare. "Please don't."

"What a memorable honeymoon, Hensley. Really, truly memorable. And completely suitable for an audience. Though they'd be bored to tears."

He pushes his foot against her back so that she falls slightly forward, her head sinking into the back of the couch. "I'm sorry," she says, her neck bent at an unnatural angle.

But he keeps his foot there, and a pain ebbs up from the pressure in the back of her head. The upholstery smells of cigarette smoke and Harold's cologne. If Lowell were a German soldier and he'd found her hiding in a trench, she could not be any more afraid. For comfort, she imagines her dear Mr. Reid, a pistol on his hip, sitting in a soggy, polluted field of mud beside her—the two of them united in their fear and conviction to survive. Grabbing the hem of her skirt as though it were his hand, she thinks to herself, *I would shoot him, Mr. Reid. I would not hesitate. Oh, give me my uniform and my boots and let me pull that damn trigger. I would aim first for his face, blast a hole through it, and then shoot him in his manly parts. Destroy that greedy, throbbing place that has turned me into this cowering girl, crouched behind her own living room sofa.*

But there is no pistol and there is no trench and Lowell is not a German soldier. He is, technically, still her betrothed.

"Leave me alone," she says firmly. "Whatever chance you thought you had coming here is ruined. I will be a newsie before I'll marry you."

Conjuring all of his contempt for her, he gathers the phlegm and saliva in the back of his throat and spits it out with a force that startles her. It lands just beside her, its yellow foam clinging to the rug in a stubborn, ugly puddle. He takes his shoes and stands at the door with them in his hand. "You will see, Miss Hensley Dench, that your gender makes you helpless. Your brother and I made a deal. We will be married."

Lowell slams the door behind him. Hensley curls up on the floor, listening to her own shallow breath. From across the room, she sees the chandelier's reflection shining in the silver goblet. What deal has Harold made with Lowell? With both of them united against her, her only hope is to disappear.

She shoves as many clothes as she can into her satchel, and on top she places the goblet. Without leaving a note, she walks out into the night.

A surprisingly cool wind blows from the Hudson, and she has absolutely no idea what to do. She has absolutely no idea what's happened to her life. How did she become this girl, homeless and pregnant and utterly alone?

The baby fidgets just under her rib cage. On the cool wind is the smell of the city's foul excretions. She stands and walks east, with her back to the wind.

Her legs move easily, seeming to know that this is all there is. This movement, this act of leaving, is everything. There is only this and she is afraid to ever stop walking.

Oh, cruel, dark night. How long before sunrise? What happens out here during the sleeping hours? Where do you gather the unwanted and unmoored?

She walks toward Marie's family's apartment on the other side of the park. It is the only refuge she can imagine, given the time of night. Hopefully nobody will chastise her tonight. All she wants is to be given a soft blanket and a pillow and be allowed to awaken to her own desperate circumstances with the dawn.

When she arrives, she rings the bell gently. But there is no reply. What now? Can she really walk all night long? She collects her satchel and descends the steps. The darkness spreads out in every direction, with no hint of reassurance. Hensley retraces her steps.

The park is lit with yellow spotlights, sending tunnels of light into the sky.

Hensley wipes her face with a handkerchief.

Taking a deep breath, she walks the narrow bricks that lead to the main tent.

Inside, all the energy of the evening's performance has been drained. Only the heat remains. The stands are empty and several performers lie across them, their makeup and costumes in various stages of removal. A dog lingers at their feet and licks their sweaty fingers eagerly. Several men push brooms across the floor, sweeping the straw and debris to the back of the tent. The smell of manure hovers beneath the sweetness of popcorn and spun sugar.

The fullness of her skirt feels too proper and her hat announces that she considers herself a lady.

"Circus is over, ma'am," a voice calls out from the stands. "Tomorrow night at seven."

Hensley blushes. "Thank you." She squints in the direction of the voice. Her own is tentative when she says, "I was actually looking for Arty. Is he here?"

A cacophony of laughter erupts from the stragglers. She realizes they probably think he's made a date with her—an upper-class lady.

When their amusement has quieted, a new voice calls out, "Second trailer on the left, out the back. The orange door."

She blinks. "Thank you," she says quietly, wrapping a protective hand across her belly. Stepping over a pile of horse manure, she crosses the tent quickly.

Outside, she is grateful to be anonymous again. Two midgets dressed in bathrobes walk across the path in front of her. Outside the orange door, Hensley takes a deep breath. Whether or not Arty says yes, at least she is certain he will not judge her. Even if he does, even if he chastises her or shames her, he will not be able to insist that she return. He has no authority over her.

Her knuckles meet the door with a surprising enthusiasm.

"Enter," he calls from inside.

Hensley is afraid he may not be decent. From outside, she calls through the door. "Arty, it's Hensley Dench."

There is silence. Then the door opens and he is standing there, his brow furrowed.

"I'm Hensley. Do you remember me?"

She finds she cannot speak anymore, but he nods. "Come in," he says, stepping back from the threshold so she can enter.

There is a small bed in the corner covered in a thick brown quilt. A little table is shoved against one wall, a cigar smoking in the ashtray.

Hensley stands there, her eyes on her own shoes.

"Would you like a drink, darlin'? Or is it another ride you've come back for?"

Hensley looks up, forcing herself to meet his eyes. "I've really fouled things up and I don't have any other place to go."

"I can't believe that's true." He winks at her and reaches for his cigar. "But it *is* how a lot of us got here."

"I've run away from my fiancé." As she says it, she laughs. Then she covers her mouth in horror. "It's not funny. Not at all."

"I can't say that I'm surprised."

"But you don't even know him..."

"No, but I saw your face in Chicago. It was not the way a girl should look on the way to the altar."

Hensley sinks into the small velvet chair just beside the door.

"Is it his child?"

She blushes. She wasn't sure he could tell. "Yes. But he doesn't care. I'm afraid my brother has misled him, made him believe in a fantasy. He wants so badly for me to be respectable that he would marry me to a murderer."

"You're in the right place," Arty says. He kneels in front of the cabinet, on top of which are his staples: a bread bag, several tins of nuts and mackerel, and a piece of cheese wrapped in mesh. From deep inside, he pulls out a tall jar of pickled onions, carrots, and green beans. He coaxes the vegetables into a pile on a glass plate. "Here you are. Besides whiskey, vinegar is the next best potion."

Hensley takes one of the carrot slices between her fingers and places it in her mouth. The vinegar singes her tongue with its acidity. Her jaw muscles tighten and her eyes water. But the sweetness of the carrot is preserved and reveals itself as she chews slowly. It reminds her of her own collection of pickles she relied upon in Hillsboro.

"I'd offer you whiskey, but I had to give it up myself. So I don't keep it."

"Too much medicine?" she asks, reaching for another carrot.

"Yep. The only difference between medicine and poison is the dose."

"These are very good. Did you make them?"

"No. A friend in Philadelphia."

Hensley nods. Feeling brave and reckless, she says loudly, "I sew."

"Do you?"

"What I mean is, I can sew well. I can repair things or make things. Anything, really."

Arty's thick eyebrows arch with understanding. "Ah, yes. I see. Practical girl. A job is what you're after, not advice."

"Of course, obviously, I could use advice. But I've got to have a roof over my head..."

"Say no more. You can sleep here." He motions to his tightly made bed.

"I didn't mean that I'd take yours; I was hoping... I don't even know how these things work, but I was hoping..."

"... to have a wagon to yourself? You mean you didn't wanna share a bed with a circus man? There are no extra wagons, Miss Dench. I'm afraid we are a full house. But my aging back actually prefers the floor. So you may take the bed for yourself. I will not add to your troubles."

Hensley hangs her head in relief. Her mouth feels suddenly raw from all the carrots. "You are very kind. I tried a friend's house, but she was not home. I know my brother will be terribly worried. Your kindness is really lovely."

"Your brother has expectations for you. I have none. The term *family* can be a sword with which we slice away those who've loved us most. Because they've also disappointed us the most. I betcha he'd be this kind to a stranger."

"Do you mean that if you were my brother, you'd marry me off to a cad, too? My shame does not offend you because you don't care about me?"

"Nope. I do care about you. But I have no memory of you as my sweet little six-year-old sis, with your dolly under your arm and your face pressed up against mine. I never confused your life with my own."

Hensley nods. She remembers playing jacks with Harold in front of the fireplace. Both of their little hands working so hard to grab more jacks than the other. Harold had a way with that red rubber ball, though. On his turn it would seem to hang in the air, as though he'd figured out a way around gravity. He won every time. But then, just as she was on the verge of tears, he'd wordlessly drop a half dozen shiny jacks into her lap. She liked the extra weight, the way they fell out of his hand and into the hollow her dress had made. But it never assuaged the sting of losing.

Arty pulls a small woven rug from another cabinet beneath the window. He unrolls it just beneath the chair where she sits. The top of his head is bald and the skin is mottled with dark freckles.

Without warning, once the rug is in place, he kicks his legs up against the wall beside her and stands on his hands. "Trade secret, Hensley. I do a handstand every night. For strength."

She replaces the jar of pickled vegetables. Removing her hat, she sets the pins on the table beside his ashtray. As she unlaces her shoes, she says, her voice trembling, "I had a place at Wellesley. Last month. My father was so proud. I was to study English literature."

Arty's toes wiggle slightly. "Instead you will study fairy tales."

She smiles and stretches out on the small bed. The baby is active, pushing against her belly with what she can only imagine are his knees, elbows, or maybe even his chin. She cradles him with her arms, loving all of his imaginary pieces already. "Only the ones with happy endings, please."

"Is there any other kind?" Arty asks, his face reddening to a surprising shade of crimson as his biceps bulge. "We'll see about some tailoring work for you. But if you'd be a part of my act tomorrow night, I'd be grateful."

"Of course I will. Yes, of course."

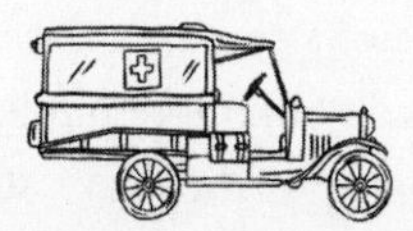

Charles cannot sleep. The whiskey has left him thirsty and restless. The bed frame makes an ugly creak as he shifts. He throws the sheet off, then shivers and pulls it back on.

Finally the room begins to fill with light. He doesn't know if he's slept or not. His pillow is hot beneath his head and it is a relief to pull his face up and away from it. He looks around, his clothes from the night before in a distraught pile, his prosthetic fallen on top in surrender. The black ink recklessly circles it.

Charles wonders if the doctor in Chicago will send him a replacement. He cringes at the thought of having to explain his own idiocy. The dawn makes him suddenly sleepy, but he wants out of the bed.

He reaches for the leg and straps it on, trying to keep his eyes from lingering on any of the words. *Let's agree to exist for each other forever.* He pulls his pants on quickly, covering this fresh pain.

On his desk, he notices a small pile of mail he did not see yesterday. Three letters, two from his cousin in California and another from France. Lieutenant Paul Rogerson.

Charles pulls out the chair and eagerly opens this last one.

Greetings from muddy hell,

How are you? I trust you are completely recuperated and hitting all the best nightspots in honor of your old pal from CCS #13. You know the news here doesn't change—fight, fix, fight, fix. I think I might be here forever. Foulsom had a telegram delivering the news that he's now a father to a chubby baby boy. It's only made him more intolerable.

During another run to the train station, I stood there smoking, avoiding eye contact with the hordes of old women and their livestock. Instead, I watched a certain bird on a branch and here's what I wondered: does that bird know how lucky it is? That effortless perch, those claws made just for that very purpose, the high view of everything, and escape just a few flaps away. No hands that might long for the cold reassurance of a gun or the lovely curve of a woman's waist (surely the source of all our troubles, eh?). This bird's head turned in small, mechanical moves from that high place and it looked just as bored as I did. Is there any joy there? I thought. And if not, if that creature is looking at our earthbound legs and long arms with envy, then we're really fucked. Just a bunch of forlorn creatures wandering the earth, longing for the attributes of others. We will never be happy.

I guess this is another way of saying that I am stuck in my own head without you here. It'd sure be nice for you to blow a hole through my amateur bullshit philosophy. How 'bout it?

In friendship,

P. Rogerson

* * *

Charles has fallen asleep in the middle of breakfast.

"Charles," his mother scolds. "I do not tolerate snoring at the table. I never have and I never will."

He apologizes and smiles at his mother, watching her sip from the delicate teacup painted with a scene of small lambs and blue flowers. "I couldn't sleep last night," he explains. He looks at his toast. "Pass the jam, please."

"You could ask the doctor for a formula," she suggests, reaching her hand across the table.

"I just have a lot on my mind. No need for medicine, Mother."

"You were not home when I went to bed. Perhaps if you need more sleep, you should actually retire at a decent hour."

"I was walking. Used to be my best medicine."

She does not reply to this. They each chew in silence. She pours more tea, methodically adding sugar and cream, then stirring it all gently with a silver teaspoon.

Charles wonders if Hensley will ever see that goblet. He didn't leave his name—would she ever know that he'd been there, that it was he who had followed her handwriting all the way to Hillsboro, New Mexico, only to return with just that silver goblet?

Suddenly he remembers something Teresa told him before he boarded his train. He didn't understand it then, but now it makes perfect, broken sense. *Whatever you find there, in New York, she wished it had been you. All along. From the moment I met her.*

Her bedroom wall, the stones, and Teresa's words all corroborated the truth of her letters. She had not been lying; it was not a ruse. He groans, as though having been punched in the stomach. "Charles Reid!" His mother stands up and comes around the table. "Are you all right? What is the meaning of this?" She places a hand against his forehead. "Are you ill?"

He takes his mother's hand in his. "No, Mother. I'm sorry. I just remembered something I forgot to do. Please excuse me." He kisses her warm skin and carefully stands. "Finish your breakfast in peace."

He returns to his room to write a letter.

New York

Dear Rogerson,

You really are thinking too much. Of course, I am in the same boat. For me, though, it is not the birds I wonder about, it is just one girl. I found her. Hensley Dench. I've found her and discovered that she is betrothed and pregnant. Can you believe it? This leaves me more bereft than did the loss of my leg. I suppose you would tell me that she was always a bit too good to be true. And, now, I would agree. Still, the pain is too real for it to have been false.

Regarding your bird and its feet: I think there is something smaller than joy, some suitability and comfort of those three small toes (?) wrapped around a lovely summer branch, that even in the middle of such a terrible war, you can admire their compatibility. There are many instances of this in our own species, but I know you may need to be reminded of them, given your current circumstances. In fact, the first you've already mentioned.

1. Our long, desirous arms do seem to be made to hold the swells and hollows of another's body.
2. Our uniquely bipedal form longs to reach for all things above our heads: crisp, red apples; the blossoms of magnolias and cherry trees; perhaps a hundred years from now, a long-forgotten bundle of letters written by an unknown man to a child's great-grandmother,

stored on a high, dusty shelf; the luminous, irrepressible stars.

3. Our words, whether formed with ink or voice, are met by perfectly undulated ears and strung into a mysterious system with which we create meaning. Are you reading this, Rogerson? Can you hear my voice? Well, if so, it is as if you are soaring just beside that bird you admired because you've managed to travel thousands of miles simply by holding this paper between your dirty—in fact, probably bloody—fingers.

There. What else can I tell you? I've decided to endure. It is the only way ahead.

Your turn. Go ahead and blow a hole through my philosophy. I look forward to it more than you can imagine. Stay safe.

In friendship,

Charles Reid

When Hensley wakes, she is not sure where she is. A series of loud cracks and whistles makes her think that she has traveled all the way across the ocean and found her way into Mr. Reid's barrack. Would he hide her beneath his blankets, give her a swig of water from his canteen, warn her—even as his eyes tell her of his relief—of the dangers of following her impulses? Would he hold her tightly until he felt the swell in her belly? And then what? With her own eyes still closed, she pulls the thin blanket tighter around her shoulders and sighs.

Soon she hears a knocking on the door.

"Hensley, you awake, darlin'?"

It is Arty's voice. Somehow this scenario is more unbelievable to Hensley than the one in which she crossed an ocean and found Mr. Reid. Has she truly run away? Is she living with the circus? In the strong man's wagon?

He opens the door, a bundle of fabric in his arms.

Hensley sits up and rubs her eyes.

"Good morning," he says, dumping the pile on the foot of the bed. "Here's your keep. Mending galore."

Hensley smiles. "No kidding. I will never see the light of day."

"Maybe not, but you will see the lights tonight." He presents her with a cup of milky coffee and a plate of toast and jam. "Don't forget. You're my grand finale."

Hensley takes the toast and coffee and eats enthusiastically. Crumbs spill on the blanket. She curls her toes with delight. "Thank you," she says to Arty, who is waxing his mustache in the small mirror over the sink.

"Pleasure," he says.

When she digs the sewing kit out of her satchel, she lets her hand linger on the letters. She does not need to open one to know its contents, but she longs to see his handwriting. Its firm, black existence. A truth. An actuality. Just the sight of her own name formed by his hand gives her a solace she cannot explain.

Long after lunch, still in her bedclothes, Hensley finishes the last repair. Her fingers are red and sore. She wishes she had her machine.

As she rests her head back on the pillow, she wonders if Harold will intercept the rest of her things for her when they are delivered. Will he store them for her until she has a proper place? When might that be?

These questions clutter her mind. She has no answers. She sits up, reaches for her stationery and a pen. With her legs still snug beneath the blanket, Hensley throws caution to the wind and begins a new letter.

Dear Mr. Reid,

She sighs. What must he think of her?

I've delayed writing this letter for too long. The explanation of my condition is shocking and tedious, both. I know you

> must hate me. When I did not receive a reply from you after my last letter, I knew you had given up on me. As you should. But now without the hope of your reply—since I have no forwarding address—I can write to you without disappointment. It is a selfish act but one I hope you will tolerate. The most amusing part of my confession is the reason why I have no address. Right now, I am working for a traveling circus in New York City—the same one that visited Hillsboro so many months ago. How I wish you could see this magical world. It is truly as though the dream world has come to life. It is certainly not where I imagined I would be when I left Hillsboro. If I thought you would ever find me—that we might ever meet, I could never tell you everything. I would protect my pride, my vanity. But I have quickly become a woman no man would ever seek.

"Goin' out. You want me to post that?" Arty asks as he pulls his jacket on.

"Could you?"

He nods. "Finish up. I will spot you the postage."

Knowing that she will never receive a reply, Hensley adds a few more lines regarding her situation, the last of which reads, *Writing to you will surely remain the closest I ever come to being with you. Allow me this consolation. I will find solace in the knowledge of some future strangers reading my words, and knowing how I loved you.*

"It's all right to be afraid, you know," he says as she is lacing up her shoes. "More drama, more tips," he adds, biting into an apple.

"How about this drama?" she says, showing him her silhouette.

His eyes grow large and he struggles to keep his mouth closed as he laughs at the sight of her. "Darlin', you are not kidding. That is an amazing display."

Hensley blushes. "The miracle of life," she says quietly, as she lets her skirt hang loose once more.

"Yep." A solemn quiet settles between them. "Every one of us. How we all started out," he finally adds.

"Yes. It is humbling to imagine our mothers, besieged by our own insistent little selves."

Arty nods and throws her an apple. "Dinner after the show. For now, just a snack."

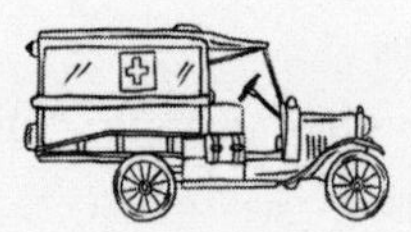

Charles stands outside the building as the crowds of men just off work shove past him. He has seen several women enter the building, but one had gray hair and was walking with the help of a nurse, and the other was a woman with a toddler clinging to her hand. Surely he will know her when he sees her, he thinks. She is not a stranger to him. But as the hordes of people diminish and very few people turn on to this block, he loses hope. He'd only wanted one glance, and to be sure the goblet had reached its rightful owner. The sun has set, his leg is aching, and he is hungry.

As he walks to the corner to hail a taxi, Charles sees the flyer. He suddenly remembers what she wrote about the circus.

I don't think I've ever felt so brave as when I sat in that chair. How silly to write that to you, I know. But with nothing save his own two hands, this man lifted me and the entire stack of chairs in one smooth gesture so that I nearly floated to what felt like the top of the world.

Suddenly distracted, he ignores his hunger and pain and enters the park. As if entering some righteous intervention, he finds himself in the middle of a haze of glistening bubbles blown by a creature dressed in feathers and silk.

"Circus! Tonight! Right here! Two dollars! Circus! Tonight!"

He pays his admission and enters the first tent. There are joyous, colorful sights everywhere. Jugglers, flame eaters, acrobats, unicycles, perfectly groomed, beribboned horses ridden by slight, upside-down ladies.

Charles joins a crowd waiting to see the appearance of the bearded lady. Soon a man appears on the stage, wearing a tuxedo, top hat, and long black beard. The crowd goes wild, cheering. Charles watches as this man removes his jacket, then shirt, revealing an ample bosom clad in a sequined brassiere. All the men clap and whistle. She shakes her shoulders and her bosoms swing naturally, confounding and thrilling the crowd. Next, she removes her pants and reveals matching sequined panties and a womanly bottom. Finally, she throws the top hat to the crowd and a mane of thick black hair tumbles down. She tugs and pulls at the beard, however, and it remains.

Charles cannot help but remember Teresa stripping down, suddenly turning from man to woman in front of his startled face. Oh, to transform so easily. To become whole in every way with just a change of clothes.

As she walks close to the front row, allowing a few men to have their chance to test the beard, which grows along her entire jawline but is combed into a long, thin growth that hovers just between her breasts, the woman collects tips in a small purse.

The little booth he intends to visit is just beside the ticket taker. **Palm Reading**, a small hand-painted sign reads. Inside, a fat palmist in a fur coat sits at a low table.

"Most people don't come in here whole," the palmist says, her thick fingers lingering on the table between them. "It's okay."

Charles takes a deep breath. "I've never had a fortune before."

The woman scoffs. "I'd say your suit cost more than I'll make in the next month. I don't give fortunes. I read the palm. It doesn't lie. People do." She coughs into her handkerchief. "Give me your right hand."

Charles places his hand on the table. The palmist looks carefully at the lines that cross his palm, then she whistles.

"Twenty cents."

Charles pulls the coins from his suit coat. He hands her the money and she nods.

Her hairline is rimmed with a perfect arc of perspiration. She drags her long fingernail across Charles's palm, tracing unseen paths. "Nothing is permanent. You see? We lose many things in life. Even love. It ebbs and flows. But when it recedes, you follow it. Like a child at the shore. When it flows, you submerge yourself. You let it take you under. It is a long line, this one. Not uncomplicated, but long."

"That doesn't sound like much," he says. "I thought you were supposed to predict something. See into the future. My future."

The woman slowly smiles and pushes his hand away. "You already know about the leg," she says, pinching at the corners of her mouth where the saliva has gathered. "You almost died. See the hatch marks here," she says, grabbing him again and pointing at a vague place on his palm. She closes her eyes. Charles watches her face change. "That's all," she says.

Charles stands. "But what am I to do now? What's next?"

The woman sighs. "Just ordinary life, pal. Your girl is right here," she says, gesturing at his palm. "She waited, huh? Lucky girl."

Charles doesn't bother to correct her. "Well, thank you, I suppose."

The woman's face does not change. She sighs heavily, the scent of onions escaping from her mouth. "I hate that bearded gal," she says and pulls her fur closer around her sweating figure. "None of us can compete with that."

Charles smiles, leaving another coin on the table. He buys a ticket for the big tent and enters, breathing deeply the myriad scents of the circus.

Inside the big tent, Hensley is transported back to the vast desert. Black-and-white clowns turn somersaults and back bends on a trailer pulled by a big white horse. One of them stands barefoot on the stallion's back, juggling luscious red balls. She expects to see Teresa dressed in her brother's work clothes and her father, his studious blue eyes momentarily carefree, as the trapeze sails above her head.

The tent buzzes with happy expectation. Ladies and gentlemen hold tightly to their children's hands, gasping at the height of the acrobats, the girth of the elephants, and the daring of the flame swallower. The scents of salty popcorn and cotton candy mingle with those of hay and animal and work. Hensley is slightly nervous. Having never before planned to be part of the performance, she's never dealt with preshow nerves.

To calm herself, she lingers near the acrobats and the sequined ladies, pinning loose straps or quickly sewing a hook and eye as needed.

Arty finds her when it is time. He is transformed once again into a performer, his mustache curled and stiff, his denim overalls revealing his gigantic arms. Under his arm, there is an oversized watermelon.

"My opening number," he says, knocking on the thick green skin.

She packs away her sewing kit and stands, facing him.

He pinches her cheeks. "You need a little color, darlin'."

She smiles.

"There it is," he says, nodding and taking her by the hand.

The stack of chairs and stools waits ominously in the middle of the stage. The stepstool is folded, resting against a column.

Hensley scans the crowd. They applaud as Arty makes his entrance, flexing his bulging muscles. As he goes through the beginning of his act, standing on just one hand, pulling apart the watermelon so it falls into a luscious mess of pink and green at his feet, breaking a chain wrapped around his chest, Hensley keeps her hands tucked behind her back. She scans the crowd, watching their faces, the men slightly chagrined, the women elated, all of them in awe. Arty is a terrific performer.

Soon it is her turn. She lifts the stepstool from its place and enters the spotlight. Placing it beside the stack, she listens as Arty tells the crowd that he will lift this young lady all the way over his head. As he extends his arm toward her, she pulls her skirts back, the abundance of her abdomen hidden by her careful tailoring. There is a collective gasp as the crowd inches even closer.

Hensley wonders if she should decline. Is this crazy? Probably it is. Reckless, surely. Potentially deadly.

But there is no time to reconsider. She climbs the stepladder that Arty has placed in front of her with a flourish and sits on the stool at the top of the stack.

"Hold on, darlin'," he whispers and then introduces her to the crowd. The baby, maybe an elbow or a knee, presses against her as if to protest. Hensley clutches the edges of the stool, which quivers slightly. Adrenaline races through her chest.

She looks out over the tent, twice as full as it was in Hillsboro. Men and women and children all enchanted by the performers with their brightly colored costumes and animated faces evoking wonder, their bodies defying all rules. Immediately, she remembers the way she felt the last time Arty lifted her high above his head. The awe from that height that made it seem as though anything might be possible. The clarity she felt, the nearness of her mother's legacy.

Now, as she surveys the tent, she wonders if there is another girl out there like her. Somebody whose past is just as damning as hers, whose life seems to be over before it has begun. Is there somebody else who will look back on this night as the last carefree moment of her life?

So far above the ground, her feet tucked into the crossbar, with a view of the entire tent, Hensley cannot be sure of anything. She sees the majestic white horses prancing around the center ring, a silver-flocked acrobat balancing one foot upon each, and wonders if the scene is real. The slippery sequins that she had to fastidiously reapply this afternoon are worlds apart from the shining figure down below. The small center holes that she slid onto her needle could not possibly add up to that shining spectacle beneath these bright lights.

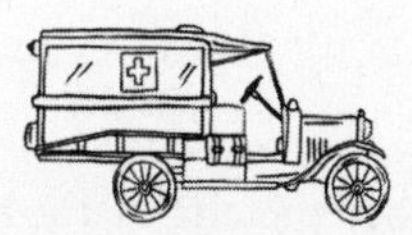

A sign above the corner ring advertises **THE STRONGEST MAN IN THE WORLD**.

A young woman smiles at the crowd, curtsies, and accepts the strong man's lips on her hand as he introduces her. "The very accommodating Miss Hensley..." He leans his ear to her mouth for a brief consultation. "... Dench."

Charles is sure he must be hallucinating. Or simply mistaken. There is no way. He's heard what he wanted to. But at that moment it doesn't matter. He cannot take his eyes off her. He watches as the strong man kneels beneath the stack. Slowly he straightens first his legs, then his arms, so that she is nearly fourteen feet above the sawdust of the circus floor. His cheeks turn a bright red and Charles backs away, trying to keep his eyes on Hensley, on that face he's imagined for so many nights. He grips his cane as though his hands are hers and his fierce hold will keep her safe.

She sits primly on the stool, high above everything. Her lips are a warm shade of red, her hair is tucked behind her ears so that the slope of her jaw and the elegance of its intersection with her neck is exposed. She is right there, still towering on top of the stack of chairs she described months ago. As though he's actually stepped into her letter and is inhabiting her very words. She looks just as brave and thoughtful as she said she felt.

He doesn't know how she could know him, but before he realizes what has happened, their eyes are locked on one another. All of it is there. Between them, in that single gaze, there is an entire history. All of those words, all of her life and his, the way it has been written and read.

Even as she floats above the circus, the noise of horns and cheers and tambourines filling the tent, she keeps her eyes on him. In an act of utter foolishness, she lifts one hand from the edge of the chair. Raising it gently above her head, she waves at him.

Charles removes one hand from his cane and waves it above his head. In that moment, nothing else matters. Not his body or hers, only that they have actually found one another. Like in so many of his dreams, he has found her and she is beaming at him, her face an expression of all that he's doubted, her outstretched arm extended toward him. Soon the crowd follows suit. They are all waving at her and she smiles even more broadly, her cheeks glistening with tears. She keeps waving the whole way down. When she descends the stepstool, she clutches the strong man's arm and curtsies.

The tears are unstoppable now and Hensley smiles through them. The crowd cheers with enthusiasm. Arty beams at her and then realizes she's crying. He pulls her close. "Everything okay?" he says, squeezing her hand. "You look like you've seen a ghost."

She nods but does not speak.

Charles has moved forward in the crowd, just a few paces away.

Hensley drops Arty's hand and makes her way toward him. He stands with both hands on his cane in front of him. Hensley, unabashedly eager to speak to him, places one of her hands on top of his. "Mr. Reid? Is that you?"

He looks down at her hand. She pulls it away. "I'm sorry. I didn't mean to be so . . . perhaps I'm mistaken." Her tears feel foolish. Her face is a mess. She fidgets for her handkerchief, but he produces one first.

It is embroidered. *CWR*. "Please, call me Charles." He cannot believe it. His throat is suddenly tight and dry.

"You are? Really?" She takes the handkerchief and dabs at her eyes. Her makeup has left its indelible black on his fine white linen. "Really?" She folds the handkerchief, trying to keep her hands from holding his face close to hers. Trying to stay subdued. She moves her foot toward his cane. "What has happened? You're hurt."

He nods. "Yes, permanently." He uses his fist to knock against the wood under his pant leg. The sound sends a shiver up her spine. She covers her mouth with the folded kerchief.

"How awful. I'm so sorry. When did it happen? How long have you been home?"

"I went to Hillsboro. You weren't there. I went to the address you left Teresa. Your fiancé's address. She found them, the goblets. She sent me with one. I left it for you."

Hensley nods. The lump in her throat seems to be expanding and preventing any air from getting to her lungs.

"You are expecting," he says, gesturing to a vague place beneath her chest.

She cannot say a word. Barely breathing, she is feeling lightheaded.

"I have something," he says. He reaches into his coat pocket. It is a small gray stone. "Here." He places it in her sweaty palm. "I didn't know I'd find you here tonight. But it's not too much to carry."

It is one of the stones from beside the gate in Hillsboro. Her counting stones. It has a date written on one side in her own hand: 7/7/17. On the other side, in his hand, is written, *dear hensley*, with a small red heart beside her name. It is what he'd told her that he would give to her if he ever had the chance. A small, warm stone from the wall, folded into her hand. This is how he'd said he would love her.

"You are even prettier than I'd imagined," he says, leaning close to her face, his breath hot on her cheek. "And that's saying something. Because I did nothing but imagine your face over there."

He turns away from her, limping away in wide, awkward steps. Hensley stands there watching him. She is paralyzed.

"Hensley," Arty says, placing his hand on her shoulder. "Remember, hold tight. Don't let go so easy."

She can barely see. The whole tent has gone fuzzy. She wraps her hand around the stone, trying to hold on. But she collapses into the strong man's arms.

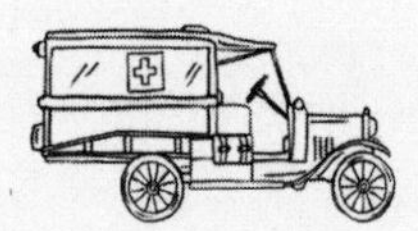

The strong man grabs Charles's arm as he rushes past, carrying Hensley. Charles follows him to a trailer, where the man lays her on the small cot in the corner. Charles places his fingers against her pale neck and feels for her pulse. She flinches. Her eyes open wide just as he finds her artery.

Charles removes his fingers. She blinks.

"Well, hallelujah," Arty says. "Welcome back to the circus."

Charles steps away and stands just by the door. "Left side is best for blood flow," he says quietly and Arty helps her shift to her side. Then he hands her a glass of water.

Looking around the small trailer, Charles notices a letter with his name on it resting on the table.

He wants to reach for it, to remember what it feels like to read a new letter from her. Instead, he looks at her again. She is propped up, the glass drained, her eyes on him. "Are you really here? Is this all true?"

Arty smiles. "Ah, the deep questions. I will let you two sort that out. Hensley, I will go fetch some supper for us. Oh, and the post was closed this afternoon. Your letter is here." He holds the envelope up, its thin rectangular existence an object of pain and beauty, both. Then he sets it down again and descends the steps of the trailer.

When they are left alone, the small space becomes even smaller. The evidence of her beating heart is visible to Charles in her pale neck. That place where he so recently had his hand.

"I've resisted for so long. But I wrote that this afternoon," she says, gesturing to the letter just beyond his reach. "How odd that you're here now."

"And how odd that you're engaged." Charles can't help himself. "And with child." The anger in his voice is surprising, even to him.

Her eyes widen and then close. She shakes her head but says nothing. Swinging her legs to the floor, she sits on the edge of the bed. "I've done absolutely nothing right," she says, opening her eyes and gripping him with their ferocity. "Nothing. But one thing is clear. I've only myself to answer to."

She stands up and walks past him, the scent of her hair soap a piece of new and treasured information. "I'm sorry," Charles says immediately. "Of course that's true. I've no right. I never asked you to wait."

"It wouldn't have mattered," she says and kneels in front of the cabinet. "Though if I'd thought it were fair, I would have. I would have waited forever." She pulls a jar of pickles from it. Removing a long, slender carrot with her fingers, she extends the jar toward him.

"No, thank you," he says. He is confused. Some of her words thrill him. Others are newly devastating.

"Do you want to read the letter?" she asks between delicate bites, studying his face. "Or do you want to just say something polite and back out of this trailer, thanking your lucky stars that my troubles are not yours."

She hands him the envelope. But he does not take it right away.

He does not want anything to change. He does not want to know the details of her unhappiness, her shame. In fact, he'd like to pretend that she is still the perfect girl who's lived in his head all these months. Instead, he speaks. "You were right about the licorice in the air. In Hillsboro. I've never breathed so deeply in my life."

Her lips curve ever so slightly. But she places the envelope back on the counter and turns away from him. "Mr. Reid. Charles," she says, her voice quivering slightly as she speaks his given name for the first time. "You must face facts. I am not the girl you thought I was." She places one hand over her belly. "I'm not."

He marvels at her spirit. She stands before him unadorned. Unlike anyone he's ever known, she is uninterested in feigning the truth. Is she really turning him away because she thinks he wouldn't want her? Doesn't she understand that it is precisely because he does want her that he is devastated? Can she not see in his eyes that he never wants to leave? That he would gladly spend forever right there in that trailer, watching her eat pickled carrots? He has found his place; that is perfectly clear. As inexplicable as it may be, he doesn't care that she is engaged or pregnant. She is still the girl whose words have brought him more comfort and joy than he's ever known. Deep in his gut, he is terrified of the heartbreak that he knows is waiting for him when the door of this unorthodox trailer closes behind him.

"Just read it," she says, extending it to him again.

He thinks of her words written on his wooden leg, hidden only by his thin wool pants. He takes the envelope from her. "Okay," he says.

It is entirely strange that he can be standing there, so close to her, and actually hold a letter she's written to him. How he's longed for such a day and yet he never imagined it this way. He never thought he would find her too late. He wants to reach out and count the freckles that march across her nose. He wants to close his eyes and just sit beside her, letting himself smell her perfume, her soap, her sweat.

He unfolds the thin paper and lingers on the salutation. *Dear Mr. Reid.*

He smiles at her, then keeps reading.

Immediately, he understands her reticence. She vividly describes the treacherous combination of her naïveté and Mr. Lowell Teagan's trickery that preceded her pregnancy. Charles struggles to eradicate the image from his mind. The anger makes it difficult to stand still. He shifts his weight, leaning against the wall. He closes his eyes and tries to see nothing. He urges it all away, but it lingers and for this he momentarily hates her. But he continues to read.

"You've left him?" he finally asks, reading the sentence over and over. He is shocked by this revelation.

She nods. "I will raise the baby somehow. Maybe in the circus."

He looks to see her smiling slightly.

"I told you I was a deviant."

Charles rubs his eyes. He sets the letter back on the table.

"Please don't feel obliged to say or do anything," she says, her voice a welcome distraction. "You have absolutely no duty here. You are home and you are healthy. You will have a wonderful life."

He takes a deep breath. "Dear Hensley," he says, "were you really going to continue to write to me? If I hadn't found you, you would have sent me letters my whole life long?"

She shrugs. "That is how I'd love you."

The words enter the small trailer so simply, without any fanfare. Without warning.

"But I did find you."

Her voice becomes sharp, pragmatic in an effort to resist emotion. "You were not looking for me. You were looking for the girl you thought I was."

He studies her face. What he's hoped for has begun to fade. She is real. This is happening and he is alive.

"It is true that I'd hoped for a less complicated situation. But you are that girl. Hensley," he says, reaching his hand out for hers. "You are still that girl."

"Like this?" she asks, holding her skirt tight against her abdomen. "Really?"

Charles imagines the child curled up within her abdomen. A child that she will hold and nurse and teach to read. A child with chubby little knees and elbows, endless questions, and arms designed to reach for what seems unreachable. "Just like that," he says.

"Forgive me if I don't believe you," Hensley says quietly, fidgeting with her fingers. "You don't know what you're saying. Why are you here?" she murmurs as she pulls the bundle of letters from her satchel. She presses them against her bosom. "After I confessed to you, your letters stopped. As I expected. But now..."

Charles furrows his brow. "Confessed?"

She nods and changes the subject. "Tell me about your injury."

They sit side by side in the circus trailer, the jubilation from the performers and the audience seeping in through the cracks, and he tells her about the day he lost his leg, his feeling of riding over the ocean and hearing her voice, so clearly telling him to survive. He tells her how he fought to return to his life because of those words. Her eyes fill once again with tears and she tells him about having a vision of him, gravely ill, just like Berto. She imagined another young woman tending to him, and she spoke to Berto the words she hoped someone would speak to Charles. She did, in fact, beg him to live.

How can they explain this? They do not try.

Arty returns with her dinner, which Charles happily watches her eat. She offers him half, but he has no appetite. He is still afraid that this, too, is a hallucination. He tells her this and she nods.

"We must devise a way to know that it's all real," she tells him. "Think."

Charles doesn't think. Instead, he does something that he cannot believe he has the nerve to do. "This has to be real," he says and then he kisses her on the cheek. The scent of sawdust and pickled vegetables clings to her skin.

When he opens his eyes, she is not smiling. "Mr. Reid," she says. "I'm emotional as well. But we cannot let ourselves forget the facts."

"What do you mean?"

She stands, placing her dinner tray beside the sink. "I've chosen this path. God knows where it will lead, but it is mine alone. I could never burden another, especially you, with this. You made it home." Her voice catches and she bites her lip to steady herself. "You must carry on. Remember, we will always exist for one another."

"You can't be serious," Charles says, standing, gripping his cane tightly. "If ever there were a reason to believe in the purpose of my survival, it is now. It is you. The letters will exist, but so must we. They are not a replacement, not a substitution."

Through tears, Hensley says, "They must be, Charles. You will have a wonderful life. Another girl will love you better."

Charles cannot respond. He imagines unbuckling his wooden leg and feeding it to the lion; stranding himself here in this trailer until he can convince her. Instead, he pulls up his pant leg and displays to her the wood. Its dull finish blackened by ink, by her words. "This, Hensley, is how I love you now. I live in the reality we created. Your words guide my every step. If they'd given me a wooden heart I would've written on that, too. I want whatever path you're taking."

Hensley bends forward, inspecting the script. It is slightly smudged but fully legible. Her lungs feel thin and empty. Those are her words. He is real and all that she'd thought he might be and she cannot ruin him. For a moment, she allows herself to imagine the place where the prosthetic attaches to what's left of his leg. It makes her cringe, thinking of his loss. She does not trust herself. Her life has become a series of mistakes, misjudgments.

"Someday you'll be glad," she says. "When you have your own child, and a wife who's not taking in mending for the circus."

Before he can reply, Arty returns to collect her empty dinner tray. He stands between them, surveying their morose faces. "So is it all decided, what's real and what's true?"

Charles extends his hand to Arty, thanking him for his hospitality. He turns to face Hensley. "I told you long ago what I believed. None of that has changed."

Hensley reaches out her hand to him, placing the stone back in his hand, "This is yours," she says, its warmth and weight heartbreaking. "I'm so glad you've survived."

Charles shakes his head. "No," he says, transferring it back to her. "Keep it. Let it be what I cannot."

That night, Hensley hides her tears from Arty.

"Courage is not my strong suit, either," he finally says, as he throws his feet against the wall into a handstand.

Hensley watches his face turn crimson. "I don't understand."

"You probably feel real brave because you're sad and you brought that on yourself. But sometimes it takes even more courage to be happy."

Hensley busies herself with untying her boots. "You are a strong man, Arty. I don't for a moment think you're a coward."

"Two different things," he says simply. "Strength is in the muscles. Courage is in the mind."

Despite his comments, and the sick feeling in her stomach, Hensley believes that she has been brave. Her arms and legs quiver as she climbs into bed, her entire body afraid of never seeing him again. She holds the stone in her hand, letting her eyes close on this most unlikely of days.

Dear Mr. Reid,

I wish I might've known more sooner. I wish I had not wasted my recklessness on Lowell Teagan. I wish so many things were different. Most of all, I wish this stone were your hand.

Charles Reid returns home, his mood fluctuating with every block. Her face—its freckles and pink lips, her slightly curved eyebrows perched atop her perfectly granite eyes—made him euphoric. Just being in her presence, sitting there watching her eat a mediocre dinner, was remarkable. For all the time he'd spent imagining their meeting, he'd never thought it would happen in a circus trailer. He'd also never thought she would be the one ashamed of her circumstances. He'd imagined she might not want to attach herself to him once she saw how much of him had been lost. But it was clear there inside the wood-paneled walls that his injury was not a hurdle for her.

When he arrives home, his father is still up, reviewing contracts in the study. "Charles," he says when he sees his silhouette in the doorway. "Let's have a game."

"I'm exhausted, actually. I really need to take the leg off."

"Do it in here. I'll not faint. I've already got my first three moves planned."

"Chess?"

"When was the last time we played?"

"The holidays, I think."

"Too long. I'll fix you a drink. You disassemble yourself."

Dutifully, Charles eases himself into a chair beside the board. He pulls up his pant leg and unbuckles his prosthetic. The release of the pressure is at once a relief and also the beginning of a different kind of pain, obtuse and vague. He massages the skin around the stump, urging it to accept its freedom more gracefully.

His father plays white, beginning with the same three moves he always does. He winds up with one of Charles's pawns and takes a long congratulatory drink. Charles's mind wanders to Mr. Dench and the chessboard in Hillsboro, his last move, and their unfinished game. He wonders what Mr. Dench would say about the wisdom of courting his daughter under the current circumstances.

"I've just about got your bishop, son. Where's your head?"

Charles blinks slowly. "I told you I was tired."

"Is it the girl? The one you mentioned?"

Charles smiles. "Trying to distract me more, are you?" He moves his bishop only slightly out of harm's way, hoping for an early finish.

"Come on," his father says. "I take offense that you would attempt to let me win. Do you think I'm so inferior?"

Charles sighs, shaking his head. "She's more than just a girl. I'm afraid I may be done."

"And yet we've never even had her for dinner? Don't be impetuous. A match is much more than romance."

Charles nods, regretting that he's begun this conversation. "Indeed. Much more."

"You are the heir to an enormous fortune, son. She must be suitable in every way. Her family, her manners, her sensibilities. Dabble in romance, but do not marry it."

With his thumb and his middle finger, Charles knocks over his own king. "Conquered," he says, reaching for his prosthetic.

"Don't be dramatic. The ending is far from foregone. I'll go easy on you."

As he straps the wooden leg back onto his body, he lets the tightness distract him from all that he might say to his father. He stands and puts weight on the prosthetic, cringing. "I think it is foregone. But not in the way you do. I'm really quite tired. Please excuse me."

His father watches him limp toward the doorway. "Charles," he says, replacing the chess pieces, "you mustn't pity yourself. There are much worse things than this."

Charles hesitates in the doorway. He knows his father must be referring to his injury, but at that moment, the only part of his life that Charles mourns is that he's left Hensley there in that trailer. He is instantly overwhelmed by the memory of her on top of that stack of chairs, so far above them all, but her smile so wide and genuine that it lit up the tent.

"You're right," Charles says, "there are much worse things." He knocks his cane once against the walnut threshold as a good night.

The next morning, Charles finds her brother in his office at the Naval Yard in Brooklyn. The smell of sea salt pervades the hallways and waiting areas.

"Captain Dench?" he says, knocking gently on the open door.

Harold's eyes leave the page and he stands as soon as he sees Charles. He invites him into the small, chilly office. "Charles Reid, sir. Served eight months at CCS Thirteen as ambulatory medic."

"Thank you, Mr. Reid," Harold says gravely. His eyes linger on the cane and he says it again. "Thank you. Please, have a seat."

Charles notices that Harold's freckles are darker than Hensley's but their placement is similar. It is a detail of their meeting he will not soon forget.

Harold makes a mark on the paper in front of him and then closes the folder. "What can I do for you, Mr. Reid?"

"First, I wanted to offer my condolences to you on your father's death. You may know that he volunteered to write letters to some of the men overseas. And I was one of the lucky ones. We were long-distance opponents in a fiercely fought chess game."

Harold's face crinkles in confusion. "My father? Sacha Dench?"

Charles has come prepared for the disbelief. In fact, he pulls one of Sacha's first letters from his breast pocket and lays it upon the desk. "Yes, your father. He was supremely generous with his pen. You've no idea how we covet mail over there."

Harold pulls his shoulders into a shrug. "Huh," he says. "No kidding. May I?"

Charles nods, looking at the stacks of folders and oversized envelopes atop every surface. The business of war. Effortless signatures authorizing—what? A few extra cartons of cigarettes? The use of cheaper gauze? Another hundred young horses? Another thousand russet potatoes?

When he's finished, Harold refolds the letter and slides it across the desk. He rubs his eyes with closed fists. When he looks back at Charles, he seems both tired but somehow more alert. "Forgive me if I seem confused. My father was an enigma, even to me. Or, especially to me. But I'm grateful that he was able to offer you some comfort while you were overseas."

"Indeed, a great comfort. Your sister, too."

"Hensley?" Harold straightens at the sound of her name.

Charles nods. "In fact, her letters continued after your father's death. And I've actually come here to inquire, if I may..."

Here Harold interrupts. Shaking his head, he says, "I will convey your greetings and your condolences to her, as well. I'm sure she will be pleased to know that you've returned safely."

"Yes, sir. I appreciate that." Charles holds his hat in one hand, his cane in the other. The sound of a typewriter reaching the end of its line emanates from another office. He turns and pushes Harold's door closed with the tip of his cane. "Sir, I've come to ask for Hensley's hand."

Harold's face twitches. His cheeks flush to a deep red. He fiddles with his pencil. "Look, Mr. Reid, I am honored by your presence and I'm sure my sister will be quite flattered, but she is not..."

Charles interrupts. "I know about Mr. Teagan. And her... condition," he says, lowering his voice slightly. Then he adds, "I adore her. I survived everything for this. For her."

Harold stands, then he sits quite emphatically back down. "You've seen her?"

Charles nods. "Last night. Quite by chance. It was extraordinary."

"Good God, man. I've not seen or heard from her since Wednesday. Is that because of you? Have you prevented her from coming to see me?"

"Not at all. I've no influence, I'm afraid."

"Where is she?" Harold stands and lights a cigarette.

"Mending for the circus," Charles says then watches Harold's face go crimson. He grips the back of his chair.

Charles stands and walks to the door and back. He taps his cane lightly against the concrete floor. "Your father told me about both of you. Of you, he wrote, *Harold has launched himself into the world with envious certainty of our democracy's impartiality.*"

Harold clears his throat and nods. "And he remained a skeptic until the very end."

"He also told me that you were as decent as they come. He said he admired your commitment to your ideals. He knew you to be kind and smart and frustrated by his own impracticality."

Harold stubs his cigarette into a brass ashtray. "He was maddening."

Charles allows a silence to stretch out and build their respective memories of Mr. Dench, so that for a brief moment he is very nearly in the room with them.

"I want to marry your sister."

Harold shakes his head. "I really don't think you understand. She's to have his child."

Charles grimaces. "I do understand."

"Well, sir, that is a generous offer, but if you've heard something about our family fortune, you've heard incorrectly. I'm not in the business of selling my sister's sin."

"Aren't you? How else did you get Mr. Teagan to agree to it?"

"Is that what she told you?"

"She didn't have to. I saw Mr. Teagan for myself. He's not the marrying kind."

Harold hangs his head. "I've only tried to do what's right for her. For this dire situation. We've not the benefit of an immeasurable fortune. But he was gullible enough to believe she'd come into one. Sometimes men need reasons to do the right thing."

On one wall of the office, there is a map of Europe, with the western front marked in small red *x*'s. Charles moves toward it. He finds Reims, Rémy, Tincourt. Using his index finger, he traces the red line from north to south. "What the hell do maps show us? Possible routes to move troops? Relative distances between battles? Areas of heavy casualties?"

Harold nods silently.

Charles continues. "The place I lost my leg cannot be found on this map. Sure, I know the coordinates. But it's just a piece of paper.

Here's the difference: I know the way the clouds looked as the rain began even before dawn that day. I will recognize the slight hills at the horizon, rimmed in a grayish lavender, or sometimes blue, until I die. I know the way the mud feels deep in my boot, squished between my toes. I know the taste of that mud because it was all over my lips. But this map is flat and useless like nobody is living or dying at all."

"Mr. Reid," Harold begins, gripping the back of his chair again.

"Please, call me Charles. Forgive me. I don't mean to pontificate. The point is, Captain, I am one of those people. 'Immeasurable' applies to me." He pauses to be sure Harold understands. Then, with an escalating frustration, he adds, "But it is as useless as this paper map if I cannot make a life with Hensley. I might as well hang it all on my fucking wall and point to it every so often, calling myself lucky." He realizes that his teeth are clenched and his voice is much too loud to be polite. He takes a deep breath. The weight of his prosthetic is pinching him, making his thigh throb. "Please, Captain, if I can persuade her, give me your blessing."

Harold shakes his head. It appears to pain him as he says it, but he does nonetheless. "There are other girls, you know. Heartbreak is . . . just part of it all. At least that's what they tell me . . ." He smiles briefly, shoving his hands into his pockets.

Charles nods. "Yeah, I've heard. They tell me that, too. But they've been wrong about so many things. I'm willing to take the risk that they're wrong about this, too."

Harold places his hand on his desk, thrumming his fingers several times. "I will have to speak to Hensley."

Charles nods. "Of course."

"Mr. Reid," Harold says, extending his hand.

"Sir," Charles says as they shake. He leaves his calling card on top of one of the stacks of brown files.

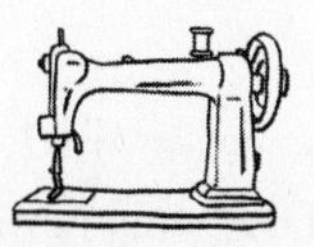

Rarely do the inhabitants of the circus trailers require any assistance before noon. Hensley uses the quiet time to slip out and across town to see Marie. The girls embrace in front of the bakery where they usually meet. Though Hensley has sworn she will not confess anything, Marie squeezes her tightly and Hensley knows she must feel the burgeoning beneath her tunic. She kisses Hensley sweetly on the cheek and says nothing.

Sharing a thick piece of bread spread with butter and jam, the girls sit on the steps of the library across the street. "Marie, I must tell you," Hensley says, licking her fingers. "I've met Mr. Reid. He found me."

Marie grabs her hand. "Oh, Hen. Is he as lovely as his letters?"

Hensley pushes her foot across a stray leaf on the step beneath her. "More, really." She blushes, thinking of the stone that is in her pocketbook even now. "But I'm leaving New York. I want you to know. I will send Harold a telegraph when I'm settled. There are other things happening, things that cannot wait. I must disappear."

Marie sets the bread down on the brown bag beside them. "Hensley, you sound so dramatic! Are you on the run from the law?"

Hensley laughs and Marie leans her head on her shoulder, relieved. "All right, then. You are not a fugitive. What could be so desperate that you have to leave?"

"Mr. Teagan. My brother. They've conspired to force me into marrying him."

"Not Harold. He's decent. Sweet, even. Why would he want you to marry that creature?"

Hensley shoos a pigeon away with her hand. "For good reason," she says quietly. When Marie puts her arm around her, Hensley's eyes fill with tears. For a long time, the girls sit together, not speaking. Hensley wipes at her tears with her linen and a far-off rumble of thunder finally breaks their silence.

Marie lets her hand fall from Hensley's shoulders. "Where will you go? With Mr. Reid?"

Hensley shakes her head. "No. I would never want him to give up more than he already has. He lost a leg, Marie. The last thing he needs is a scandal. The thrill of actually finding me, or perhaps his sense of chivalry, has made him say he doesn't mind. But if I've learned anything, Marie, it's to be wary. Our own sympathies can be used against us."

"Oh, Hen," Marie says, pulling her shawl closer to her body.

"Let's walk," Hensley says, standing up from the step. "The storm is coming. My friend Teresa, from Hillsboro, has written. She is settled in California. Just up the coast from where my mother was born. I've a place with her. She's never been much for convention anyway."

"When?"

"Tonight. There's a Twentieth Century Limited. Please don't tell anyone. At least not for a fortnight. I will write as soon as I'm settled. There will be lots of news, I'm sure."

They are standing beneath an awning just as the first drops of rain fall. Marie is nodding. "But you love him, don't you? From the first time you showed me his letters, I could tell."

Hensley scoots closer to Marie to keep out of the rain. "I'm afraid I lost my chance at love. But you haven't. So choose wisely, my dear friend. Don't marry a man for the shoes he can get you," she says, smiling.

Marie points her toe out from beneath her skirt to show off her new blue leather pumps. She laughs.

The girls embrace once more. Marie lets her hand rest on Hensley's waist. "Take care of yourself. I'll miss you dreadfully."

Hensley kisses her once more before darting out from under the awning into a taxicab.

When Harold visits the circus that evening, he ends up standing in Arty's trailer, watching the strong man wax his mustache. Hensley has already gone.

"Where? You must tell me where," Harold says, looking around for some hint of his sister.

"I believe she's decided to run her own life," Arty says, choosing an apple from the basket on the counter.

"But what can that possibly mean? She is barely eighteen. Tell me now, or I will have you questioned by the authorities."

Arty bites into the apple, smiling. "I've no idea, Mr. Dench. Your sister is remarkably independent. More than you'd like to think."

"Did she have any money?"

Arty nods. "We gave her two weeks' wages. She mended everything within sight."

"So she's gone out into the night with a couple weeks' wages from the circus. I suppose that fills you with confidence?"

Arty picks up a scrap of lace from the floor and places it on the table beside the door. "It did her."

Harold sighs, clasping both hands behind his head. "Damn it," he says quietly.

"She's not reckless. She's got that baby on her mind, that's all..."

"If she did, she'd be married by now."

Arty shrugs. "I lost my wife to a lion tamer. It's a good story. True, catchy, cautionary. But in reality, I'd lost her long before." Arty takes off his shirt and pulls the overalls up over his bare torso. "I've made a lot of mistakes, Mr. Dench. No denying that. When these muscles get too old, who knows where I'll end up? I've not your station in life, and there's probably not much we'd agree upon, but marrying a man like that would never have ended happily. Now, if you'll excuse me, I'm due in the big top. Good luck to you," he says and ducks through the doorway out into the noisy night.

Around her neck, Hensley wears a delicate piece of lace, hand-sewn into a little pouch. It hangs on a piece of black satin cord. She managed to salvage the lace from an irreparable costume belonging to one of the acrobats. Inside, she has tucked the small stone that Mr. Reid found and marked and brought back to New York City. As she stands on the train platform, waiting for the doors to open, she places her fingers on it.

Despite her worries, nobody arrives to stop her. The crowd moves around her, oblivious to her troubles. When the conductor calls out her train's boarding, she eagerly leaves the platform, afraid that if she'd had to stand there one more minute, she would run back to Harold's apartment and throw herself at his mercy.

Instead, she settles herself into the sleeping car that she managed to afford with the money her father had hidden in his desk, those crisp bills she carried with her all the way from Hillsboro and handed to the ticket agent without hesitation. She slides the door closed and collapses next to the window, thinking only of the west; those vast, blue skies and brown earth cracked through with a desperate longing.

When they are whizzing through the Pennsylvania countryside in the dark, and the only view in the glass is of her own tired face, she finally closes the curtains. Just as she stretches out on the berth, a piece of mail slides beneath her door.

They've not stopped since New York, so it wouldn't be a telegram. Perhaps it is the next morning's dining menu. Or a weather report. Her head rests heavily on the pillow; she is too tired to move. A stray tear cascades down her cheek. In an effort to keep her maudlin thoughts at bay, she places her feet on the cool floor and reaches for the delivery.

At first, she does not trust her own memory. But his writing is so familiar—she'd know it anywhere. *H. Dench* is printed in black ink on the envelope. She opens it and sees his slanted salutation.

> Dear Hensley,
>
> I, too, have chosen my own path. Would you be willing to join me for breakfast in the dining car?

The train's motion adds to the feeling that she is falling. Reaching for the wall and steadying herself, Hensley is sure that she is dreaming when another slip of paper skims beneath her door. This one is without an envelope, but it is folded over.

> Dear Hensley,
>
> Eight o'clock suits me. I know you've no obligation to do so, but it would make the day so nice to have breakfast with you in, what will it be, Ohio or Indiana?

Hensley sits and presses the papers against the floorboards. She tries to see a shadow beneath her door but cannot. Is he right there? Could he be standing just outside, the train vibrating through him just as it does through her? She must be dreaming. This is not possible.

Then, as though she is still a part of some act in the circus, another piece of paper slides beneath her door.

Dear Hensley,

This is real.

Afraid of disturbing whatever alchemy has occurred, Hensley sleeps on the floor just beside the door. When she wakes, her back is bruised but the sight of the three pieces of white paper against the dark wood floor assuages the pain. She looks again at his writing and then at her father's pocket watch she's inherited. There are only twenty minutes until eight.

Hensley replaces the loose skirt and tunic she wore to board the train. Her condition is still partly hidden by her own desperate alterations. She combs her hair and powders the dark circles beneath her eyes. Utterly unsure of what she will find in the dining car, she embarks nonetheless.

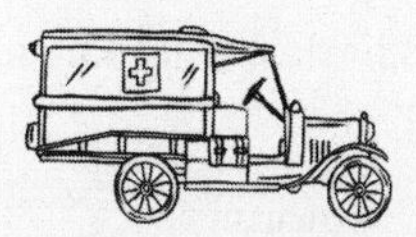

At a small table on the northern side of the train, Mr. Charles Reid is ignoring the newspaper in front of him and, instead, staring at the door. When he sees her, he gives a casual wave, as though they've done this a million times before.

Without a thought, Hensley raises one hand and acknowledges him. Still not knowing if it's real or imagined, she chooses to believe.

With the help of his cane, he stands and pulls back her chair for her. "Good morning," he says, smiling from ear to ear.

"Good morning," she says quietly.

They sit across from one another as the wheat fields on either side of them burst with golden sunlight. Finally, Hensley says, "I apologize for being so blunt, Mr. Reid, but whatever are you doing on this train?"

"I'm headed west," he says, offering her tea from his pot. "And you must call me Charles."

She smiles. "Of course you are. But why?"

"The University of California. Medical school. My path."

Hensley nods. "So it is mere chance that we've ended up here together?"

"Sometimes chance needs a bit of coaxing."

"Marie?" Hensley says, stirring sugar into her tea.

Charles shrugs. Yesterday, after he'd seen Harold, Charles returned home to find his mother sitting in front of the fireplace, the thunder outside forbidding.

She called to him. "Charles, where have you been? I missed you at breakfast."

"Just walking again, Mother."

"In the rain? Hm," she said, opening her catalog again. "I do wish I'd learned to paint when I was a child. Maybe you should take up painting, Charles."

He let his fingers move across a piece of ash that had found its way onto the marble mantel. Smudging it, letting its char trace his fingers' path, he thought of telling his mother everything. How scandalized she would be that he'd fallen for a girl who'd been seduced by an actor. A girl who'd had a place at Wellesley! How disparaging she would be of any girl who'd written to him without a proper introduction. She would attempt to cast off his scorched heart into a pail, as though disposing of the fireplace ashes. *There, now,* she might say, *let's not see any more of that.*

"Remember Tux, Mother?"

She furrowed her brow. "Of course. What a sweet dog. You loved him more than any of the others." She sighed.

Charles nodded. "And do you remember what you told me when Father took him to be put down?"

Her face relaxed. "No, I've no idea. What was it?"

Charles looked at the soot-stained tips of his fingers, almost as though he'd just written a long letter. "You told me that it was better for us to suffer than the dog."

"Of course," she said. "Because we can understand suffering. An animal only feels pain and doesn't know why. It cannot be told that it will end, or what it all might be for."

Charles nodded. What it all might be for. The phrase echoed in his mind, taunting. *And what is that, please?* he wondered. *Has she seen the ledger book keeping track of suffering and happiness, the balance due on each account?*

Charles realized he knew nothing of his mother's suffering beyond his own injury. He wondered if there had ever been another suitor, one besides his father. Had her heart ever felt like this, as though it may fatally shatter while the world carries on? If she had, surely she would know that there is no comfort. "And maybe they know just as much as we do," he said, retrieving his cane from its place beside the couch. "Because certainly it's all for naught."

Just then, the bell rang.

"You've a good friend in her," Charles says now, sipping his tea.

"Or do I?" Hensley says.

"I've no intention to force myself upon you. Nor even in front of you. But I could not let you leave New York alone, unaccompanied, distraught. Despite your recent admonishments, we are friends. I've documentation," he says, patting the pocket of his suit jacket.

Hensley blushes. "Oh, Charles. This cannot be happening. I mean, I don't know what to think."

"Let's have breakfast," he says simply, handing her the menu.

By the end of the meal, she knows that he likes his eggs poached and his bacon flimsy. He prefers rye toast to all others, but an inordinate amount of butter is required upon all his bread. He takes his coffee with milk, no sugar. His tea with sugar, no milk. His favorite fruit is a crisp, cold apple, but he enjoys melon and oranges, too. He always waits for her to lift her fork before he lifts his and even when silence stretches out between them, it is different from any other silence and neither seems to mind.

"What's your very favorite sound?" he asks when they've moved to the observation car, each of them nursing a cup of coffee.

"Let me see. I do love the way hot butter in a pan greets nearly anything. That sizzle. It's mouthwatering."

Charles smiles. "And it's usually morning. And the house may still be slightly dark, the windows open. A cool breeze is the only assertion of the world outside."

Hensley closes her eyes and nods. Before she knows what she's said, she adds, "And I wouldn't mind at all if you sat at the table with your paper and quite ignored me."

"Never," he says, touching the handle of her coffee cup with his fingers as gently as if the curve of it were the curve of her waist.

Hensley opens her eyes on the blur of Illinois' vast plains. She remembers observing the very same view as she sat beside her father so many months ago. The distance she has traveled can be tallied, but it means nothing. Numbers, calculation, logic of any kind could never have brought her to this moment. "But the upside of being ignored—if there is one—would be the regularity of my presence. It would mean each day began just so and that there was no reason to think it might not always."

He lets his fingers linger on her cup as she reaches for it. Their skin touches and at first, the heat of it silences them.

Then Charles says, "I met your brother yesterday."

"Harry?"

He nods. "You've the same freckles. Rather, the very same pattern to them."

Hensley blushes. "How is he? Terribly angry?"

"I don't know. He seemed concerned, surely."

"Why ever did you go to see him? I certainly hope it was not regarding me. I've had quite enough of men making arrangements behind closed doors."

Whatever moment of solidarity they've shared has gone. Hensley turns her body back toward the window.

"I offered him my condolences. For the loss of your father."

"Oh," she says, pulling a loose thread from her shawl. "That was kind of you."

Charles sighs. "And, I must confess, I followed a societal convention regarding the proposal of marriage. I asked his permission."

Hensley turns her face to his. "Marriage?"

Charles nods. "My greatest fear, Hensley, was that this injury might cause you to reject me. And, honestly, I don't suppose I could fault you. I will never run, never get on one knee, never lift a girl high above my head. I am crippled..."

Hensley interrupts him. "Oh, but I'm so much worse than crippled. Charles, your injury is a testament to your bravery. I've nothing to recommend the situation in which I find myself. Nothing. It only reveals my shocking naïveté and lack of character."

Charles looks out the window. He is moved by the sudden brilliance of the fields. It reminds him of driving across muddy roads with Rogerson, the sun setting behind them, the day's casualties waiting for them and the innocent French fields still bursting with color.

"There were these purple flowers in France. Lots of them. And sometimes yellow. A beautiful red one, too. Maybe poppies? I don't think I ever saw them up close. Just from the road," he says, his eyes still on the landscape beyond the glass. "It never made sense to me. Nature so adamantly cheerful in the midst of such assault."

Hensley leans her head against the seat. "Mmm. I suppose that would be awful. In New Mexico, the landscape reflected my own desperate misery."

Charles smiles. "I find it reassuring now. The important things carry on. The sun continues to warm and feed those things that want to live. Let's not be arid and bleak, Hensley. Let's not spend these days withering and dying. Let's carry on, shall we?"

"Of course we shall," she says, looking straight ahead. "But you mustn't add to your misery."

"Here is where you have lost sight of what misery means."

Hensley takes her eyes off the passing scenery and looks at him. He has not had a good shave this morning and there are whiskers on his chin illuminated by the sun's glare. "I assure you, I know misery, Charles."

"But my misery, Hensley Dench, is looking ahead at a life without you. Regardless of your condition. Regardless of your mistakes."

Hensley moves her eyes back to the window, then closes them. His words have dislodged something that she's worked so hard to contain. Her fingers vibrate with the possibility of loving him. "Please," she whispers, her eyes still closed, "let this be real."

In the darkness of her own mind, she feels him lift her hand and the tender weight of his lips upon it. She dares not open her eyes. Instead, she exists there, with the train's unceasing motion beneath her, and Mr. Charles Reid's breath making her fingers warm.

The baby's head is becoming heavier against Hensley's groin, but she does not mention this. She tries not to imagine all of the things that can still go wrong. Walking the length of the dining car carefully, mindful of the narrow space between the tables, she glances at other couples and marvels at the simplicity of it all. Hensley and Charles eat dinner slowly and watch the landscape turn from its often breathtaking striations of blue and gold and green to a blur of dusky shadow and, finally, to a looking glass reflecting their own familiar faces.

When it is time to retire, they walk along the passages, lingering between cars where the wind whips at their cheeks and they can briefly let their hands lock and, occasionally, their lips touch, each invariably tasting of sugar and soot.

In the mornings, Hensley has taken to writing notes while still in her nightclothes. The porter doesn't come until eight o'clock to replace the berths. She sits in her bed and composes something brief. *Dear Train #25, You are the favorite piece of steel I've ever met. Carry on.*

Then, without having even brushed her hair, she sticks her head out into the passageway, sneaks out, and slides it beneath Charles's door, three to the west. Moments later, she can hear him pull open his door and, then, with a beautiful, dry crescendo, the paper reappears in her compartment. It reads, *Dear Admirer, I'm not sure I'll ever live up to your adoration. But I will carry on.*

A few more times before eight o'clock they are able to deliver these notes undetected.

I had a dream that your joints were made of poppies. We kept watering cans on every ledge.

Couldn't sleep. The porter brought me a whiskey. I saw a shooting star out the window.

Does it hurt?

Not too bad usually.

I'm sorry.

You should be, because if you could have seen that leg…

Was it the most handsome part of you?

By far. Definitely. No way you'd ever resist me. No way.

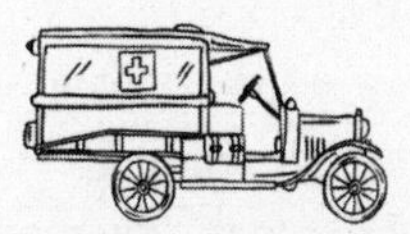

Charles has found a small bungalow with jasmine vines growing across the front porch to rent near his medical school. It has two small bedrooms, a bright kitchen, and a living room with a fireplace. Each morning, he listens to the hammering of a resident woodpecker searching for its breakfast and wonders if today he will have a telegram.

Ever since the impossible afternoon on which he disembarked three stops before Hensley, they've continued to write letters. She is staying with Teresa, who traded the goblets for a dairy farm outside of San Marcos.

> She was standing upon the platform in all of her womanly beauty when I arrived. Her long dark hair contrasting starkly against the white blouse she had tucked into blue dungarees. Berto was waiting for us in the truck, similarly transformed into a strong, capable man. The only evidence of his bout with polio is a pronounced limp. I told him that all the best men have one these days. They remain grateful to you for your care.
>
> I exist outside of their routine. They rise long before the sun and by the time I wake, there are gallons of milk jugs already emptied, ready for the afternoon. Occasionally Teresa

allows me to prepare their lunch, but mostly she insists that I spend the mornings on the porch watching the black-and-white herd meander across the green hills. I do so dutifully, losing myself in the memories of our train journey. I've already written to Marie, conveying my endless gratitude for her tenacity and loyalty.

The landscape here is so green and soft. It reminds me of my mother. As I walk, I close my eyes so that I can imagine the tender breeze is her touch. There is a border of cypress trees that cast steep shadows in the morning and evening and I step into and out of their darkness, mimicking a sort of shadow tag that I remember her playing with us in the park. The rosemary plants coax me back toward the house, as well as the scent of Teresa's lamb stew and blistering, buttered tortillas.

Charles spends each evening reading her letters, closing his eyes against the night air and imagining what he would tell her if she were next to him.

I've never been so lonely in my life. That you are just a hundred miles away is torture. I'd gladly trade the smell of the sweet jasmine for the smell of manure if it meant I were closer to you. I wish you would allow me to be there. Each evening I worry that the next day's news will be unwanted. I try to stay focused on the stack of books they've supplied me with here, but inevitably my thoughts turn to you and your well-being.

Your mother's memory will serve you well. After all, you are standing in the same dirt that she once did, my dear Hensley. We both know that the mystery of this absurd continuum called life will remain unsolved. But the mysteries contain comforts, too.

After dinner one night, Hensley takes a walk by herself while Teresa and Berto help themselves to another piece of pie. The pain started that morning, a sharp, ebbing ache. But now it radiates from her thighs through her back and beneath her rib cage. Walking only keeps her from falling down beneath the intensity. She does not want to worry these two who've given her so much, but she is sure she must be dying.

As she turns the corner of the pasture, she can no longer pretend that she wants to be alone. Her throat is dry and her legs shiver with exhaustion. "Teresa," she calls out, moving slowly through the pain.

Teresa is ready, meeting her at the bottom of the porch steps with her hair tied back. She puts her hand upon Hensley's back.

"Oh, Teresa," Hensley whimpers. "Help me. I am dying. Help me," she cries, leaning into her.

Teresa takes her elbow and somehow maneuvers them both up the two steps and into the house. Hensley closes herself in the bathroom, hovering over the toilet, buckled over in pain, wondering how long she has.

From just outside the door, Teresa's voice calls to her. "I'm coming in, Hen."

Before she can answer, something within her bursts. Her skin erupts with goose bumps and her legs quiver as the warmth trickles down the inside of her thighs, past her knees to the white tile floor. A new pain begins, hard and focused and insistent.

"Teresa," she calls, "I can't. I can't." She leans against the wall, her face drained of all its color. Her lips move soundlessly. "Please," she finally says, her voice thin and terrified.

Teresa already has towels in her arms and she places them on the floor. "You can," she says, calmly, easing her onto them and handing her a wet washcloth, which Hensley clamps her teeth upon, sucking the water out. "You can and I will help you."

"Teresa," Hensley says, her eyes shut tight, "you must tell Charles. Tell him that even when he goes on without me, we will still exist. He loved me just as I'd thought he would."

"Hensley," her friend says in a calm and certain voice, "you are not dying. You are going to deliver your baby. Like your mother before you. And her mother before that. Just breathe. Try to focus your mind." Teresa pushes Hensley's hair away from her face and watches her lips come together in an intentional exhale. "That's it. Nice and slow. You are just fine."

Darkness settles over the farmhouse, making her efforts seem louder than they are. Teresa is unfazed by the blood and fluid and the intensity of her moaning, but when she sees the dark hair on the crown of the baby's head, so startling and perfect, she is momentarily silent. Then, finally, she begins again. "Hensley. Keep going. Push again," she says, her voice drowned by Hensley's.

When the baby's head is in Teresa's hands, it is only another moment before the entire child, slick and warm and miraculous, has fallen into her arms. A girl. Her eyes blink slowly and a nice, healthy protest begins in the back of her throat.